Re-Enchant

Dark Fantasy Stories of Magic and Fae

Edited
by
Kelly A. Harmon and
Vonnie Winslow Crist

Pole to Pole Publishing
Baltimore

Re-Enchant
Dark Fantasy Stories of Magic and Fae
Copyright © 2018 Pole to Pole Publishing

Published by Pole to Pole Publishing
Edited by Kelly A. Harmon and Vonnie Winslow Crist

Cover layout copyright © 2018 Pole to Pole Publishing
www.poletopolepublishing.com
Cover Art Copyright @ Subbotina Licensed via DepostPhotos.com.

ISBN-13: 978-1-941559-28-4

The Grammarians' Grimoire ©2015 E.E. King, first published in The 3288 Review.
Dust ©2001 James Dorr, first published in Strange Mistresses: Tales of Wonder and Romance.
A Half Dime Adventure ©1996 Don Webb, first published in Asimov's Science Fiction
Aftertere's Eyes ©2000 "Mattie" Brahen, first published in Scheherazade Magazine.
The Well ©2015 Gregory L. Norris, first published in Coven.
Vasilissa the Fair © W.R.S. Ralston
A Thing at the Edge ©2012 Kai Miro, first published in Night Gypsy: Journey into Darkness.
The White Wood ©2011 Jude-Marie Green, first published in Beyond Centauri magazine.
My Muse Wears Combat Boots ©2011 Christine Lucas, first published in Murky Depths magazine.
When Phakock Came to Steal Papa ©2016 Ace Jordyn, first published in On-Spec: The Canadian Magazine of the Fantastic.
The Stone Gift ©2003 Robert N. Stephenson, first published in Forever Shores: Fiction of the Fantastic.
Color ©2010 Alma Alexander, first published in Human Tales.
Any Kiss Would Do ©2018 Kelly A. Harmon, first published in The Pale Leaves magazine.
Justice ©2017 Vonnie Winslow Crist, first published in Devolution Z: The Horror Magazine.
The Wild Swans © Hans Christian Andersen
The Way of Sisters ©2013 April Steenburgh, first published in Fight Like a Girl: A Short Story Anthology.
A Lantern Maker of Ai Hanlo ©1984 Darrell Schweitzer, first published in Amazing Stories magazine.
Black Angel ©1995 Nancy Springer, first published in Orphans of the Night.

Library of Congress Control Number: 2018960347.

Re-Enchant

Storybook pages abound with all manner of magic...

– Tony Di Terlizzi

Table of Contents

The Grammarians' Grimoire
E. E. King

*S*hirley picked it up at a Sunday rummage sale at the Waterford library. It was so old and worn that the title had been rubbed away. She imagined it was a children's book because of its detailed and colorful illustrations, one in the series of color-named fairytale collections she remembered from her youth. This cover was a blend of every hue conceivable. Shirley could not recall a rainbow volume, but there must have been one and this must have been it. It was dog-eared with use.

How come no one ever says 'cat-eared,' Shirley thought? *My Tom has ears as mangled as any dog.*

It was an unusually fanciful idea for Shirley. Normally she didn't consider the words that ran through her head. They were as unremarkable as the buses that passed the library every fifteen minutes, as stale as the bread at Maggie's Day-Old Bakery across the street.

Shirley was a charwoman. She made a steady income scrubbing the library every night, working from closing time at 6:00 PM till 1:00 or 2:00 AM. As a result, she arrived home just a few hours before the sun peered over the horizon and slept late, usually waking at noon. It was a solitary life, cut off from her mates by her vampire's schedule. Her parents were long dead. Her only regular companion was old Tom, her ginger cat.

Generally, Shirley was not interested in books. They collected dust. They sat on the shelves, silently berating you with your ignorance.

No matter how many you read, there were always more: more words, more ideas, more dust.

Shirley had dropped by the library Saturday afternoon to pick up her check and to buy some scones from Maggie's. But, on her way out, the bright clutter of old books had made her pause. The book she believed to be *The Rainbow Book of Fairytales* had whispered like a secret. She scooped it up. It nestled in her palm, familiar as an old friend.

She certainly didn't need it, but it was only ninety pence, and she wanted it. She rarely wanted anything. She was fair, fat, over forty, and content. She rented a neat, book-less, dust-free cottage, walking distance to the library. Her only causes for concern were the night meanderings and occasional battles of old Tom.

Shirley bought some scones and walked home, the book in her bag heavy as a promise. Once home, she carefully wiped it clean and set it over the mantel.

The next night when she returned home from the library at 2:00 AM, a card was pinned to her door. It was handwritten, a rare thing these days, penned in rust colored ink. The card was woven of heavy parchment. The ink had caught in the fibers, splattering the card.

"Thomas Conner, Grammarian," it read. Lines swirled beneath, ending in graceful snail shell curves.

Shirley examined it. The name seemed slightly familiar but she couldn't place it. She rubbed it. It was both soft and rough. She didn't know what it meant, but she took it inside and laid it next to the multicolored book on her hearth.

There was a sound at the door. When Shirley opened it, there stood Tom. He strolled in as if he were the one who owned the cottage and yowled for food.

Dogs, Shirley thought, *you house 'em, feed 'em, love 'em, and they worship you for it. But Cats, you house 'em, feed 'em, love 'em, and they expect you to worship them.*

She sighed, filled Tom's bowl with food, and absently stroking his battered head.

"I'd be careful of that book if I were you," Tom said.

Shirley froze, hand hovering over Tom. She held her breath, time appeared to stop.

"It's okay," Tom said. "All cats can talk. Even some dogs, though truth is they don't have much to say. Nasty empty minds most have, full of food, disgusting scents, and human worship."

"If all cats can talk," Shirley whispered, "then why don't they?"

"Why spoil a good thing? You humans need to feel superior and in control. Just look at how hard you fought against the notion that the earth was the center of the universe. No, humans like to feel that we need them. It works out best this way."

"So why," Shirley whispered, "are you talking now?"

"Because you picked up a grimoire somewhere, and a very powerful one. I have a feeling all kinds of unpleasant creatures will be calling soon."

Shirley remembered the odd calling card.

"What's a grimoire?" Shirley asked.

"A grimoire," Tom said, slowly blinking his golden eyes, "is a textbook of magic. They contain instructions on creating magical objects, how to perform magical spells, and how to summon supernatural entities. In many cases, yours being a case in point, the book itself has magical powers.

"And it is yours, bought and paid for. The book can only transfer ownership if you choose to sell it, and some form of payment must change hands."

There was a knock on the door.

"Also," said Tom, "if anyone comes to buy it, I would not let them across the threshold. People have been known to lose their souls over less."

A half-moon shown through the window, Tom leapt out; the curtains billowed in his wake like a ghost. Shirley shivered. Her door creaked open. A tall darkness stood in her doorway. A chill filled the room.

"I believe you have something that belongs to me," said the darkness.

Shirley swallowed.

"I realize," said the voice, slightly nasal and whining a little, "that you didn't mean to steal it. I will take that into account when reckoning the price."

"I didn't steal nothing," said Shirley, proper grammar leaving her head like an ill wind.

"Ah-ha," said the voice "Double negative—that means you *did* steal something."

Shirley remembered the voice; it was Old Master Conner's, Latin and English instructor at Chelsea Primary School where Shirley had gone as a girl. She had failed his class. It had sealed her fate. He had labeled her unable to learn, possibly dyslexic, certainly not public school or university material. Shirley's parents, and Shirley herself, had believed him. She had left school as soon as it was legal, and began cleaning.

But Master Conner was long dead and buried, so why was he still here bothering her?

"If you think I stole it, why are you offering to buy it?" Shirley asked. She was not brave, but she was not imaginative either. It is only those who envision consequences that are easily scared.

"Because certain bookssssssss," the darkness hissed the word like a serpent. "Certain books need purchase."

Shirley considered. "Sounds like you have a cold," she said. "I didn't know the dead got colds."

"What you don't know could fill all the libraries of the world, and there would still be enough ignorance left over to fuel an election," the darkness sniffed. It, or he, definitely sounded plugged up.

"No need to be snide," said Shirley. "I ain't your student anymore."

"*Not*," wheezed, the darkness. "You're *not* my student. 'Ain't is an ungrammatical construct—it means nothing."

"Well, if it means nothing why are you getting so upset about it?" asked Shirley.

"I despise ill usage," the darkness said. He coughed.

Shirley wondered if dead germs were contagious.

"Why are you lurking in the doorway?" Shirley asked.

"I'm not lurking," the darkness sputtered. "I'm hovering, and I'm hovering because the rules plainly state that I'm not allowed entry unless invited in."

Shirley considered. Conner had always been a bit of a bully. He'd often managed to reduce other, more sensitive students to tears, but never Shirley.

"Sounds like you could do with a nice mug of tea," she said. "Tea, honey, and lemon, maybe even a shot of whiskey to kill that cold." She walked to the sink, filled the kettle and put it on the stove.

"You stupid cow," the darkness squeaked. "I'm dead. I can't ingest tea, and even if I could, I can't cross your threshold unless invited."

"No need to be rude," sniffed Shirley. "You'll never get an invite talking like that. Still I bet…"

She drifted off. The kettle was already screeching. It had boiled faster than usual. *Maybe,* thought Shirley, *it was the presence of a ghost that made it burn hotter than usual, though you'd think that would lower temperature not raise it.*

"Fire can't be hotter than fire," the darkness was almost weeping with rage.

So, thought Shirley, *you can hear thoughts then?*

"Yes," said the darkness, "It's one of the benefits to non-corporealness."

"Even if you can't drink it, perhaps just smelling the steam and all could do you some good," Shirley said. She bustled around the kitchen, adding the best Earl Grey, her finest honey, and a splash of the Michael Collins Single Malt she had gotten herself for Christmas.

It was true that Master Conner was rude, *but how often,* thought Shirley, *do I get visitors?* Usually her only companion was Tom who had, until tonight, always been rather taciturn.

Conner, or rather the darkness where she supposed Conner to be, made a sniffing sound.

"That's very nice, thank you," said the darkness. "I died with a cold, and I haven't been able to shake it. You'd be surprised how few people sip tea by open doors, or windows on a cold night."

Shirley wasn't surprised at all.

She put the tea on the mantel, then pushed the small round table over to the doorway. She pulled up two chairs and laid two saucers on the table, carefully setting them on a delicate lace doily. Even if Conner couldn't drink, Shirley imagined, it would be nicer for him to have his own place. She filled a second cup with Earl Grey honey, lemon, and a healthy shot of Michael Collins Single Malt, and laid it on the table.

The darkness sniffed, "Do you know," he said. "I think it's working."

Of course it was working, thought Shirley. *Imagine being surprised that people didn't sit by open windows; imagine not realizing that a cold, even a deceased one, could benefit from tea, honey, lemon, and whiskey. Academics—always so lost in their heads, even when they weren't dead and still had bodies.*

"Perhaps you'd like a nice buttered scone?" Shirley asked.

The darkness sighed. "Do you know how long it's been?" he said. He sounded close to tears.

Shirley bustled back into the kitchen, first removing a day-old scone, then after a moment's consideration, two. Even if Conner couldn't eat, it seemed rude to make him smell hers. She heated them in the microwave. After a minute, she carried them to the table along with sweet butter, clotted cream, and her best semi-sweet orange marmalade which she laid out on thin china bowls, delicately rimmed by blue flowers.

She cracked open the scone, buttering it generously, adding a liberal dollop of cream and a heaping spoonful of the marmalade. She didn't usually have such sumptuous teas, but this was a special occasion.

"Just a tad of marmalade for me, please," sniffed the darkness.

"Perhaps you'd prefer something sweeter, I have just the thing." Shirley rose from the table scuttling over to the cupboard. "Blackberry preserves," she said.

"Yes, please," said the darkness.

"I knew it," Shirley ladled the thick purple preserves into her last matching blue flower rimmed china. She carried it to the table and, after buttering and ladling clotted cream onto the second scone, covered it with blackberry. "It's always the studious skinny ones that can get away with eating whatever. Just sit on their duffs all day and never gain a pound."

Shirley couldn't actually remember if Master Conner had been skinny or not, but who didn't like being told they were told they were thin?

"Bet you like yours sweet, am I right?"

If darkness could have blushed, it would have. The darkness inhaled, groaning with pleasure.

"What's so special about this book?" Shirley asked.

"It's an extremely significant grammar," said the darkness. Shirley thought he sounded considerably clearer.

"I was told it was a grimoire," Shirley said. "Though it looks like a book of fairy stories to me."

"Who told you that," the darkness said sharply.

"Old Tom, my cat," said Shirley, delicately dabbing a sticky, curling, rind of marmalade off her chin.

"Cats," hissed the darkness, "they think they're so clever. Well, as it happens, Old Tom is wrong…or at least partly wrong. It's a grammarians' grimoire, the most precise dissection of magic in existence. It diagrams the structure of spells; it's *The Fowler's Modern English Usage* of spells!"

Shirley was unimpressed. She didn't know magic and had never been able to analyze a sentence; the combination seemed an unpleasant one.

Outside, the sun stretched fingers of light above the horizon. The darkness in the doorway paled. "Thanks for the tea and scones," whispered the fading darkness.

Shirley cleaned up the tea things and went to bed. She awoke at 3:00 PM. Tom was sitting on her chest, carefully gnawing his saber claws and spitting old sheaths onto Shirley's comforter.

"Oh, Tom," she sighed, "Where have you been?"

But Tom only purred. Either the question did not warrant a reply or, most likely, it had all been a very odd dream. It was impossible to be sure. There were no signs of a late-night tea party, but Shirley was a good housekeeper. She had put the room to rights before bed.

True, there was the book, back on the mantel, and next to it the odd card, but that was not proof. Shirley sighed. At 5:00 PM she left for work.

At the library, she scrubbed the bathrooms, wiped sticky fingermarks off the seats in the children's corner, and then began the endless dusting.

Her habit was to begin at one end of the library and work her way through. It took about a month for her to complete the cycle. Tonight, she began in the L's. L was apparently a popular letter; there were books on Lancing, Lasers, Lassoing, and Lazarus; volumes on Legends, Lepers, and Lewis and Clark; treatises on Lost Artifacts, Lords, and Lourdes. Shirley was just reaching up to replace the tome on *Lost Artifacts of Ancient Religions* when a worn paperback tumbled down and landed at her feet. It was *The Secret Spells of Syntax and Structure*.

As if she had opened the back of the book deposit, manuscripts began to leap from the shelf, crashing round her sensible brown oxfords. They raised a small whirlwind of dust. Shirley was embarrassed that so much dirt had been hiding on the shelves. She glanced around, hoping no one would see, but of course she was alone. It was, after all, the middle of the night. Suddenly, just then, as if to reassure her, the clock struck twelve.

She heard a rap at the library door. The door was heavy oak with chessboard sized windows of glass. Shirley peered through the pane. At first glance she spied no one, but when she squinted she saw a tall shadowy darkness deeper than the rest of the night. It looked vaguely familiar.

"Collins?" she asked.

She heard a cough. "Oh no, I really thought that tea had helped," she said. "That's a killer of a cough you've got." She considered her words. It was perhaps not the most tactful thing she could have said.

"Look," she called through the door. I can make you a cup here, but it will just be some P&G, nothing fancy. If you join me at home later I can make you a proper tea just like last night."

"Do you know what you've unearthed, woman," a voice from beyond the door cried. "It's the lost treasury of the magic of lexicology."

"What?" said Shirley. The door was thick, and there was a shrill wind blowing outside. Conner, or rather the darkness-that-had–been-Conner, had a cold, and besides Shirley wasn't sure what lexicology was.

"Lexicology, woman, the study of words, their nature and function as symbols, the relationship of their meaning to epistemology in general, and the rules of their composition from smaller elements. Let me in and I can explain."

Shirley doubted that. She had never understood Conner when he was alive, and she was skeptical that death had improved his powers of communication.

He coughed again.

"Oh, you poor, poor, ma…uh…ghost; just wait right there and I'll bring you a spot of tea. Then, I'll hurry up my dusting and you can follow me home for something more substantial."

"Bollox the dust, bollox the tea, you have just uncovered…" The darkness' stream of vituperative words was interrupted by a bombardment of hacking.

"There now," said Shirley, "serves you right it does when all I'm trying to do is make you better."

The darkness sulked a bit. "Sorry."

"As well you should be. Now, just hold tight." Shirley filled the electric kettle. It boiled almost instantly.

"I'm afraid all I have is Chamomile," she said.

"It's all right," the darkness said in a slightly muffed voice.

Shirley opened the heavy door. She had planned to put the cup just outside, but on second thought decided to leave it on the threshold. The wind was blowing vengefully, and so Shirley picked up some of the books that had lemminged off the shelves and shoved them in the crack of the door.

"Noooo!" the darkness yelped as though it was in physical pain. Shirley wondered if that were possible. She had always supposed that pain dissolved in death.

"Those manuscripts contain the key to glamouring grammar," a shadow reached out of the night.

Shirley slapped at it. "Not without a library card you don't," she said. She had never had one herself, not much caring for books, but rules were rules.

"My card has expired," wailed the darkness.

Shirley sighed. "Well, how about I put them on hold for you, and…" She considered. Conner could hardly return and get a new card. After all you needed to show a utility bill as proof of residence, and Shirley doubted that the water bill for the graveyard would work.

"Tell you what. I'll apply for one myself, but you have to promise me—cross your heart and hope to…well, you have to promise not to stain them, and to return them on time. I can't afford to be paying fines for you."

"But Shirley, these don't belong to the library, at least not to this library. Don't you understand you have opened a magic hole, an arcane vault to lost treasures of syntax and glamour?"

"That may be as it is," said Shirley, "but what's in the library stays in the library, unless it's checked out proper."

Shirley noted that Conner had called her by her name for the first time and was pleased.

"Now, if you'll stop all your bother, I can finish up and we can go home."

"Let me in and I'll help?"

Shirley considered. This was after all not her home, but what did a ghost know about cleaning? He was dust—the opposite of clean. And Master Conner had never been the neatest even in life. Also, she distrusted his apparent hunger for those odd texts. She sighed. She hated to deny him, but… She hustled around and even so left half an hour before her usual time, something she had never done before.

She tried to put *The Secret Spells of Syntax and Structure* and the other books back on the shelf where she supposed they had come from, but they kept vaulting from the shelves, landing at her feet like trouble. Finally, she swept them into a bag and left them behind the front desk.

After cleaning up Conner's tea, she applied lipstick, a fresh coat of powder, and walked to the front. The bag was blocking the entrance. She tried to step over it, but the bag twisted loops round her feet like a newly leashed puppy. She untangled her feet, but the bag, though it did not appear to grow, or move, continued to thwart her departure. With a sigh, she picked it up and crossed the threshold, vowing to return and apply for a card tomorrow.

As she stepped into the night, or rather into the wee hours betwixt midnight and dawn, the wind screeched. A shadow loomed beside her.

"Give me the books, Shirley," it whispered. Then, it coughed.

"Enough of that now," said Shirley, and she walked home, the darkness sniffing behind her. It was nice to have a companion in the darkness, even if the companion *was* darkness.

Once home she put on a kettle of tea. While it was heating, she rummaged through her cupboard. Way at the back she felt what she wanted, it was an old charred pan that she had meant to be disposed of long ago.

Taking a tissue in her right hand she struck a match with her left. She lit the corner of the tissue, watching as it burnt to cinders. Ash and smoke rose into the night.

"What are you doing?" the darkness asked.

"Well," she said, "you are dead, dust, ashes to ashes and all that, right? So perhaps you can use the ash of a tissue and finally get a good blow."

The darkness was silent. A sound like a fog horn split the night. "You know," said a muffled voice. "It works."

Shirley smiled and put the bag of books on the mantel. They barely had time for tea and toast before the sun peeped over the horizon and started heading east. Shirley fell into bed, rising late, hurrying to ready herself for work. She felt bad that she would not arrive early enough to apply for a card. She felt guilty about the borrowed books, and resolved to leave a note explaining what she had done.

Tom vaulted though the window and glared at her. His left ear was nicked and there was a fresh scratch across his face.

"Oh, Tom," Shirley said. "Have you been fighting again? Let me clean you off."

Tom struggled halfheartedly as she cleaned his wounds with alcohol and iodine. Then he ate, curled up on the foot of the bed, and went to sleep.

Night at the library passed without incident. No books cast themselves from the shelves, no ghosts rapped at the door. But when Shirley closed up and crossed into the night, a damp coolness linked through her arm.

"How's the cold," she asked?

"Much better, thanks," said the darkness.

"I was thinking." The darkness cleared its throat. "Perhaps I was hasty."

Shirley waited.

"Perhaps I, well…perhaps I underestimated you. Burning that tissue was a very good idea you know."

The darkness was silent for a moment. "You're wasted as a charwoman, why with thoughts like those…" The voice drifted off,

"I don't mind being a charwoman," Shirley said. "It's what I know."

"Well," the voice began again. "I was thinking. Perhaps you could…well someone really ought to…I need an amanuensis."

Shirley waited.

"Amanuensis," said the darkness. "A literary or artistic assistant, one who takes dictation or copies manuscripts."

Shirley smiled. *So, the man, or rather ghost, was too grand for the word secretary?* She pictured herself spending the lonely wee hours of the night uncovering secrets with a companion. The night would be lonely no more.

Thus it was that Shirley left the library, winning acclaim as a scholar in the arcane art of spells and syntax, at an age when most people were retired. She always insisted that she had a silent partner, crediting a mysterious 'Thomas Conner' as co-author and chief researcher of all her works, but most supposed that this was some odd form of modesty.

Tom, who disapproved of spirit scholars, moved next door.

In spite of his departure, Shirley always followed Tom's advice. She never let Conner cross her threshold. She wasn't certain that she had a soul, but just in case she did, she'd prefer to keep it. Each night, bundled in a down parka, a wool hat, scarf, and open fingered gloves so she could type, she sat in the open doorway, taking notes, warming herself with tea and malt, and warming Conner with the aroma of tea and malt.

She did not fear catching her death of cold. She knew this was a partnership that would only be strengthened by death.

Dust

James Dorr

A lma shivered despite the warm night air. She did not like
spiders. Where she had been brought up, on the high,
dust-filled Castilian plateau, her father a soldier, they had a saying:
Kill a spider and it will bring rainstorms. Her summers of girlhood,
sweating—as she did now—in that land's furnace heat, had been spent
seeking and killing as many of the eight-legged creatures as she could
find, yet never once did it bring the rain's coolness.

And here, in Seville, or rather outside the city itself in the
garden of the Marqués Sebano, she found herself surrounded by spider
webs, sprinkled with gold dust to glitter and shine in a soft summer's
moonlight. The Marqués was wealthy—or so the rumors she and her
mistress had heard in the gaming establishments had it. His taste in
outdoor decorations proved it.

And that was why Doña Carlotta pursued him.

"A sherry, milady?" a voice whispered to her. "*El vino de
Jerez?*" She glanced to see a liveried servant thrust a tray toward her, the
glasses it held also sprinkled with gold dust, as least on their outsides,
so all would be known by the golden sheen of their lips and fingers as
guests of Sebano. She shook her head. No. Her duty here was not to
enjoy the party.

Rather, she watched. She watched Carlotta, not standing too
close, yet not too far from the lady either. She watched as the Doña

danced and spun, her voice tinkling laughter over the music. She smelled the lady Carlotta's perfume as it vied with the flowers that grew high on trellises under the golden webs.

She watched Sebano as, finally, he noticed the lady's milk-white skin, the scarlet silkiness of her hooped gown, the black of her hair—as raven-wing black as the lace mantilla that failed to conceal the curve of her bare shoulders. She watched as Sebano whispered, bowing, gesturing to where the musicians were playing, and thought of the work she had done that morning to gain her and her mistress's invitation.

She looked at her own skirt of brown, supple leather, but thick—and *hot*. The waistcoat she wore cinched over her linen shirt, studded with rivets that held plates of thin iron beneath its dark red velvet.

She thought of her father. She thought of two fathers, one a *grandee* and the other a soldier, and of the arrangement they had made between them that made her the guardian of a lord's daughter. She, who was scarcely even the age of her charge, an armored *dueña*—a "lady in black," whose job was to keep a young woman from trouble.

A woman who *gambled*, then often as not made up to the men she met at her dice tables, exchanging, perhaps, a kiss for her losses.

She hated Carlotta!

But, no. Alma shrugged. She reached to the pouch that hung from her belt as the servant approached again, this time with brandy. Instead she withdrew a short *cigarrillo*, then flint and her tinder box. Striking a spark, she drew on the Turkish weed, letting its rich smoke escape from her nostrils. It was not as though she lacked her own addictions.

She drew again on the dried, brown weed, letting its ash whirl away as so much dust. The dust of the *Levante*, she thought—of the Eastern lands where the weed had its origins and where, someday, perhaps she would visit—she and Carlotta who so disapproved of her breathing the sweet smoke as unfit for ladies, if Spain grew too hot for them. Or dust of the high, arid plains of Castile, where she as a girl had once hunted out spiders, now to come south with her mistress to *this* place where webs flecked with gold dust beset them on all sides.

"Milady?"

Again, the servant approached her, this time from behind. She turned to wave him off—then saw he held not a tray but a sword.

He and two others spread out to surround her, their swords drawn and weaving. They no longer spoke now as, jumping back, she drew her own sword—a short, soldier's sword, edged on both sides but built chiefly for thrusting—clattering from the belt-rings that held it. She glanced back, once, to confirm that Carlotta was still in plain sight as she wove her own traps about Sebano, then, noting that many of the guests had left by now, she laughed with a shrieking laugh.

This she was trained for—her father's daughter. As, clearly, the men who opposed her were *not.*

She thrust forward, twice, with short, mincing thrusts as she gathered a part of her skirt in her left fist to free her ankles, then whirled and thrust rightward, forcing the first man—the servant—backward. She nicked his shoulder, she heard his soft cry of pain, but was already back facing the other two, forcing first one, then the other from her as well.

Then—a louder scream! This from the serving man, now behind her. High in its terror. Thrusting again she nicked another of her assailants as both he and his companion cried out, too, then suddenly turned and ran. Taking another step in their direction, she crouched and, warily, slowly looked back toward the first man she'd wounded.

She saw he had stumbled when her point had struck him. In his attempt to regain his balance he'd staggered backward into one of the decorations, pulling the golden web down around him. But this was a web that was still in the weaving. Its makers were still there, the spiders now streaming over the man's face, biting and stinging him as he screamed louder. As he attempted to claw them from him.

She winced as she struck home—one quick thrust as an act of "mercy"—then turned once again to be sure the other two had, indeed, left the fight. Satisfied at least for the moment, she stood still and listened, hearing the distant sounds of two pairs of feet still running. That much, then, was over—but *why?* she wondered now. Why had these men attacked her in the first place?

Then she realized: From the pavilion where guests had been dancing, there was no more music.

She whirled now, quickly, to where she had last seen her mistress, Carlotta. The lady had vanished, along with Sebano. She wiped her sword, then hung it back on her belt, while, with her left hand, she reached to her pouch.

No! she thought. She dropped the Turkish weed she had instinctively drawn out from it and crushed it beneath her foot. No, she thought again—time for vice later, even that one which her mistress so frowned on. As much as she wished to breathe in the relaxing, perfumed vapor, she could not until she had found Carlotta.

And never mind whether her mistress, Carlotta, at that very moment might be with the Marqués enjoying her *own* vice.

§

Unladylike, that was what Carlotta called it. This lighting of weeds and breathing its vapors. But Alma, too, could be a lady, despite her low birth and a childhood spent under the wing of her father. Her skill with a short sword and her love of riding. Still, could she not be so?

The iron of her vest itched, even through linen as, heated now more from her fight with the ruffians than the warm night air, she crept unseen into the Marqués's palace. She could, perhaps. Still…

She thought of Carlotta: How *she* did comport herself, though, even in this Andalusia—this land of strangers. Her bobs and her curtsies, her hoops and her ruffles, her combs and mantilla, her breasts' ivory globes as, unblemished, they peeped from the top of her bodice. While Alma, laced tight, armor pressing her own breasts, her boots—*not* fine slippers—pinching her feet, struggled not to allow her sword to clank too loudly against its rings and harness as, squinting, she let her eyes adjust to darkness.

The palace was unlit, the most of it anyway, but also, luckily, nearly deserted. She traced what she thought were the steps a lord might take escorting a maiden to…

Alma blushed. Perhaps a bedchamber? But no—not Carlotta. In time, perhaps, if she did not come to her mistress's rescue but first, more likely, a gaming parlor. Which would be…where?

A lady might know. But a palace this size? She saw now in the far-off light of a low-burning hall sconce what looked like a scratch on the smooth marble floor. A scuff mark, perhaps?

Or dirt from a garden?

She looked beyond it. Another dark speck—then, far in the distance, a larger darkness. Struggling to retain her silence, she crept up to it and saw she had found Carlotta's mantilla.

She picked it up. Yes. She put it around her neck. But where she stood now was on a staircase, not leading up, but down. Into the wine cellar?

Doubling back, she took the candle out of the hall sconce and used it to light her way down the steps to a dust-laden corridor rimed with spider webs. Shrinking into herself she followed now-visible footprints to another staircase, this one also downward, but twisting and narrow.

She followed it also, her candle stub nearly burned down to her fingers, and entered into a wide, low-roofed chamber of tables and shelves, of books—*real* books with words written in Latin and in other tongues that used strange, angled letters—and stone bowls and glassware. A room not for gaming, but…

Stifling a cry, she dropped her candle—a wind had blown its hot wax on her sleeve where it soaked through the linen, burning the flesh beneath. Stooping, she tried to pick it up, but it rolled away from her. Guttering to darkness.

. . . an alchemist's chamber?

Squinting again, she made out a soft, red glow to her left, through the arch of a doorway. And now she *heard* something, too. Far in the distance, she heard a scuffling. Mice perhaps. Or the sounds of a struggle!

Then it *was* a bedchamber Sebano had led Carlotta to, alchemist's or not, perhaps on the promise of trying out a fine *vino de*

Jerez. Her father had warned her—there were men like that, and not just in the army. Noblemen, even, like Carlotta's father, were known to fall prey to the lusts of the flesh and, forgetting themselves…

She ran as silently as she could to the distant red glow. To the sounds, now, of panting and muffled curses. She burst now into an eight-sided chamber with dust at its edges—dust piled in heaps glowing yellow in torchlight—and in its center a pit and a chimney, above and below it, the pit edged with chalk lines describing a circle, superimposed with points and angles. A circle of magic.

A circle not as mere alchemists made, but…

El signo de brujo!

The words escaped from her—*the sign of a warlock!* Across the circle Carlotta answered —most unlike a lady—with screams and curses. Alma blinked twice, her eyes dazzled by brightness, and saw now the Marqués, his own eyes glowing, approaching her mistress while Carlotta spat on him, holding a dagger. Defending herself, yes, but…

Ah, he was handsome even now, Alma thought—handsome at least to one like Carlotta. His slick black hair, his epaulets showing the breadth of his shoulders, his waist trim and narrow. His thick mustachios curling just so as Carlotta, weakening, took one step, then two, back toward the circle.

Alma drew out her sword, letting it clatter as loud as it wished to. She circled the pit, avoiding its chalk lines that now, as she passed them, whirling around them, resembled a vast web. She thrust at Sebano, wide to the left, but making him dodge as she grabbed for Carlotta.

Sebano backed, warily, as she circled, Carlotta in one arm, her sword in the other, back toward the entrance to the chamber. "Now run!" she whispered.

Carlotta blinked. "What?"

"He's woven you in his spell," she whispered. "Or would have, had I not come to save you. I saw you faltering."

Carlotta nodded. "I had just hoped to regain my money—the money *we* live by. I'd lost at table…"

Alma glared at her. "I know," she said. She glanced across the pit to Sebano who, she could see, had opened another doorway behind him. She saw his hand reach inside.

"Hurry," she said. "Get out of the palace. I'll meet you outside where the horses are stabled. And take your knife with you—you may yet need it. Where did you get it?"

Carlotta blushed. She cast her eyes down toward the cleft in her bodice, then back up at Alma. "You have my mantilla?"

"Take it!" Alma said, thrusting it toward her. "Sebano approaches. Run now. Quickly!"

She shielded Carlotta as the other dashed through the doorway, then turned to the Marqués, her sword at the ready. She forced him again, back, a quarter…halfway…around the circle, but this time he opened his hand and blew in it, muttering as he did, blowing a powder into the pit's center.

Smoke rose up to fill the chamber—and then the Marqués was gone! As the smoke cleared, the far door Sebano had reached in slammed shut. The other, still open…

But now a shadow descended toward her from the chimney above the pit.

Alma stepped back. Above was a *spider*. Huge as a man, it hung from a golden thread, mandibles clashing, swinging slowly in ever widening circles toward her.

She thrust at it with her sword. Once. Again. And each time the sword's tip glanced off its shell as if it were plate steel. Taking a chance, she swung with the sword's edge as the creature continued downward.

She heard a loud laugh—then a sickening *snap!* as the blade of her sword first caught, then broke, on an outthrust ridge in the creature's chitin. Then the words of Sebano, still laughing, far in the distance. "If not for me the Doña Carlotta—then you…*doncella!*"

The final word stung. *Lady's maid? Serving girl? House drudge? Virgin?* Yes, Alma thought, the insult meant all of these. But at least a live virgin she would remain for now, as would her mistress if she could help it. She knew, from tales she had heard as a child, of the *things* warlocks liked to do with virgins.

But, as for spiders—the creature was now just above the pit rim and, even as she looked, its metal-sharp pincers were reaching to her. She threw her sword hilt at where she thought she saw eyes, trying to buy time. She needed to think. It hung between her and the one open door, swinging on its shimmering thread. Back and forth. Slow. Like a spell. Relaxing…

By instinct her left hand reached…

"*Yes!*" she shouted. She backed to the wall and dumped out her pouch in the glittering dust heaped at the room's corners. She grabbed up her flint. A *cigarrillo*. She struck the stone, once. Twice. A spark. An ember.

She puffed it to brightness.

"Ah. Now!" she shouted. Leaning as far as she dared, she thrust the burning weed-end forward, not at the spider, but just above it.

She smelled the stench as gold-flecked silk began to smolder, then pushed at the spider, again taking chances, but spinning it so its mandibles faced away. Over the pit edge.

She shouted again as the thread burned through, hearing the spider shriek in answer as scrabbling legs tried to grip the pit's rim, smearing the chalk lines. As, overbalanced, the creature fell, screaming, into darkness.

And golden rain fell from the chimneyed ceiling.

Kill a spider…

"Yes," she whispered. She reached to the corner, refilling her pouch as quickly as she could, then inched around the room's angled perimeter. Now it rained fire too, at first in the room's center, over the pit alone, but, even as she looked, the flames were spreading.

She reached the door and slipped quickly through it, then ran through the corridor, through the shelved and tabled chamber, not daring to pause but crashing through webs -- the webs of *ordinary* spiders—pursued by the heat from the pit-room behind her. She laughed high and loud as she plunged up the stairs, brushing the small creatures out of her hair, then up the second stairs to the main hallway.

And then out the doorway and into the garden as flame licked higher, increasing in brightness, still lighting her path as she looked for the stables. Where she found her mistress impatiently waiting.

§

She *hated* Carlotta!

Carlotta had laughed, a ladylike laugh, while Alma—*doncella*—had saddled their horses. "So once again you have rescued my virtue," Carlotta had said—the Doña still did not know what the Marqués *was*. "But can you always? Especially now when we have no money?"

Carlotta had giggled, and wrapped her mantilla around her shoulders as, mounting, they looked back once more toward the palace, now all but engulfed in a storm of fire, then turned their horses onto the road away from Seville to the port of Málaga. "And where is your sword?" she asked. "Alma, you're so careless. Why did you leave it? As if gold were picked from trees!"

Alma had shrugged as she reached to her pouch, but she did not answer. She thought about dust, as well as her mistress's disapproval. The world was but dust, the philosophers said. The dust of the high plain. The dust of a windstorm. The dust of a lady's corpse long in its tomb. But she and the lady were still quite alive -- and there was another dust as well.

She shook her head, sighing. She would have to beg the Doña to purchase her more of the *cigarrillos*, she having emptied her pouch's contents back in the palace to make more room in it. Not to mention to buy a new sword too.

But not a new knife—or a new mantilla. She thought of the knife, where her mistress had hidden it.

She loved Carlotta.

31

But daughters of *grandees*, she knew, loved the yellow dust that glittered so when she had stuffed her pouch with it nearly to bursting, back in the cellar of Sebano's palace. And sighing once more as they rode through the darkness, she handed it over.

A Half-Dime Adventure
Don Webb

I'd found me a pan with no holes in it. I'd already plucked the chicken. I washed the pan in the creek scouring it out with sand. I made a little fire and hotted up the pan. I put pieces of the chicken in. Sizzle, sizzle. Pour in a little water. I would make a mulligan that the yeggs—a yegg is a professional criminal—and the bindle stiffs would remember til their dying days. They'd cough out pieces of their lungs in cold hobo jungles and say, "That was fine. That was sure some mulligan Tim Wilson cooked us the night before we stole the circus train. That was the best mulligan I had in my life."

"You can smell that chicken for a mile." It was Half Face Joe. A railroad cop pushed him off a speeding train deep in the Yukon. He fell into the rocks doing forty. He left half of his face there. He even has a hole on the ugly ruin of his head which you can stick your finger in and feel his brains. He charges a quarter for this entertainment. I only had the stomach to do it once and it was cold in there. Cold like the Yukon snows. I told Half Face he'd better hope for Heaven because his brains would melt in the other place. He carried a sack of vegetables.

"You buy those things, Half Face?"

"I jes stuck my head in the store and they gimme those things."

We sorted out the rotted from the clean and I cut up the clean. Carrots. Turnips. Celery. Tomatoes. This will be a superior mulligan. Half Face carried the rotten things off. I suspect he ate 'em. He's none too cleanly. It was boiling a little too hard and I tossed a little dirt on the fire.

Moses Donelly walked up. He kept body and soul together by DDing. Being a Deaf and Dumb man. He'd go to a pharmacy and buy some lavender cologne, then he'd soak several envelopes with it. Then he'd go door to door with a card, "I am Deaf and Dumb from birth. I need money to go to my cousin's funeral in Laramie. Would you buy a packet of lavender from me?" Sometimes he'd run into a real dummy who made with the hands. Moses would sign back. 'Course Moses' signs were pure bunkem. The dummy would know it but everybody would think, "There's two dummies talkin' to one another. Ain't it a miracle? God's in His Heaven and everybody's happy."

Moses parted the grass in front of him and soon was standing by my mulligan.

"It'll be dark soon and this jungle will be full. I want to be sure you get this." He pulled out a Dr. White's four-bit mickey. I put it in my shirt pocket.

"Moses Donelly, you are a gentleman."

"I remember when you sprung me from the railroad jail in 'Frisco. If I can ever help you. Let me know. I'm your man."

"You can help me now by filling this coffee can with water and then by setting beside me for a spell."

Moses was back in a shake of a cow's tail. I poured the water into my mulligan. Poured and stirred. Poured and stirred.

Moses undid his bindle and handed me a can of pepper. I peppered my mulligan just so. There were other fires being lit in the jungle.

"Tim Wilson, you reckon we'll steal that circus?"

"I reckon we'll try. Some of us may get killed but that's the same as any day. Any day you wake up you may get killed. These jungles are full of ghosts."

Just as I said that a cool breeze began to blow through the jungle as though the dead hoboes and yeggs were raising to my call, which is just as well. I'd rather have ten hobo ghosts with me than one live citizen. Maybe some of those ghosts would take the bullets for us tonight. They don't stand nothing to lose, if you think about it.

Parsimonious Pete was brewing coffee. It would be weak coffee brewed from grounds that had already had three chances to swim. Nobody needed money as bad as Parsimonious. If he couldn't talk you out of it, it would just sort of gravitate to him. I once saw him pick up a dime by just touching it with his elbow. He was magnetic for silver. He'd probably talk some greenhorn into buying his coffee tonight. If anybody ever found out where he hid his money they'd crack his ugly mug. It'd be easier to find out what grows on the dark side of the moon.

Someone got a pot to boil clothes and all the bindle stiffs were gathering around. Moses took my spare outfit down. A fight started about then. One of the brass peddlers, a seller of "gold" jewelry, turned out to be lousy. Dead lice roiled in the laundry pot. I could hear some of the boys cursing Brass Bill. The curses would lead to shoves, shoves to a fight, and a fight to somebody getting killed. That would queer the whole business. All the hoboes would leave the jungle as soon as somebody got killed (even if they just got drunk and fell in the fire). I hoped Preachin' Ivy would show up. This whole caper was his idea and he could settle a crowd the way an egg can settle coffee grounds.

Moses came back with my clothes. "They're raisin' a fight. I didn't want to put these in the pot because someone's sure to turn the pot over."

Sure enough, just as he said those words there was a great whoosh of steam. Somebody pushed Brass Bill down in the mud and embers. He screamed as he was getting scalded so somebody tapped his head with a brick. I reckoned he was done for because I heard them dividing up his loot—even his 99¢ a dozen brass rings that he dropped for a dollar or more. He shouldn't have come into the jungle lousy.

"You know, Tim Wilson, it's a mean world."

"Compared to what, Moses? Compared to what?"

Night came and about half the camp left on account of Brass Bill. Ivy still hadn't showed. He was supposed to be in town getting rods. If he didn't come in an hour or so we'd head out figuring the town bulls had jailed him. I poured my mulligan into cups and cans and everybody agreed that it was the best mulligan anybody had had for quite some time. Some of the boys were pulling out their mickeys, but I didn't drink none because I knew Ivy wouldn't hand out any rods to drunk men.

A stool pigeon moon came up. Half Face suggested we bury Brass Bill or at least drag him away from the jungle. We got up a burial party and they drug him off to cover him with leaves.

"Where the hell is everybody?" Preachin' Ivy carried a crate under his right arm. He walked up to the fire and helped himself to my mulligan. "Ain't nobody here."

"Brass Bill got himself killed and everybody lit out."

"How many are left?"

"Ten counting you and me."

Ivy thought awhile. "We can still have a damn good time with ten men. We'll just take the last eight cars."

He opened his case. He gave a gun to Moses and me, one to Parsimonious Pete and Half Face and kept one for himself.

"I bought these from Judge Cooley so ditch 'em if you get caught. Judge Cooley told me he'd hang anybody who showed up with his guns."

The burial party made its way back singing a low, mournful tune. As soon as they saw Ivy they shut up. Ivy's thinking all the time—there's a fire inside his brain and sometimes you can see that fire through his pupils. Stops a man to see that fire 'cause he always realizes he's in the presence of a man who is a little quicker than he is.

"The train will be along in two hours. Formeter's Circus will be in the last sixteen cars. We'll take the last eight. When the train starts up the big grade it'll slow down to two, three miles per hour. Parsimonious and Half Face will take the eighth car and unhook it. The cars will start rolling backwards. Everybody else will be on their cars by then. Our mulligan-maker and Moses will take the caboose. The railroad bull will be there with the circus strongman. Take 'em out. I'll take the fourth car. The money box. I'll cut up the payroll ten ways. The cars will roll for twenty miles. We'll get the circus to put on a little show for us—then we'll let the cats loose as a little gift for John Law—then we'll ride off in ten separate directions on the horses the circus has so kindly provided for us. By the time they've sent a train to pick up the uncoupled cars we'll be forty miles away. Boys, we'll go down in history."

There was some questions and some answers. Everybody speculated on what we might find. One man had seen a hootchy-kootchy dancer in a circus at St. Louis. He picked up a rag and danced round the fire to show us what kind of gyrations to expect. Another had seen a talking dog.

Stumps Magee asked that if we came across a talking dog we should give it to him as a talking dog would be a great aid in his begging. We took a vote. A talking dog for Stumps.

A third man had had his fortune told. A gypsy woman had dealt the cards. You will travel the country whole and not die until very old.

Parsimonious Pete said, "You mean they'll be gypsies on this train? I don't like it. Gypsies can hex you bad."

"Oh, I've got something stronger than gypsy curses," said the man who just told the story of his fortune, and he pulled from his vest pocket a wooden pig about two inches in length. "I've got this pig and when I'm getting shot at I say, 'Little pig, little pig don't let me get shot at 'cause if they get me who's gonna take care of you?' or, if I'm in court I say, 'Little pig, little pig don't let me go to jail 'cause if I go to jail you'll go to jail, too.'"

"Where'd you get the little pig?" Ivy asked.

"I found him in the hands of a dead hobo. He was the oldest 'bo I ever saw, so I figure he's got to be lucky."

The man polished the pig and returned it to his pocket. I could see the fire in Ivy's eyes. He was thinking about that little pig.

Half Face Joe doused the fire. It was time to take our positions. As we walked to Dead Man's Hill, I thought I saw Half Face open his four-bit mickey and tip it into the hole in his head. I swore that if I get out of this caper, I would stay among men that were fully alive.

We crouched behind bushes and trees. They were running two engines on the train, which was one too short for the grade. Most of the train was still on the valley floor when the engines labored past. Sixty cars would have to pass before the circus would've begun to pass. Moses was coughing heavy in the coal smoke.

He was still coughing when our time came. The train was going maybe four miles an hour—still strong enough to knock your wind out if you catch wrong. We all sprang out. Moses came from one side and I from the other. I knew they could hear him coughing so I pushed him ahead of me into the caboose. The railroad bull was up and firing. He sent two slugs into Moses and Moses wounded him in the shoulder. The strongman tried to squeeze himself between a side bench and the ceiling. Half Face and Parsimonious had uncoupled the car because suddenly we began rolling backwards. Moses and the bull went down. I put a bullet in the bull's neck and then I plugged the strongman in the chest—just above a leopard spot. I never saw a man so surprised to die. He stepped off the bench and raised his arms as though to yawn and then he fell on the card table busting it to flinders.

I checked out Moses. He was dead. I heard a shot from up the train.

We were gaining momentum. Moon-silvered trees blurred by. I went through Moses' pockets. Two five-dollar gold pieces and some silver. The strongman didn't have anything but a bar of some soft metal doctored up to look like steel. It was easy to twist around. I pocketed it—figured I could win a few bets. The guard had three paper dollars and a brass token for a drink at Sally O'Mara's in Denver.

I tossed the bodies of the guard and the strongman off the train. Then, I realized that I'd tossed out the guard's gun, as well. Your own dumbness always trips you up. We were in the valley now all scrub oak and tall grass. The train rolled on at about twenty per and we were beginning to slow. I lay Moses out on a bench. His eyes jerked open and I thought he might be alive so I talked with him a spell.

"Sorry that cough killed you. A cough's a terrible thing. My mother died of a cough. She kept coughin' and coughin' and my dad got her some capsules. Four grains quinine and one sixth a grain morphine. To be taken at bedtime. These didn't do a damn bit of good. She kept us up all night. Cough, cough, cough. Me just thirteen and going to read my Caesar every day. *Omnia Gallis est divisa in partes tres.* And Dad a-laboring in his pharmacy. We just couldn't take it. The sleeplessness. Know what I mean?"

Moses nodded or maybe the train just jiggled his corpse. I started to break off the legs of the card table. I'd get some linen from the back of the 'boose and soak it with coal oil. We'd need torches when we stopped.

"Poppa and I wore pretty thin. Everybody said that whole Wilson family weren't nothing but a pack of ghosts—no offense Moses—so Poppa compounded a new remedy. Five and one sixth grains of morphine. No quinine. Stopped Mother's cough right away. Same way sixty grain of lead stopped yours. If you see Mother, tell her that I love her."

The train was down to two-three miles an hour. Parsimonious applied the hand brakes on the first car. Its wheels shot sparks into the frosty grass. Then the second threw his brakes, then the third, and so on up to me. The train shuddered to a stop. The air smelled of hot iron. An elephant trumpeted. I began lighting my torches.

Preachin' Ivy jumped off and shot his revolver in the air.

"I don't want nobody moving excepting my men. If anybody sticks his head out of a car. I'll blow it all the way to Dead Man's Hill."

I jumped off the caboose carrying all four torches blazing together. I handed one to the wooden pig man, who stood between the second and third cars, one to Ivy, one to the hootchy-kootch man, and one to Half Face.

"Moses didn't make it to the promised land."

"Well, there's a little more for us. We'll have a moment of silence for Moses."

The elephant ruined the moment of silence by trumpeting again.

"Open up that damn car. Let's see that elephant. Maybe we can cut its tusks off for ivory."

The wooden pig man opened the ride door of the tall boxcar. Loose straw drifted out along with the smell of a hundred barnyards. Someone had already tusked the elephant. The elephant couldn't stand up all the way and sort of crawled forward. His big yellow eyes looked scared. He was looking for someone. It lurched out of the boxcar with a half-liquid motion. The pig man wasn't quick enough. The elephant's front foot smashed the pig man into the frozen ground. This really scared the elephant. He trotted a few yards away from the boxcar. Ivy shot the elephant's rear. It bellowed and went crashing off into the scrub oak.

"Damn murderin' elephant."

The pig man was a breathing bloody mess. There would be no getting up for him—no way to separate the flesh and the earth. Ivy walked over to him. The pig man nodded and Ivy let him have it through the heart. Then Ivy bent down and pulled the wooden pig from the dead man's vest and put it in his own shirt pocket. The elephant bellowed again.

"Can't ever have too much luck," Ivy said. "Let's open the other cars one by one and see what we've got."

"Let's divide the coin first," said Parsimonious Pete.

"Eight ways comes to seventy-five dollars apiece." Ivy started laying the gold and paper in neat piles. Counting out loud where everybody could see. Then we went forward one by one and claimed our share.

The first two cars held the horses. Half Face opened 'em up and peeked inside. Tack was there but the saddles must've been in the main train.

One of the bindle stiffs opened the third car. Eight chimpanzees came stirring out. Parsimonious started shooting, but

Ivy yelled at him to stop. Couldn't he see that they were doing no harm? The chimps made a four-three-one pyramid. Then they leapt off and tumbled and scrambled over the cars. One of them stole Parsimonious Pete's cap and was shot for his trouble. At the sound of renewed gunfire all the chimps jumped off the train and into the bushes. They vanished almost instantly but we heard their chatter as long as we were there.

Half Face went into the chimp car. There were eight little desks with eight little typewriters. Each of the chimps was turning out a five-cent novel. *Frank Reade and his Steam Man of the Plains, Frank Reade and his Steam Horse, Frank Reade and his Steam Team, Frank Reade Jr. and his Steam Wonder, Frank Reade Jr. and his Electric Boat, Frank Reade Jr. and his Wonderful Airship, Frank Reade Jr. and his Electric Velocipede.* In stacks of crates along one side was the whole of the Half-Dime Library. Nowhere was indication that the hard-working apes had received a penny for their labor. In fact, it wasn't clear to us whether the chimpanzees were the authors of these works or were merely typing them up from memory as a sort of entertainment. Parsimonious felt badly about shooting one as all yeggs and hoboes have a soft spot for literary men. Ivy told him not to take it so hard. It was a well-known fact that Mr. Edison was working on a device to produce half-dime novels automatically. Ivy had been to Menlo Park and had not only told us of the coming light bulb, but had stolen one to show us. If he could have only stolen a method of electrifying it—it would have been quite the novelty.

Parsimonious left the monkey car. He was outside, bawling his head off and looking for coin in the pig man's pockets.

The next car had held the lucre. Now the only thing of interest was a dead bearded lady and her pearl-handled six-shooter. The hootchy-kootch man asked Ivy if he could have the gun and Ivy said sure, why not? One of the other men said it must've been hard to shoot a woman and Ivy looked at him. I wouldn't've wanted to be on the receiving end of that look. It was a special Ivy look and there was death in it. Ivy said, "If it's got a beard it ain't a woman."

I said, "Ivy, we've made real history. Even the James brothers never stole the train."

Ivy smiled and we all breathed easier. The moon was going down. Bloating near the horizon.

The next car had held the elephant. We collected Parsimonious, all covered in blood and tears. Half Face opened the sixth car. It held a tank and three cages. We each walked through the length of the car—passing the torches backwards so each man got a good look. It was early morning now and much colder so our breath and the breath of the animals steamed considerably. After this caper we would each ride off in different directions, but I knew in a few weeks we'd all be heading south.

In the tank: A half-man/half-fish swam in stagnant green water. It looked as though someone had hollowed out a thirty-pound albino catfish and stuffed a baby in it. The arms and legs were well-formed— just like a baby's—except covered in scales, each about the size of a dime. The head was large but fishlike. Its silver eyes were scaled over. I think it was blind, but it sensed our passage with its whiskers. Its little mouth worked. O. O. O.

In the first cage to the left: A two-headed black rooster beat its wings at us. It looked just like the chicken that I'd cut up for my mulligan (save for it's having two heads). The left head had been fighting the right head. It had pecked out the closer of the right head's eyes. I think we all had to fight to keep our mulligan down—except for Half Face. He was the last one through. He couldn't stand to see this creature with two faces, when he had one half of one. He opened the cage and grabbed the rooster. He wrung both its necks in contrary directions, then he threw the bird out in the cold. It ran around in the frost with both heads trailing.

In the cage to the right: A rose bush bloomed. Each blossom was perfect and lime-green. The hootchy-kootch man reached into the cage to pluck a rose for his lapel. Two branches swished forward raking his hand with thorns. He gave a squawk and pulled his hand back. The branches resumed their normal position. Blood dripped down into the terra cotta pot which housed the rose—enriching its soil.

In the second cage on the left: Only musky straw—a sexy-musky smell. Each man shuddered as they wondered what had been here—what kind of ghost the cage held. We were glad for the cold outside air.

We all regrouped outside. There was one unexplored car. We heard a train whistle from far away. That would be the train backing down Dead Man's Hill looking for its lost cars. More-n-likely it also meant John Law.

"Time to mount up, boys," said Ivy.

"Not me, boss," I said. "I'm going to see what's in that last car."

The train whistled again and the elephant trumpeted as though calling to its mate.

"Give me your gun then. I told Judge Cooley that I wouldn't let any of his guns fall into lawman's hands."

I hated to be without the gun, but I knew Ivy would take it if I didn't give it to him.

"Here."

"It's your own funeral, Tim Wilson."

The boys were mounting up—heading off in the direction Ivy pointed. I opened the last car. There was a long glass case in the middle of the car. In the case still as death lay a young red-haired woman. If it was a mannequin it was the most perfect mannequin I'd ever seen. She was dressed as a bride. She held a bridal bouquet of silk flowers—roses and daisies. A small plaque on the side of the case read, "The Amazing Sleeping Beauty. Miss Daisy Miller fell into a hypnotic trance in 1893 while watching a traveling mesmerist's act. Her parents have taken her to the most expensive doctors in Europe and America to no avail. What does this sleeping girl dream of? What sustains her in her five-year sleep? Will she ever awaken?"

I opened the case. I felt her cheek; to my surprise it was warm. I bent over and listened. I couldn't hear any breathing. I had to get all the details. I could live off this story the rest of my life.

I took a long pull on my four-bit mickey to sweeten my mouth.
I kissed her. Full on the mouth.

Hell, what would you do?

She smiled a little, but she didn't awaken. I heard the train whistle—much closer this time. I left Miss Daisy Miller and ran to the horse cars. The horses were all gone, but there was a zebra gelding left. I put a bit in its mouth.

We rode east toward the rising sun.

Afertere's Eyes
Marilyn "Mattie" Brahen

Carina was dressed before him, and as he finished, pulling on his shirt, she drew the ring off her right forefinger and handed it to Alowyn.

He held it gingerly, examining it in the full moonlight. Its two emerald stones sparkled strangely. A golden glint, like a pupil, seemed to flame within each stone's center.

"Is it magical?"

"My great-grandmother named it Afertere's Eyes. When it's passed on to someone you love, it grants each new owner an honorable wish."

"And when you received it? What did you wish?"

"I wished—" she started, her cheeks dimpling,

"—for true love!" She laughed, pouncing on him, seeking his lips with boisterous determination.

He fended her off, holding the ring aloft. "Stop! You'll make me drop it!"

She sat up, smoothing her skirt around her raised knees. "You're always so serious. I would have found it, had you dropped it."

"Are your eyes that keen at night?" He reached for her and pulled her down to complete the kiss he had thwarted. They broke apart and sat up, Alowyn's arm around her.

Alowyn stared at the dark-haired girl he had deserted his own family for. He studied the ring.

"My betrothal gift to you," she said. "To you who left your home and kin to learn the music of the Wandering Folk and to become my husband."

"How does this magic work?"

Carina paused, quietly meeting his gaze. Tangles of damp hair fell heavily across her eye. "It must be worn before you can make your wish upon it. Worn on the right forefinger, which leads to the heart."

He smiled at her tutorial tone. "And if it doesn't fit that finger?"

"Then, it isn't meant for you, and you have to give it back."

Alowyn slid the ring along his right forefinger. It passed the knuckle easily, fitting perfectly. Carina sighed her relief. "Now shut your eyes and make your wish, asking that Afertere grant it."

"Out loud?"

"It doesn't matter…but I would like to hear it."

Alowyn closed his eyes, concentrating, pale brows furrowing. "I wish to become the greatest musician, so great, the gods themselves will covet my music. May Afertere grant my wish." He lifted his eyelids, and laughed, delighted with her gift. "Have I asked for too much?"

Carina stared back, shivering in the cooling night air. "I don't know. We'll have to wait and see. No one has ever wished for such a thing before."

§

The Chieftain of the Wandering Folk tied thongs of leather about their wrists, declared them mated, and welcomed Alowyn into the tribe through marriage.

Wine flowed lavishly as the Folk toasted the new bride and groom, then laughing banter and fine belches filled the early evening as they gathered round tables laid out with the wedding feast of cheese, bread loaves, slabs of roasted meat, and fruit. Night came on. They lit torches and lanterns, and passed around tankards of warm ale to the adults, and cups of sweet cider to the youngsters.

Alowyn took his flute and drew it to his lips. A piping melody emerged, as sweet as a bird's song in the dawn. The Wandering Folk joined in. Soon the sounds of guitar and fiddle, tambourine and drum swelled into the night air. What began as a light refrain grew rapidly into a quick tempo jig. Dancers filled the meadow clearing where the Folk had camped and now celebrated. Their feet stepped in lightning rhythm. Their faces flushed with sweat and delight. Swirling and twirling fetchingly was Carina. The skirt of her silken green wedding dress danced upon the air around her legs, showing off the shapely, sturdy contours beneath the fabric.

The spirited music faded to an end, and tapping, kicking, leaping feet ebbed to stillness as exhausted dancers sat or sprawled on the damp grass. As Alowyn tuned his mandolin, a hush fell over the camp, and he began to sing a haunting madrigal of love gone awry.

Carina tucked her legs beneath her skirt, leaning on one hand on the grass, listening. Alowyn bent over his mandolin, a waterfall of sparkling notes cascading from its strings, his voice more resonant and richly controlled than it had ever been before.

The last verse Alowyn sang drifted off into the night wind, poignant and sad, and his fingers plucked an exquisite finale from the mandolin. The momentary quiet was quickly replaced by fervent prolonged applause. High praise from the Wandering Folk, famous across the entire continent for their own music and dancing.

The deep baritone of Sofar, Carina's father, interrupted the enthusiastic clapping and noisy hooting approval. "Your performance skill seems to have increased at least threefold." He sat near the central fire pit, his tapestried robe, threaded with gold and silver, glimmering in its light.

His eyes spied the gleam of the emerald ring on Alowyn's right forefinger, but he said nothing further, simply glancing at his daughter with raised brows.

"Only enhanced by thoughts of love and other skills," Alowyn answered with a sly wink. A gale of ribald laughter erupted among the Folk. Sofar smiled, but didn't join in.

§

Within one year, Alowyn's extraordinary performances, sought by the richest nobles, brought him widespread acclaim. Gold and favors were liberally bestowed upon him. Gold filled the pockets and purses of the Wandering Folk as well, as they accompanied him both in travels and instrumentally, from castle to castle, from stronghold to stronghold. Carina often danced to the beautiful music Alowyn coaxed from a variety of instruments, his abilities increasing with each cycle of the moon. He need only be shown an instrument and, given an hour, played it fluently. His expertise now extended beyond flute and mandolin, to harp, guitar, fiddle, and harmonium.

But if Carina's fine looks and captivating fluid dancing were the wick to Alowyn's flame, she went unnoticed in the comparison. The High King Yuoric soon ordered Alowyn to journey to Drissandere, to reside at court, and to study and perform with the royal musicians.

Privately, the message-bearer confided to Alowyn that only Carina could accompany him to the High Court. The Wandering Folk took the news with snide humor. They, too, had an aversion to the simpering manners of royalty. Good-naturedly, they helped Carina and Alowyn prepare supplies for their five-day journey, and the Chieftain himself gifted them with two strong mares to carry them to Drissandere.

Once at court, Carina found herself surrounded by finely-dressed ladies who advised her insistently on style and etiquette.

She soon resembled them in dress and manner, fitting in outwardly. But in her heart, she missed the wide spaces, the travels, and the unencumbered freedom of the Wandering Folk.

Alowyn, fawned and fussed over, settled in eagerly, spending many hours with the court musicians, discussing theory, learning from them, and performing with them.

But whatever he was taught, he soon exceeded those who taught him. Gossip flitted around Drissandere: Alowyn was either genius or bewitched, perhaps both. Such talk broadened his mystique and popularity, fueling his creative ego. He began to compose original music, works born of fiery visions that assaulted his brain and left him no peace until they were written down in musical script, a skill King Yuoric's court composer had instructed him in.

A date and time were set for him to perform his brilliant work before the court. In the throne room, they erected a second dais to accommodate Alowyn and a small quintet of accompanying musicians.

Finely-attired lords and ladies took their seats expectantly, and Alowyn, seated beside a golden harp, motioned the other musicians to begin.

His fingers plied the harp strings, and an achingly exquisite melody arose. Behind him, flute and harmonium lent subtle accents to his sure handiwork. The audience sighed as the music caressed their ears and souls, and Carina sat in the front row, tears flowing from her eyes.

Then, chaos erupted. Five men and four women fell heavily from their chairs in the audience, fainting. Servants carried them away. A muted buzz of consternation filled the throne room, quieting as the program resumed, undisturbed to the final note played.

It was later discovered that all nine fainters suffered from long-standing physical malaises, and that all nine were healed completely by week's end. Alowyn's music, the court whispered, was the cure.

The High King Yuoric brought Alowyn before him. "The nobles are arguing whether your music stems from divine or demonic influences," Yuoric, with a gleam in his royal eyes, confided. "I do not care myself, as long as the effect it has is for the good!"

Alowyn replied with quiet earnestness, "It is the gods' influence, my liege."

Yuoric smiled. "Perhaps. I like a good tonic as well as the next man. You might, however, in your future compositions, create music a bit less stimulating?"

"As best I can, my liege," Alowyn promised.

But at his next performance, nearly half the audience fell down in religious ecstasies, calling out the names of gods, some even taking on the persona of a god or goddess, singing praise for Alowyn's music in unnatural voices before losing consciousness. Alowyn played on as if nothing untoward was happening, even when his accompanists set aside their instruments in confusion and terror.

Upon awakening, none of the afflicted remembered their words or movements while entranced. Nor did any healing or other beneficial effect follow their entrancement.

King Yuoric, unaffected by the music, called for his High Priest, Maelric.

Maelric touched Alowyn's chest and forehead simultaneously, chanting a long string of indecipherable words, and rocking back and forth with his eyes raised to the heavens. He slowly steadied himself, staring with both horror and adoration at Alowyn.

"He is beloved of the gods!" Maelric shouted, releasing Alowyn. "And most favored by Afertere, the goddess of music and dance, for through his music, he honors her."

Carina, standing nearby, stared down at the golden ring Alowyn wore, its twin emerald stones, and the strange golden mote within each.

Maelric took sudden notice of her. "It's said that the Wandering Folk are favored by the gods. While composer Alowyn is not of their blood, his lady is. Have you bewitched him, my lady? Perhaps called upon Afertere to bless him?"

"No...no!" Carina stammered.

"Then you must relinquish him," Maelric said in a tone that held no sympathy for her fears or the suffering she felt. "He no longer belongs to you. Afertere is the favorite of Nekeras, the father of the gods, who has decreed that any mortal she covets is beholden to her until released by death. Alowyn will be anointed and cared for by my priesthood, as one cherished by the gods. Afertere has claimed him."

"But he is my husband!"

"No longer," Maelric repeated. "Would you defy Afertere?"

Carina turned beseechingly to Alowyn. Her heart chilled, seeing what remained of him. His eyes gazed into her own without feeling, and then turned upward into their sockets, showing empty white. A frightening golden aura shone like dust motes around the edges of his open lids.

King Yuoric laid a gentle hand on her shoulder. "My heart goes out to you, my lady. You are most welcome to remain here at court, under my protection, if you wish. But neither you or I can fight the will of the gods."

Carina gripped the unmoving Alowyn's right hand. "This is my betrothal ring to him," she explained. "I would have it back."

She tugged and pulled, but the ring would not slide free.

"It is not meant to be," Maelric told her.

"Perhaps it is meant to stay with him," Yuoric said soothingly, "that a part of you will stay with him as well."

"Alowyn!!" Carina cried out, as if her shriek could pierce the veil over his heart. But he neither heard nor responded, as Maelric grasped his arm and led him without resistance from the throne room.

§

Carina refused Yuoric's offer. He provided funds and an escort and returned her to her people. Her solitary arrival went unquestioned, for the Wandering Folk have long ears and glib tongues. Over tankards of ale, Sofar had discussed Carina's transfer of Afertere's Eyes to Alowyn, had discussed his fears concerning Alowyn's wish upon it. As events now played themselves out, Sofar's fears proved well-founded.

Further word came that Maelric's priests had built a temple for Alowyn, where supplicants could hear his strange musical renderings and pray to Afertere, yet no man nor woman among the Wandering Folk ever advised Carina to abandon her loyalty to her lost husband. The way of the Folk was to mate for life.

In their travels, the Folk ofttimes passed near the Temple of Afertere where Alowyn resided, meeting with pilgrims coming and going from the shrine, seeking cures or craving the ecstasies Alowyn's performances often brought. Many reported that his music frightened them—discordant and powerful, seeming to split their very souls open and fill them with its sound. "It's meant for the gods' ears, I suppose," one pilgrim told them, "but no matter. When I woke from my daze, my leg no longer pained me and could bear my weight!"

When they passed closely enough, Carina traveled to the temple to visit Alowyn. Sometimes his gaze settled on her and he seemed to know her. Once, he smiled, then sighed. Several times, he wept. But then his music called. His eyes would cloud over; recognition fled like a small bird that would not be contained, even by a warm, imploring, outstretched hand. He would sit by the harp, or grasp the mandolin, or raise a flute to his lips, his sightless eyes upon the statues of Afertere and the other gods that stood within the temple, and he would play.

And so Carina would leave him, her heart still burdened, but glad to have seen him and shared what little communion they could.

Ten years passed. Her faithfulness both a blessing and a curse, she had aged, no longer strong, but her frailty held an aura of quiet patient beauty about it. A great weariness wore her down, and a desire to be with and commune with Alowyn, in whatever way she could, grew within her.

The Wandering Folk were traveling in the opposite direction, and so she saddled a horse one night and rode alone towards Drissandere.

She reached the Temple of Afertere as the sun rose, its rays bathing the marble-columned entrance. Carina stepped into the dark interior, empty save for a lone figure hunched over a harp, asleep against its frame.

She stared sorrowfully at the man, now aged and disheveled, whom she had never ceased to love. His hair, once blonde and shimmering in rich waves, was thin and white, matted and filthy upon his head, his clothes, soiled remnants of finery ill-cared for.

"Alowyn," she whispered.

He stirred, his head lifting. "Carina?"

He had spoken her name!

"Yes! It's me! Do you remember me, Alowyn?"

"Long ago, in a dream I had nearly forgotten."

"I have never abandoned the love I have for you," she said simply, glad again to share her heartmost feeling.

"I cannot remove the ring," he said dully, "nor the wish I made upon it."

"Then, play for me. I cannot blame Afertere for loving you," she answered, glad for the shadows that hid her tears, "You are worthy of the love of a goddess. Play for me and let me pray to Afertere."

Even in the dusky chamber, she saw joy suffuse his face. With trembling hands, he grasped the harp. Music swelled from its strings. Major chords mixed with minor melodies. Rhythms switched—fast, moderate, slow as a dirge. Notes clashed, stood alone, and harmonized with other notes. Somehow, the seemingly incongruous composition melded together, built upon itself, and fit itself into place. From beginning to middle to end, it carried the thundering strength and the airy laughter of the gods conjoined.

Alowyn let his hands fall from the harp.

Carina, eyes still shut, still upon her knees, head bent in supplication, finished her prayer to Afertere. She lifted her head. "Your finest work," she said, through tears of amazement, for she had understood, and the work was beautiful.

"What did you pray for?" he asked.

"It doesn't matter. A prayer never granted."

He stepped slowly over to her and took her hand in his ringed right hand, bringing it to his lips and kissing it. "Forgive me," he said, and his arms went around her, drawing her close. "I have never forgotten. Deep within, you are remembered and cherished. But the visions of the gods come upon me and mask all memory. It is the price I pay for the wish."

Against his embrace, Carina felt sharp despair sting the final remnant of her hope. "Afertere," she called out, "why have you never heard my prayer? You are the patron goddess of dance and of music. Will you never end our pain? I shall never dance as wondrously as you, nor shall Alowyn sing or perform as wonderfully as you. But can you not restore us in some way that Alowyn and I might sing and dance together once more, and both of us pay tribute to you?"

Silence and darkness.

She pulled away from Alowyn's arms. "I dare not return to you again," she said. "Each parting becomes more painful. Good-bye, my Alowyn. Remember me, as I shall you."

She walked woodenly towards the portico.

"Afertere!" Alowyn shrieked into the darkness. "I beseech you! Is there not a way in which we both may glorify you!?"

A light grew, warm and golden, casting shadows, filling the chamber with inhuman radiance. Carina turned back and stared at the stately female figure from which the radiance emanated. The goddess—for it could be no other—stood before the marble statue cast in her likeness, a cold and drab icon compared to her brilliance. The delicate drapery of her gown seemed spun from stars, her hair the color of the sun at midday. And her eyes! Green as meadow grass with glimmers of molten gold at their core. Her lips were pale as she spoke, her voice held the timbre of a different world, a different time. "There is a way," Afertere said. "A way in which Alowyn can create a different eternal music, and you can dance an eternal dance. But you must sacrifice the forms in which you now clothe your souls." The goddess paused and regarded Carina knowingly, almost, it seemed for a second, wryly. "Will you accept both sacrifice and transformation?"

Carina knelt before Afertere, eyes shut, hands clasped forward. "I accept!"

She felt a hand, long, thin, and warm, upon her shoulder, and knew it was Alowyn's.

"Wait," he said, and to Afertere, "Is there no other way?"

The goddess turned to him. Her eyes seemed to soften with empathy. "How can there be? You have been touched by the gods; your wife has borne heroic suffering for the sake of the gods' will. Were I to restore you to your mortal lives, they would be tainted by the past and bitter, walking among mortals, outcast, neither belonging with them nor any more with the gods."

"Will we know one another, Carina and I?" Alowyn's hand clasped Carina's. A small tug, and she rose to her feet beside him.

"Yes," Afertere replied. "You shall know one another intimately."

"Then, I accept, also, and give you my trust and faith."

Alowyn drew Carina to him for one last mortal kiss. They drank hungrily of each other, their long-parched thirst finally sated.

As they embraced, their skin began to tingle, dissolving without pain. For both, their fleshy covering seemed replaced by something cool and soothing. But, for Alowyn, the coolness was fluid and in motion. For Carina, the coolness was light, nearly without substance, yet it, too, had direction and motion, as her essence danced within it.

§

The lovers vanish from the story at the end. But those of us with sight and ears to sense hidden magic might chance upon the signs and recognize them.

Alowyn became a wide brook running through a forest that still shades the land where Drissandere once rose in all its finery. The brook still sings upon the stones and the water currents, and beasts and birds of the forest come and lend their music to its own. Carina is the wind that still dances through the trees and stirs the leaves of that forest.

They are still there, and shall remain there, forever.

Yes, sit beside the brook within the forest that once bordered lost Drissandere. Listen. The branches of the trees along its bank may start to weave, their leaves swirling as the wind leaps and dances to the singing of the brook.

The Well
Gregory L. Norris

*C**raig woke to an absence of sound, the silence telegraphing* that, true to their threat, the power company had turned off the juice. In the terrible moment that followed, he realized the obituary was official. This was the first of his last days on the Vel Kief family farm. The end.

He heated water in a pan on the gas stove, poured it through fresh grounds, and created something like coffee. Close enough, he thought while drinking the bitter brew. On this morning, beggars were schooled about choosing, and coffee was a luxury. He showered, using the last of the hot water in the tank, dressed, and went about his tasks in the hope that feeding the chickens with their spring chicks and checking the seedlings in the greenhouse would help him to hold things together. The idea conjured a humorless chuckle.

"Because everything's falling apart," Craig said aloud to the otherwise silent house.

He thought about offering up a prayer to whatever deity or divine presence might be listening, only he'd already exhausted his faith, and the prayers would go unanswered because they went unspoken.

§

The barn needed painting. The voice inside his head growing steadily angrier argued that painting the barn was the least of his concerns. First, there were a thousand other more immediate repairs in the house—a new roof, plumbing, replacing a furnace that had maybe a year left to it. Not that he or the farm would be around a year from now. Already sixty-three days past due on the mortgage, in a year the bank would have taken possession and chopped up the eighty acres of farmland and old growth woods into a development of new homes. A gigantic chunk of the greenbelt on Erie Land had already vanished in the land grab of the late 1990s, the Claren and Kalispell farms gone, claimed by housing developers from out west.

He watered the tender green sprouts, but the certainty that pumpkins would mature and rot in the vast patch without him, that corn would be enjoyed only by deer and squirrels, and that nothing mattered, for everything was doomed, drove him out of the greenhouse and into the woods. A long walk through the dense thickets might help. He doubted it, and was right.

§

Thoughts of Dex plagued him, as Craig knew they would. Dex was dead, but relics of his life prevailed in all directions years after the deed was committed, the dead truck parked at the edge of the wood line they'd used to haul firewood only the first and most obvious. A plank nailed into a thick pine trunk, all that remained of an attempt at building a boyhood tree house, also drew Craig's attention. Sunlight cascaded through the canopy, reflecting off the brown glass of a broken bottle, further proof of Dex's existence. His brother had left a lot of broken bottles in the woods.

Craig wandered along the trail. The early May warmth performed its usual magic trick, conjuring fresh green leaves and buds everywhere he looked. Lady slipper orchids flashed haunting pops of pale pink color along the ancient farmer's wall snaking over the ridge, a wall that Terek Vel Kief, the first to farm this land, had constructed. Their mother had loved the orchids. A wave of renewed sadness slammed into him. His mother was gone. So was Dex. Craig didn't want to think that his older brother had cursed him, but it was the truth, and the truth was damning.

The coffee in Craig's stomach turned to acid. He doubled over and vomited. The sound of a snapping branch reached him through the retches. Hands on knees, he focused beyond the watery veil superimposed over his eyes and tensed. A man walked down from the ridge.

"Who—?" Craig started, the lone word tasting foul.

He wiped his eyes and recognized the interloper. Rage replaced remorse.

"Hubbard," Craig spat. Righting, he charged and drove his body into the other man's.

The scrum was brief. In focusing on Domenic Hubbard, Craig failed to remember that the lowlife never traveled alone. Two sets of hands pulled him off the man who had murdered his brother. Craig struggled as Hubbard picked himself up and wiped pine needles off his clothes.

"Settle down, egg man," Hubbard said, adjusting his crotch. "I come in peace."

"You'd better hope your boys don't let go, 'cause you'll leave in *pieces*."

Hubbard snorted a chuckle. "I didn't kill Dex."

"You sold him the stuff that did."

"Says you. Your brother OD'ed—that was all him."

Craig barked a rosary of expletives, threw an elbow into the muscles of the soldier at his right, and gained some freedom, though not from the left. The two Orkutt brothers again contained him.

"Cut the talk and listen. *Listen*," Hubbard shouted. Then he grabbed hold of Craig's ear, making it impossible not to. "I know you're upset. I'd be, too—especially if my older brother blew the family fortune on recreational snow."

Hubbard let go and gently caressed both sides of Craig's face, which proved more painful than having his ear yanked.

"I know you're hurting. And that you're up the creek because of Dex. I'm here to help you fix this lousy dilemma."

"Help?" Craig parroted. "*You?*"

The slippery smile on Hubbard's face evaporated. "I plan to grow a little garden myself this summer. About an acre should do. Bright, sunny acre in an out of the way corner of your land. A private garden. You'll be paid well for this rental agreement."

Craig insulted Hubbard's mother in his response.

"You're acting like you have a choice," Hubbard said. He tipped a nod with his chin at one of the Orkutts. The younger, Frank. The man released Craig and, lightning-quick, fired a punch into the meat of his guts. The world before Craig's eyes erupted in red. A cyclone stole all the breath from his lungs. Craig fell and continued to plummet even after his physical body struck the ground. The world spun around him.

From miles overhead, Hubbard said, "I'll be in touch, sharecropper. Here's something for your trouble, a small down payment."

Something fluttered onto Craig's face. When he caught his breath enough to drive the miserable reds apart, he saw that it was a thousand dollars, doled out in hundreds.

He picked himself up, tasted fresh blood as well as stale vomit. Hubbard and the Orkutt brothers were gone. The money remained. Craig kicked at it. The world as he knew it was over. The Vel Kief farm, which had prevailed for over two hundred years on Erie Lane, would soon disappear, following other, greater palaces and city-states and entire collapsed civilizations into the ether. Life was done, but the afterlife was not, and Craig had no intention of spending it in league with the devil.

A sound reached his ears through the hammering cadence of his heart, soothing, seductive; the soft gurgling giggle of moving water. There were two brooks running through the woods, a lesser stream that wound close to the pumpkin patch and the larger, deep in the primeval woods, neither close enough to hear.

Craig turned toward the rolling gurgle. He shot a look at the money—dirty money still wet with blood, *Dex's blood*—and left it where it had fallen. Crooking an ear toward the surrounding woods, he pursued.

§

Once, when he was a teenager, a terrible winter had piled snow and ice deep along the sides of Erie Lane, making the walk to school treacherous. Craig had struggled to keep up with Dex and his friends—the Orkutt brothers, Reggie Claren, and that no-good shithead, Domenic Hubbard. Falling behind was worth the risk of falling on his face.

Dropping back from the older boys, he noticed that a steady rivulet cut through the ice sheets at the side of the road. The water giggled as it tumbled, carrying stones and sand and bottle caps along, its current infused with the sun's light. The image of the golden-kissed stream brought a smile to his face and, for reasons he hadn't known until that afternoon in the woods, he'd sensed that he was looking at magic, real magic, manifested in the water.

Wiping at his mouth, Craig continued around the ridge, toward the place in the woods where the trail forked right, toward a patch of new, green growth. Halfway to the oasis of bluettes and brambles, he caught a flash of dappled liquid gold. A small stream whispered through the forest, one where none should be.

Craig's first impression was that sunlight, not water, tumbled over the ground, meandering around a copse of red birch, and through a glen of hemlock trees. But the water simply reflected the sun. Upon his approach, he saw that a bed of golden sand formed a base beneath the brook's course. This was Northern New Hampshire, though the sand instantly called to mind distant deserts, those of Egypt or Mongolia or some other mysterious, arid realm. He followed the current out of the woods and into the greening meadow and saw it reached all the way to the farmland, where corn and tomatoes and pickling cucumbers would flourish in any other year, but probably not this coming season or the ones to follow.

Intrigued, he reversed course and wandered back into the woods, tracking the stream to the hemlocks and red birch, through a bed of skunk cabbage toward a cluster of hillocks covered in moss. Golden light glinted off the current, a reflection of sun and sand. The giggling gush intensified. The source of the water, he guessed, was close.

A fresh water well, it had to be, Craig thought. Maybe a minor earthquake or blasting at one of the new home developments that used to be farmland or wilderness had caused a shift or a slide, tectonics aggravated, the orbit of the Earth upset. Then, he caught a flash of rich green color among the gold, and nothing after that was so simple to explain.

The green pop pulsed, tumbled. Craig followed it along the stream's course, green glass reflections strafing the tree trunks as it rolled past. Craig caught up with the reflection. Leaning down, he saw the object that had created so much dazzle was a ring.

He reached into the water and plucked it from the stream. The ring bore an emerald, the largest Craig had ever seen, the stone an Asscher-cut like the one his Grandmother Vel Kief had been buried with, set in a filigree band of gold. Impossible, it couldn't be, only it was. Craig doubted the ring was a fake, given the exquisite design and detail. It looked antique, almost ancient, probably worth a small fortune. Craig held it in his palm. The flesh beneath grew warm from the treasure, which had absorbed the sun's energy.

Maybe he'd banged his head after the cheap shot by Hubbard's goon, he reasoned. A concussion, delivered by one of the Orkutts. It had to be. The ring would vanish the moment he blinked. Only it didn't. Another effulgence cut the gently rolling gold, this time silver in color. Craig glanced down to see a trio of coins tumble past. He caught up and pulled them from the stream. The coins looked like U.S. silver dollars, only different from any that had been issued in his lifetime. The dates stamped onto them corresponded with the Civil War. Civil War silver dollars.

"Take only what you need," said a feminine voice, sunny and warm like the water that captured the daylight. "Take all that you need, but no more."

§

Craig stared at the odd collection of treasures assembled on the scratched top of the old dining room table, around which generations of Vel Kiefs had sat. The emerald ring and coins shared the space with a small bronze statue of a horse and a necklace that bore a single pink stone, teardrop-shaped; a diamond, he'd discovered after running it along one of the greenhouse windows. As the sun set, how long he'd sat bewitched by the collection sank in. The dying daylight glittered off the objects, creating a prism on the dining room's faded pineapple-print wallpaper.

He'd followed the course of the stream around the hillocks to a section of stonewall that had tumbled off the ridge, the large rocks forming an imperfect circle. At the heart of that geometry, a freshwater well had sprung forth from deep in the Earth. The bubbling waters glowed with a preternatural golden glint. Sand billowed up with the current—and there were things swirling in the sand, colorful, valuable things. He found the primitive bronze horse sitting half-submerged in the bottom of the stream's source. While leaning down and whispering a tentative, "Hello?" the diamond necklace had pulled into view, rising on a fountain of light and water. He'd snagged it by its golden chain.

"Take what you need," the woman's voice repeated, only the words seemed to emanate up from the well with the sand, relics, and water, a voice he felt more than heard. "But remember this warning— only what you need, no more than that."

He took the horse and the necklace, pocketed the ring and the coins. At eight that night, he wandered upstairs to his bedroom and fell asleep in the dark house, serenaded by the chirrup of crickets and other night insects, convinced the entire episode was either wishful thinking or from that knock to the head.

§

Craig woke and wandered downstairs, his eyes full of sleep. Pinching them, he saw the mysterious objects were still on the table, bright against the drab gray morning light.

"No way," he gasped.

Pulling on his boots, he exited the house and marched toward the tree line. By the time he reached the trail through the woods, Craig was running.

Sweat poured down his forehead. Craig had worked the farm for all of his twenty-nine years and had played baseball in the summer, hockey in the winter. The deluge was the result of nerves more than physical exertion.

He turned right at the ridge and followed the rock wall. The happy giggle of flowing water reached him through the cadence of his pulse, beating at his ears. The golden glint of the stream teased the corners of his eyes. He turned. It was still there.

Craig drew in a breath, held it, and then let it sail. He wandered over to the water and leaned down, partially hypnotized by the effulgence of dappled reflections. As he waited, a pop of rich blue color pierced the gold. Something lay in the sand, partially submerged. Craig dipped his fingers into the water and worked it free. The blue stone began to tumble. Craig followed it as the current carried it another yard or so, caught up, and grabbed hold. The stone was a star sapphire, twice the size of the thumbnail that had dislodged it. It sat warm in his palm.

"Take only what you need," the dreamy female voice again warned. "Never more than that."

Smiling, Craig said, "Thank you," and bowed his head. The water answered with a joyous laugh, and the well sent other treasures tumbling up from its depths, including a pale pink aquamarine gemstone, an ancient coin with a lion's face etched on one side, a tribal mask on the other, and a primitive Buddha head carved out of jade.

§

Sweat poured down his spine, soaking his back. The late spring sun beat down on him, transforming the seconds into sums of time that felt more like minutes. Hours. The pay phone's heavy black receiver grew oily against his cheek.

"Thanks for holding," a man said.

"Yeah, my name's Craig and I'm in a bit of a, well, a really lousy financial situation."

"You and most of America. What can I do for you?"

Craig choked down a dry, mildly painful swallow. "I'm losing my house. I have some family heirlooms," he lied. "Antique jewelry, mostly. Some coins. How does this work?"

"Bring them in and I'll give them a look. If what you have is worth anything, we pay you on the spot."

"Cash?"

"If you want. Ask for Matty."

"Matty," Craig said. "I'll see you soon."

Sooner than Matty suspected, thought Craig. He hung up and turned. Across the street, on the second floor of a converted house, a lit neon sign proclaimed that Three Guys Gold was open for business. Craig hurried across the street, clutching a brown paper bag against his chest.

The man behind the banker's window—bulletproof glass, Craig assumed—eyed the emerald ring warily before shooting him a look.

"Family treasures, huh?" Matty asked.

Matty, with his severe expression and hairy, thick fingers covered in gold rings, was not the sort of man Craig wanted to cross.

"My grandmother's," he said, which wasn't so much a lie as an edit to the story—she had owned such a ring, and this ring had risen up on a surge of golden sand and glowing water on the Vel Kief farm. "It's breaking my heart to part with this stuff."

Matty narrowed his gaze but didn't blink, as though dissecting him through glances. "I'll bet. These coins your grandmother's, too?"

"The silver dollars were my dad's."

Matty snorted, indicated the ancient coin. "What do you know about this?"

"Not much."

"It's Etruscan. Do you know how rare it is?" Before Craig could answer, Matty educated him. "They didn't dig the idea of coin money, only started making it after the Greek's conquered them and forced them to. This coin isn't just old, it's museum-quality. So is that little bronze horse. Roman, if I had to guess."

"My grandfather brought them back from Europe after the Big One."

Big lie, yeah, his inner critic taunted. It shocked Craig how easy it had gotten to skewer the truth in so short an amount of time. He stood instead of sitting in one of the sweaty-looking chairs with the torn fake leather cushions in the claustrophobic anteroom on the customer's side of the window. Behind the glass, a secretary with long nails and a tan typed at a computer. Various government rules as related to the exchange of gold, silver, and similar valuables were posted on walls, within clear view. Shelves containing buckets of expensive trinkets hid mostly out of view behind a room divider upholstered in gray industrial carpet.

"You got more of this stuff at home?"

Craig nodded. "A few pieces, yeah."

Matty's eyes locked with Craig's. Instinct told him he mustn't blink first—to do so would result in conflagration. He faced Matty directly. The other man balked.

"I find out any of this stuff is stolen and I'm gonna come down on you hard personally."

"It isn't. It's my birthright." And that, Craig knew, was the truth. The well had given him a long-overdue second chance to save the farm and the land he loved and was so close to losing.

"You've got some of the most amazing pieces I've seen, and given this shitty economy, as you can imagine I'm seeing a lot of desperate folks."

He wrote down a figure, more money than Craig had known since discovering that Dex had inhaled the last of their bank account.

"You can try Aalseth's up the road, but I guarantee you he'll offer less."

"No, this is great," Craig said.

"And if you have other pieces you want to part with of equal or better quality, I'll see that you get treated fairly."

"That works," Craig said.

Steeling himself, he willed his hands to steady by clasping them behind his back and waited for Matty, who dipped behind the half wall, to return. He did, with a stack of hundred-dollar bills in his meaty hand.

"Cash?"

By the end of the afternoon, the lights were back on. The refrigerator hummed, and the TV again worked. Craig turned the tube and the lights off, listened to the sounds of the farm at night, and slept solidly for the first time since Dex's death.

§

They were gathered around Hubbard's car, a new Mustang, slick and white, the two Orkutt giants who'd been with him in the woods, a woman nursing on a beer bottle, and Hubbard behind the wheel.

Craig walked up to the car, but only got as close as the trunk when the Orkutts formed a living wall between him and his target.

"Let him through," Hubbard said, exiting the Mustang.

The men parted. Craig moved past.

"Hubbard," he said.

Hubbard smiled and extended his hand. "I see that you've wised up about our new business arrangement."

"Yeah, I have."

Craig reached into his front pocket. One of the Orkutt goons grabbed his hand by the wrist, but released it after seeing it held a wad of cash, not a weapon. A thousand bucks, to be exact.

"What the hell is this?" Hubbard demanded, his smile gone.

"Your money," Craig said. "I don't need it, and I wouldn't stoop so low even if I did." He tossed the bills at Hubbard's feet. "Come on my land again and I'm gonna shoot to kill, you hear me?"

Not waiting for a response, Craig about-faced, pushed through the two men, and walked away.

§

Water tumbled out of the woods and into that patch of farmland he'd let go wild again to meadow; from the meadow into the pumpkin patch, where the tended earth absorbed it. The farm was also absorbing sunlight and happiness from the whispering water, Craig thought while looking across the Vel Kief land with fresh eyes. Had the place ever seemed so beautiful or happy, so alive?

Earlier in the morning, he'd not only paid the back due mortgage, but had brought the payments forward by half a year and had thrown five thousand more at the principle. There was even some left over, enough to replace the food lost in the fridge during the power outage and maybe attend to one or more of the house repairs. Not to replace the roof or furnace, but to buy paint, maybe patch up the plumbing issues.

He followed the brook in reverse, toward the source of the well, loving the way the water giggled as it gurgled along, and the warm sunny glint off the sand. Craig remembered that other stream from that different spring. At a clearing in the woods that formed a private bower, he sat beside the water and watched it flow past, his eyes growing heavy, hypnotized by the glitter, his ears bewitched by its liquid laughter.

Craig stretched out beside the magical currents and drifted into a state not quite asleep, less than awake.

"Take only what you need," the female voice said, adding another level to the spell.

"Who are you?" Craig asked. The words emerged sounding distant, disconnected. An echo beneath the water.

"I am ever-moving, never still," the voice answered. "I spill out of the sky, scatter across the earth, picking up momentum and gathering trinkets from the world of men. Silly little things that men covet. Pretty baubles. I don't mind sharing the toys."

"Who…"

Craig forced his eyes open. His gaze fell into the water; his thoughts followed. The stream carried his consciousness along through abandoned columns and colonnades; Doric, Ionic, and Corinthian styles, the latter capped in elegant embellishments of carved acanthus leaves; along ivied granite mausoleums and forgotten sepulchers; past pyramids in Egypt and Mexico; through temples in ancient China and Greece; around obelisks and terraced cities, some still hidden beneath caps of ice and a mile of ocean trench, others worn down to pebbles by the universal solvent's constant, laughing caresses. Craig blinked, and the fountains and aqueducts and flower-wreathed wells evaporated in a rush of golden flashes. He woke fully beside the stream, at peace.

"Only what you need, never more."

Craig dipped his hand into the water. Deeper, into the sand. The soft grains tickled his flesh with pleasant sensations. He sifted. Sand and the forest's top layer of decay clouded the water. A vibrant eruption of red color followed. Craig withdrew his hand, at first thinking he'd been cut, that he'd taken more than he was due.

Then he saw the fat ruby, the gem in a shade of pigeon's blood, and understood that he hadn't broken the rules. A ruby, a strand of pearls—black—and a small statue of a cat, seemingly simple but certainly quite old, Egyptian or possibly Mexican, tumbled out of the well and into his grip. A new furnace and roof, some money thrown at the town for property taxes, would be more than enough. With that bit of breathing room, the Vel Kief farm would again flourish. He'd make up the difference with the pumpkin and corn, the fresh vegetables and fruit at summer farmer's markets.

As if reading his thoughts, the well rewarded him with a golden bar, imperfect in shape, something he could easily imagine coming from the spilled guts of a sunken galleon.

"No more," the voice said.

"Understood. And thank you. Thank you so much for sharing your toys. Your generosity saved me," he answered.

The water giggled in response. Holding the treasures, Craig turned, intending to head home and replace the furnace, the roof, to return to turning the soil, feeding the chickens, and harvesting the results of his hard work, as his family had done for generations.

Only blocking his way were Domenic Hubbard and the two Orkutt brothers.

"Hubbard," Craig gasped.

The incredulous look on the other man's face, shifting between the treasures in Craig's hands and the stream, sharpened into a dangerous grin. "Now it makes sense. Why you didn't need my money, my help—because you got your own treasure mine back here."

"Get the hell off my land," Craig barked.

"No," Hubbard said and brushed past, grabbing the bar of gold from his hand.

Craig dropped the other treasures in the struggle that ensued. The two giants overwhelmed him, one knocking him out of the fight early with a cheap shot to the jaw. Craig landed, rolled over, and watched what followed with the sky and the earth having changed positions.

Hubbard strutted over to the stream, hunched down, swore. "What the—?" He scooped his hand into the dappled water and drew back a water pitcher made from solid gold. "Karl, Frank—get over here and help me dig!"

The two Orkutt brutes joined Hubbard at the water. In pain, Craig watched them scoop out strands of platinum and gold, lockets and antique cameos, and a particularly impressive amethyst bracelet.

In his haste, a canopic jar of lapis lazuli tumbled out of Hubbard's hands and shattered on the ground.

"Only what you need," Craig heard the voice threaten and now, through the filter of his own agony, it sounded angry. "And no more!"

In their excitement, Craig imagined that Hubbard and the brothers didn't hear the voice from the well. Or they did and didn't care. A little statue made of obsidian stone in the shape of a head; a gold pocket watch; a handful of doubloons. Though gazing upside down, Craig saw that their careless pawing had turned the water cloudy, dirty. One of the Orkutts, Karl, was jumping around, splashing water everywhere. The happy laughter of the current was gone. It seemed to scream.

Craig rolled over, coughed out blood. "Stop," he called.

"Do you believe this?" Hubbard asked Karl Orkutt, his fingers full of gemstones and strands of gold chain. "Do you?"

The man who had murdered his brother turned away from the well and toward the mouth of the stream, where the scream was building, clearly quite audible now to all.

The arrogant smile vanished from Hubbard's face. Then Hubbard, too, disappeared as a wall of dark water devoid of all sunlight, all joy, rushed through the trees, scooping the three men into its clutches. The wave crashed at the stone circle. Terrified shouts continued for another second or two, only to fade completely, replaced by the placid melody of the spring woods.

Craig stood and staggered over to the brook. A damp depression was all that remained. Clutching at his stomach, he worked his way around the hillock, the lush green tufts of skunk cabbage, and to the section of collapsed stonewall. The rocks were still there in their imperfect circular geometry, but the ground beneath was solid again, a damp mess of dead leaves and pine needles. The well had dried up, taking Domenic Hubbard and the Orkutt brothers with it to some unknown place deep beneath the earth.

Righting, Craig started back toward the house, unable to feel any remorse for the three men. A glint of golden energy at the periphery drew his eyes to the ground and, for an instant, he thought the well had reopened. But the source of the reflection was the golden bar. The ancient cat statue and other priceless relics lay beside it, where he had dropped them in the fight.

Craig smiled, gathered up the treasures, and ambled along the trail, headed toward home.

Vasilissa the Fair

A Traditional Russian Folktale, collected by
W. R. S. Ralston, M.A.

In a certain kingdom there lived a merchant. Twelve years did he live as a married man, but he had only one child, Vasilissa the Fair. When her mother died, the girl was eight years old. And on her deathbed the merchant's wife called her little daughter to her, took out from under the bed-clothes a doll, gave it to the child, and said, "Listen, Vasilissa, dear; remember and obey these last words of mine. I am going to die. And now, together with my parental blessing, I bequeath to you this doll. Keep it always by you, and never show it to anybody; and whenever any misfortune comes upon you, give the doll food, and ask its advice. When it has fed, it will tell you a cure for your troubles." Then, the mother kissed her child and died.

After his wife's death, the merchant mourned for her a befitting time, and then began to consider marrying again. He was a man of means—it wasn't a question with him of girls with dowries. More than all others, a certain widow took his fancy. She was middle-aged, and had a couple of daughters of her own just about the same age as Vasilissa. *She must be both a good housekeeper and an experienced mother*, he thought.

Well, the merchant married the widow, but he had deceived himself, for he did not find in her a kind mother for his Vasilissa. Vasilissa was the prettiest girl in all the village; and her stepmother and stepsisters were jealous of her beauty. They tormented her with every possible sort of toil, in order that she might grow thin from over-work, and be tanned by the sun and the wind. Her life was made a burden to her.

Vasilissa bore everything with resignation, and every day grew plumper and prettier, while the stepmother and her daughters lost flesh and fell off in appearance from the effects of their own spite. Notwithstanding, they always sat with folded hands like fine ladies.

But how was this possible? Why, it was her doll that helped Vasilissa. If it hadn't been for it, however could the girl have gotten through all her work? It was that Vasilissa would never eat all of her share of a meal, but always kept the most delicate morsel for her doll. And at night, when all were at rest, she would shut herself up in the narrow chamber in which she slept, and feast her doll, saying the while:

"Here, dolly, feed. Help me in my need! I live in my father's house, but never know what pleasure is. My evil stepmother tries to drive me out of the world. Teach me how to keep alive, and what I ought to do."

Then, the doll would eat, and afterwards give her advice, and comfort the girl in her sorrow, and next day it would do all Vasilissa's work for her. She had only to take her ease in a shady place and pluck flowers, and yet all her work was done in good time: the flower beds were weeded, the pails were filled, the cabbages were watered, and the stove was heated. Moreover, the doll showed Vasilissa herbs which prevented her from getting sunburned. Happily did she and her doll live together.

Several years went by. Vasilissa grew up and became old enough to be married. All the marriageable young men in the town sent to make an offer to Vasilissa; but at her stepmother's daughters not a soul would so much as look. Her stepmother grew even more savage than before, and replied to every suitor—

"We won't let the younger daughter marry before her elders."

And after the suitors had been packed off, the stepmother beat Vasilissa.

Well, it happened one day that the merchant had to go away from home on business for a long time. Thereupon, the stepmother went to live in another house. Near that house was a dense forest, and in a clearing in that forest there stood a hut, and in the hut there lived a Baba Yaga. The old Baba Yaga never let anyone come near her dwelling, and she ate up visitors like so many chickens.

Having moved into the new abode, the merchant's wife kept sending her hated Vasilissa into the forest on one pretense or another. But the girl always got home safe and sound; because the doll showed her the way, and never let her go near the Baba Yaga's dwelling.

The autumn season arrived. One evening, the stepmother assigned work to the three girls; one she set to lace-making, another to knitting socks, and the third, Vasilissa, to weaving. Each of them had an allotted amount to do. By-and-by, she put out the lights in the house, leaving only one candle alight where the girls were working, and then she went to bed. The girls worked and worked.

Presently the candle wanted snuffing. One of the stepdaughters took the snuffers, as if she were going to clear the wick, but instead of doing so, in obedience to her mother's orders, she snuffed the candle out, pretending to do so by accident.

"What shall we do now?" said the older sisters. "There isn't a spark of fire in the house, and our tasks are not yet done. We must go to the Baba Yaga's for a spark!"

"My pins give me light enough," said the one who was making lace. "I shan't go."

"And I shan't go, either," said the one who was knitting socks. "My knitting needles give me light enough."

"Vasilissa, you must go for the spark," they both cried out together. "Be off to the Baba Yaga's!" And they pushed Vasilissa out of the room.

Vasilissa went into her little closet, set before the doll a morsel saved from supper, and said:

"Now, dolly, feed, and listen to my need! I'm sent to the Baba Yaga's for a spark. The Baba Yaga will eat me!"

The doll fed, and its eyes began to glow just like a couple of candles.

"Never fear, Vasilissa dear!" it said. "Go where you're sent. Only take care to keep me always by you. As long as I'm with you, no harm will come to you at the Baba Yaga's."

So Vasilissa got ready, put her doll in her pocket, crossed herself, and went out into the thick forest.

As she walked, she trembled. Suddenly a horseman galloped by. He was white, and he was dressed all in white. Under him was a white horse, and all the trappings of the horse were white—and the day began to break.

She went a little further, and a second rider galloped by. He was red, and dressed all in red. He was seated on a red horse, and all the trappings of the horse were red—and the sun rose up.

Vasilissa went on walking all night and all the next day. It was only toward the evening that she reached the clearing on which stood the dwelling of the Baba Yaga. The fence around the clearing was made of dead men's bones. On the top of the fence were stuck human skulls with eyes in them; instead of uprights at the gates, there were men's legs; instead of bolts there were arms; instead of a lock, there was a mouth with sharp teeth.

Vasilissa was frightened out of her wits, and stood still as if rooted to the ground.

Suddenly there rode past another horseman. He was black, dressed all in black, and seated on a black horse. He galloped up to the Baba Yaga's gate and disappeared, just as if he had sunk through the ground—and night fell. But the darkness did not last long. The eyes of all the skulls on the fence began to shine and the whole clearing became as bright as if it had been midday. Vasilissa shuddered with fear, but stopped where she was, not knowing which way to run.

Soon there was heard in the forest a terrible roar. The trees cracked, the dry leaves rustled. Out of the forest came the Baba Yaga, riding in a mortar, urging it on with a pestle, sweeping away her traces with a broom. Up she drove to the gate, stopped short, and, snuffing the air around her, cried, "Faugh! Faugh! I smell Russian flesh! Who's there?"

Vasilissa went up to the hag in a terrible fright, bowed low before her, and said,

"It's me, Granny. My step-sisters have sent me to you for a spark."

"Very good," said the Baba Yaga; "I know them. If you'll stop awhile with me first, and do some work for me, I'll give you a spark. But if you won't, I'll eat you!"

Then she turned to the gates, and cried, "Ho, thou firm fence of mine, be thou divided! And ye, wide gates of mine, do ye fly open!"

The gates opened, and the Baba Yaga drove in, whistling as she went, and after her followed Vasilissa; and then everything shut again. When they entered the sitting room, the Baba Yaga stretched herself out at full length on the couch, and said to Vasilissa,

"Fetch out what there is in the oven; I'm hungry."

Vasilissa went outside and lighted a splinter from one of the skulls which were on the fence, and then began fetching meat from the oven and setting it before the Baba Yaga—enough meat had been provided for a dozen people. Then, she fetched from the cellar kvass, mead, beer, and wine. The hag ate up everything, drank up everything. All she left for Vasilissa was a few scraps—a crust of bread and a morsel of sucking-pig. Then the Baba Yaga lay down to sleep, saying,

"When I go out to-morrow morning, mind you cleanse the courtyard, sweep the room, cook the dinner, and get the linen ready. Then, go to the corn-bin, take out four quarters of wheat, and clear it of other seed. And mind you, have it all done before I get home. If you don't, I shall eat you!"

After giving these orders the Baba Yaga began to snore. But Vasilissa set the remnants of the hag's supper before her doll, burst into tears, and said:

"Now, dolly, feed, listen to my need! The Baba Yaga has set me a heavy task, and threatens to eat me if I don't do it all. Do help me!"

The doll replied, "Never fear, Vasilissa the Fair! Sup, say your prayers, and go to bed. The morning is wiser than the evening!"

Vasilissa awoke very early, but the Baba Yaga was already up. She looked out of the window. The light in the skulls' eyes was going out. All of a sudden, there appeared the white horseman, and all was light. The Baba Yaga went out into the courtyard and whistled, and before her appeared a mortar with a pestle and a broom. The red horseman appeared, and the sun rose. The Baba Yaga seated herself in the mortar, and drove out of the courtyard, shooting herself along with the pestle, and sweeping away her traces with the broom.

Vasilissa was left alone, so she examined the Baba Yaga's house, wondered at the abundance there was in everything, and remained lost in thought as to which work she ought to take to first. She looked up; all her work was done already. The doll had cleared the wheat to the very last grain.

"Ah, my preserver!" cried Vasilissa, "you've saved me from danger!"

"All you've got to do now is to cook the dinner," answered the doll, slipping into Vasilissa's pocket. "Cook away, in God's name, and then take some rest for your health's sake!"

Towards evening, Vasilissa got the table ready, and awaited the Baba Yaga.

It began to grow dusky. The black rider appeared for a moment at the gate, and all grew dark. Only the eyes of the skulls sent forth their light. The trees began to crack, the leaves began to rustle, and up drove the Baba Yaga in her mortar. Vasilissa went out to meet her.

"Is everything done?" asked the Baba Yaga.

"Please to look for yourself, Granny!" said Vasilissa.

The Baba Yaga examined everything, and was vexed that there was nothing to be angry about. She said, "Well, well! Very good!" Afterwards she cried, "My trusty servants, zealous friends, grind this my wheat!"

There appeared three pairs of hands, which gathered up the wheat, and carried it out of sight. The Baba Yaga supped, and just before going to bed, again gave her orders to Vasilissa: "Do just the same tomorrow as today; only, besides that take out of the bin the poppy seed that is there, and clean the earth off it grain by grain. Someone or other, you see, has mixed a lot of earth with it out of spite." Having said this, the hag turned to the wall and began to snore, and Vasilissa took to feeding her doll. The doll fed, and then said to her what it had said the day before:

"Pray to God, and go to sleep. The morning is wiser than the evening. All shall be done, Vasilissa, dear!"

The next morning, the Baba Yaga again drove out of the courtyard in her mortar, and Vasilissa and her doll immediately did all the work. The hag returned, looked at everything, and cried, "My trusty servants, zealous friends, press forth oil from the poppy seed!"

Three pairs of hands appeared, gathered up the poppy seed, and bore it out of sight. The Baba Yaga sat down to dinner. She ate, but Vasilissa stood silently by.

"Why don't you speak to me?" said the Baba Yaga. "There you stand like a mute creature!"

"I didn't dare speak," answered Vasilissa, "but if you give me leave, I should like to ask you about something."

"Ask away. Only, it isn't every question that brings good. There's an old saying, 'Get much to know, and old soon you'll grow.'"

"I only want to ask you, Granny, about something I saw. As I was coming here, I was passed by one man riding on a white horse. He was white himself, and dressed in white. Who was he?"

"That was my bright Day!" answered the Baba Yaga.

"Afterwards there passed me another rider, on a red horse. He was red himself, and all in red clothes. Who was he?"

"That was my red Sun!" answered the Baba Yaga.

"And who may be the black rider, Granny, who passed by me just at your gate?"

"That was my dark Night; they are all trusted servants of mine."

Vasilissa thought of the three pairs of hands, but held her peace.

"Why don't you go on asking?" said the Baba Yaga.

"That's enough for me, Granny. You said yourself, 'Get too much to know, old you'll grow!'"

"It's just as well," said the Baba Yaga, "that you've only asked about what you saw out of doors, not indoors! In my house, I hate having dirt carried out of doors; and as to over-inquisitive people— well, I eat them. Now, I'll ask *you* something. How is it you manage to do the work I set you to do?"

"My mother's blessing assists me," replied Vasilissa.

"Eh! Eh! What's that? Get along out of my house, you blesséd daughter. I don't want blesséd people around here!"

She dragged Vasilissa out of the house, pushed her outside the gates, took one of the skulls with blazing eyes from the fence, stuck it on a stick, gave it to her and said, "Lay hold of that. It's a light you can take to your stepsisters. That's what they sent you here for, I believe."

Home went Vasilissa at a run, lit by the skull, which went out only at the approach of the dawn; and at last, on the evening of the second day, she reached home. When she came to the gate, she was going to throw away the skull.

"Surely," she thought, "they can't still be in need of a light at home." But suddenly a hollow voice issued from the skull, saying,

"Throw me not away. Carry me to your stepmother!"

She looked at her stepmother's house, and not seeing a light in a single window, she determined to take the skull inside there with her. For the first time in her life, she was cordially received by her stepmother and stepsisters, who told her that from the moment she went away they hadn't had a spark of fire in the house. They couldn't strike a light themselves anyhow. And whenever they brought one in from a neighbor's, it went out as soon as it came into the room.

"Perhaps your light will keep in!" said the stepmother. So, they carried the skull into the sitting room. But the eyes of the skull glared at the stepmother and her daughters, then shot forth large flames and burned them. They would fain have hidden themselves, but run where they would, everywhere did the eyes follow after them. By the morning they were utterly burnt to cinders. Only Vasilissa was none the worse.

The next morning, Vasilissa buried the skull, locked up the house and took up her quarters in a neighboring town. After a time, she began to work. Her doll made her a glorious loom, and by the end of the winter she had weaved a quantity of linen so fine that it might be passed like thread through the eye of a needle. In the spring, after it had been bleached, Vasilissa made a present of it to the old woman with whom she lodged. The crone presented it to the king, who ordered it to be made into shirts. But no seamstress could be found to make them up, until the linen was entrusted to Vasilissa.

When a dozen shirts were ready, Vasilissa sent them to the king, and as soon as the courier had left, she washed herself, and combed her hair, and dressed herself, and sat down at the window. Before long there arrived a messenger demanding her instant appearance at court. And when she appeared before the royal eyes, the king fell desperately in love with her.

"My beauty!" said he, "never will I part with thee; thou shalt be my wife." So, he married her, and by-and-by her father returned, and took up his abode with her. And Vasilissa took the old woman into her service, and as for the doll—to the end of her life Vasilissa always carried it in her pocket."

A Thing at the Edge
Kai Miro

I *saw a thing today,"* Angie sang into her tomato soup, the spoon held clumsily in her small fingers, "at the edge of the yard." The spoon fell, splashing Angie's muddy yellow t-shirt. It'd been a busy morning digging up wild flowers in the small woods outside the yard with Charlie, their shepherd. Sunlit daffodils and daisies, wild pink roses, and violet morning glories littered the kitchen table. Angie took the straw out of her strawberry milk and put it into the soup, sucking up the soup noisily.

"What was that?" Isabeau was washing the morning dishes. Outside the kitchen window, a summer breeze danced the blue-headed wild geraniums and tickled the small green and gold leaves of the birch trees. A dog barked, and Isabeau scanned the carefully landscaped yard for Charlie.

"A *thing*," Angie said. "I saw a thing and it kissed my finger."

Where was that dumb dog? Isabeau turned towards her daughter, her hands still in the cooling dishwater. Angie was now cradling her soup bowl with her left hand while trying to suck it up with the straw. Orange tomato soup spilled onto the table. She held her right hand in the air. Her forefinger was missing to the first knuckle. Dried blood mixed with dirt on the rest of her hand.

Isabeau felt faint. Numbly, she pulled her dripping hands from the dishwater. Her voice shook only a little. "Angie, how are you feeling?"

Angie looked up, smiling sweetly, her teeth holding the straw in her mouth. "Good Mama. How are you?"

§

"The doctor could not fix it," Isabeau told Roger on the phone. "She will have to just live without it. Without part of her finger, like a tail that will not grow back." It was late now on their end. Isabeau'd tucked Angie into bed hours ago. But it was morning for Roger. "I want you to come home."

Roger sighed. "Izzy, you know I can't." Isabeau answered with silence. "It was probably just a dog."

"That doesn't help. Dogs carry rabies and speaking of dogs, Charlie is missing."

"He probably chased it off. Now, doesn't that make you feel better?"

"Non," Isabeau's accent returned. "I do not feel better now."

Voices came up on Roger's end. He spoke to someone there, "Yes, of course, I'll be right in." To Isabeau, he said, "I have to go. If I'm late for another meeting, Jason will have my head. He insists that Bron's people are taking us to the cleaners. He wants me to fact check every line twice, leave no clause unturned."

"Jason wants you," Isabeau said, tiredly, "I want you, too. Angie needs you. We want you back home."

"I will always be there for you, Is," Roger sighed, "but this is work." A male voice became more insistent in the background. Isabeau recognized Jason's rapid-fire Chicago delivery. "You're going to have to deal with this yourself."

Isabeau remained silent. Angry. Listening, not listening. Her heart thundered in her ears.

"Isabeau, I'm doing this for all of us. Izzy?" Isabeau hung up on him, cutting him off. Roger didn't call back. They'd had this discussion before.

Isabeau walked down the dark hallway towards Angie's bedroom. Despite the warm night outside, the house retained a chilly coolness that on most nights Isabeau found refreshing. Tonight, she did not. Tonight, it felt threatening, predatory. Isabeau crawled into bed with her daughter, curling up behind her and pulling her in tight. She listened to Angie's calm soft snoring and waited for dawn.

§

Golden sunlight splattered the yard, gilding every grass blade and highlighting the peony and hardy rose bushes surrounding the house. It felt hollow and desperate to Isabeau, though. The skies above were pulling in darker clouds, promising a summer shower. It was strange when it happened like that. It was if the weather was caught between two thoughts, torn in half, unwilling to give way to either.

"Was it here?" Isabeau asked her daughter. She stood on the bright green lawn, facing the dark woods. She hated those woods. From the very beginning, she'd loved the red brick and white wood house. She'd loved the maintained yard and brightly decorative garden. But, those woods. Sunlight never pierced it, and Isabeau was half convinced that bears and wolves roamed it. Jason and Angie loved the woods. They reminded Jason of the wild freedom of his boyhood. And Angie, she was five years old, Isabeau told herself, too young to realize the dangers. For Angie, it was a fairytale land, princess magical and Disney World happy. *Maybe not so much now*, Isabeau thought with a small bit of righteous satisfaction, *maybe not so much when it bites off fingers.*

Only the missing bit of finger didn't seem to bother or slow Angie down at all. If she was feeling any pain or fear, nothing showed. In fact, if anything, Angie seemed even more fearless and bright.

Angie cocked her head sideways, examining her mother. "No, Mama, not there…"

Isabeau swallowed and took two steps closer to the woods. She tried to hide the trembling in her legs. "Was it here?"

"No, Mama…" Then Angie shrieked, jumping up and down, clapping, "Yes! Yes! It *was* there!"

Angie ran past Isabeau. She entered the woods and for a moment, she disappeared. Isabeau cried out. *Non*, she *knew* Angie was right there. She could hear her sunny laughter. And then, there she was, her round face beaming the brightest smile, her tiny hands, one hand with a bandaged finger, clutching a white bark birch.

But, for a moment, the woods had swallowed her whole.

"I was here Mama!" Angie shrieked from the woods. "I was right here and the thing was right where you are now!"

Isabeau swayed, the heat swelling up on her, closing her throat. "You come now, Angeline. Come out of there this instant." One hand on her breast and under that her heart roared, racing towards a terrible finish line, and the other hand held out towards her daughter. She took a hesitant step forward, the woods nearly pulling her, the lawn trying to drag her down.

I go forward, I go down, all at once, Isabeau thought, nearly giggling. And then, the thought came to her: the thing had stood between Angie and the house. She waved desperately towards Angie to come, come along now. They really needed to get back to the house right now. The house was safe. Nothing could happen to them in there.

Angie pointed past her, to a point behind Isabeau. "Oh, look, Mama."

Isabeau whirled, nearly losing her step again. *When had the lawn grown so uneven?*

Halfway back to the house, in the dead center of the beautiful lawn, a dark mass lay. Charlie. He wasn't moving. It was hard to tell in the distance if he was even breathing, but Isabeau knew he wasn't. Once black and tan, Charlie was now mostly a mottled gray-black. A breeze tried to stir Charlie's clotted fur, but the blood had stiffened into cement. A moan escaped Isabeau. Charlie'd not been there when they'd come through a few minutes before. "How...?"

Angie thought her mother was talking to her. "The thing brought him. It waved at us. Didn't you see it, Mama?"

Isabeau tried to control her breathing and just smile. But it was a funny smile: lopsided and shaky, threatening to slide off her face if pushed any further. Angie laughed to see it, her tiny hands, one in bandage covering her mouth politely. The wild childish laughter echoed, seeming to surround Isabeau and come back at her mockingly from all around the lawn.

In a cheerful happy voice, Isabeau said, "Let us play a game, *chérie*. Let us run back to the house as if something were chasing us."

"What about Charlie?"

"He's sleeping."

"Won't he wake up if we run past him?"

"I hope not." Isabeau meant it.

Angie thought on that and finally nodded. "What about the others?"

Isabeau's smile twitched, promised to crack wide open. "It's a game, petite. We will pretend not to see it or the others."

"'Kay, Mama!" Angie screamed happily, darting past Isabeau to the house.

Isabeau spun around, hesitating a moment, and searching the lawn. The green was darker now, fuller and lush. The gathering rain clouds had pulled in a humidity that vibrated the air, crisping the colors of the flowers and warming their scent. Nothing else was there. Not it. Not others. Just a dog that crawled up to die on the lawn while her back was turned. A poor sweet dog hit by a very real car. A normal everyday accident. At the kitchen doorway, Angie waved. "I won! I won!"

Isabeau found her breath and started walking quickly to the house. "Yes, darling, you win…"

And at the corner of her eye, dark movement. Isabeau turned her head, following. She could not see it dead on. But there, at the corner, it danced and moved, always both within and just out of sight. It seemed unwilling to let itself be seen or yet unseen. It remained in-between. And there were others. Isabeau ran to the house, scooped her daughter up without breaking stride and slammed the door shut, locking it firmly behind them.

§

Isabeau found the gun easily enough but it jammed when she tried to load it. A frustrating hour later, she got the chamber unstuck and calmer now, reloaded it. Then, loaded with a bag of peanut butter cream cookies, a couple of ham sandwiches quickly prepared, a pitcher of tangy orange drink, the small tv, and the telephone, they settled into Angie's bedroom to wait things out. That's it exactly, Isabeau thought, we're waiting *things* out. Waiting them out. They'd have to go away. It wasn't like they'd always been there, just out of sight, living in-between the house and the woods, right?

It was useless to call Roger. He was always there, just out of reach.

Who else was left? The police? To say what? Something at the edge of my eye killed our dog and took my daughter's finger? And now it has friends and they're all outside on the lawn? What? You can't see them? Try not looking at them. Then, they're clear as daylight. Better to just sit tight and wait it out 'til the end. She was on her own. Like always. She'd deal with it alone, calmly, logically.

The day passed slowly. Angie sang to her shows and ate the cookies and sandwiches. Isabeau couldn't touch either. Her stomach was in knots. They drank the orange juice drink from Angie's teacup set, pretending it was High Tea. Then, later when the news came on, Angie and Isabeau read stories from Angie's bookcase. Angie fell asleep soon after night fell outside her window.

Isabeau was torn. She wanted to keep the light on but then, what if they came inside the house? She thought of turning the light off so her eyes could grow use to the darkness but then, again, what if they came into the house? The light stayed on and so did the nightlight and eventually, crawled up around her daughter, Isabeau fell into a troubled, deep yet restless sleep.

§

In the dream, Isabeau walked up to a blackbird in the middle of a dirt road. She peered down at it, admiring the shining blue-black feathers. It cawed at her, preening, carefully cleaning itself. Then, a touch of white crawled out from under one of the beautiful wings. The white thing crawled out and Isabeau saw it was a maggot worm. Others followed and the black bird rolled its black eyes in horror and shock towards Isabeau, its beak open but cawing soundlessly. The bird collapsed, fighting itself, seeming to crumble from within and the white maggot worms burst free like a pie exploding.

Isabeau woke with a muffled scream. Outside the window, a calm cool silence promised an early dawn. It was all going to work out. As soon as it was light, Isabeau would load Angie into the car and they'd drive into town. It was ridiculous. Why had she panicked? She'd had the car all this time. They could have slept in a motel last night. Not that she would have had to do that. It'd all been stress. Jason working all the time, Angie's finger, the dog dying. All of it had gotten to her, made her hallucinate.

She pulled Angie tighter to her. Angie was cold, so cold. But, then, so was the house. It was strange how cold the house got at night, especially considering how it was still July. Holding her close to her breast and carrying her, Isabeau managed to gather some of the blankets from Angie's bed. Angie made a strange sound when Isabeau settled them both back down on the floor. *Was she sick?* Isabeau held her out to look at her.

It was not Angie she held.

It was some sort of horrible doll made of dried woven grass, yard clippings, animal bones, feathers, various teeth and decaying flowers, held together with bits of string, matted organic matter and black dried blood. Its mouth was open and within the blackness, something roamed. When that rolling thing within the doll got to the holes of its eyes, Isabeau dropped the doll and stood up, slowly, crippled with fear. The doll looked up at her with malevolent glee, a weird life animating it from within. Stiffly, jerking, the doll lifted its arms towards her. Isabeau took a step backward.

"Is a game, Mama."

Isabeau screamed and kicked the doll in the belly. It flew across the room but then, faster than she could watch it from the corner of her eye, it ran back at her, striking at her breast. Isabeau screamed again, clutching her chest. Her hand came away bloody. She looked down. Her shirt was torn and blood ran from the gaping hole where her left breast had been. Isabeau fell against the wall, a sudden wooosh in the front of her head making her feel lightheaded and faint.

Across the room, the Angie doll waved a bloody shred of flesh in the air shrieking, "I won! I won! I WON!"

It then ran out of the bedroom and down the hallway. Distantly, Isabeau heard the front door open. Afterwards, the door slammed shut and opened a few more times. The sounds of nails on tile, weird giggling, and then rapid footsteps on carpeted floor followed.

Isabeau slid down the wall, her hands leaving bloody tracks. She sobbed, trying to catch her breath. The hole in her chest wheezed, sucking in air, and suddenly Isabeau couldn't breathe at all. There was pressure within her chest and throat, liquid filling her and she vomited up blood and orange drink into her lap. Isabeau hiccupped air, trying not to choke on the blood, bile and juice in her throat. Her stomach bloated before her eyes, filling like a balloon.

The pain wasn't terrible, just uncomfortable. Mostly, it was the fear of what would happen next. Isabeau didn't want to see what her body would do. It wasn't hers anymore. It was other now, beyond her control. She could feel what it was going through. She would know… but she would not be able to help it or stop it. Her body belonged to that place outside of her. Her body belonged to them. And she wasn't really sure where *she* would go, where *she* would be. *Its kisses are poison.* Tears filled her eyes. Worse, they had her child. Her beautiful, bright, sun-lit summer child.

Isabeau noticed out of the corner of her teary eye that her bloated belly had burst open and was now waving white maggoty worms and the tiny wet heads of baby blackbirds. Angie's bedroom door opened. With her head turned sideways, Isabeau could see all of them. She closed her eyes.

And now they had her.

§

It was 8 p.m. Sunday night when Jason got home. The house was dark and quiet. Strange. Isabeau always left the front porch light on for him. She was afraid of the dark. She was afraid of silence. Jason couldn't remember a time that the tv or radio wasn't on, along with all the lights in the house.

Once inside, the scent of wild roses, lilacs, clover, violets, and freshly cut grass was overwhelming. Jason turned on the foyer light. This was really strange. Isabeau had filled the house with pitchers of flowers and potpourri of scented herbs and grasses. He stood there a moment, enjoying it. Isabeau was not a gardener. She liked the appearance of it but when it came to the actual work, she'd rather spray the smell and hire the help. Maybe Izzy was finally taking root here.

"Jason?"

Jason grinned and walked through the foyer, living room, past the candle-lit kitchen and dining room. The table was set with a large fresh salad and a wide array of fruits in large bowls. Isabeau had been busy. There was a smell of meat roasting with root vegetables in the kitchen. Delicious. Jason could smell the blood simmering, the fat crackling. It was mouth-watering.

"Isabeau?"

"In here, *chéri*," Isabeau called to him from the family room. While the house reeled with the scent of fresh flowers, grass and woodsy potpourri, it was the family room where Isabeau's new green thumb really took off. The room had been turned into a greenhouse. Planted flowers and dried herbs hung from the ceiling. Small slender trees were potted in various parts of the room. Ferns and flowering plants dotted areas of the bookshelf and areas of the floor. The room was warm, inviting, green, and fresh. Jason breathed it all in deeply.

Best of all, Isabeau and Angeline were sitting on the floor playing board games. The large flat screen TV was missing from the wall. Instead, a large mirror took up its place. Jason liked the way the mirror displayed all of them. They looked so happy.

"What are you playing, baby?" He asked Angie.

"Chutes and Ladders."

"You know, that's a really old board game. It was called Snakes and Ladders when I was young."

Isabeau smiled at him, her dark eyes glittering. "And before that, it was called something else. It is a very old game."

Jason leaned down to kiss the top of her head. She smelled sweet and musky, like citrus and woods. He murmured, "What're you cooking?"

Isabeau's smiled deepened, displaying her small white teeth. "Some meat we had hanging around. We need to eat it before it spoils rotten."

Angie giggled behind her hands. Jason's smile drifted slightly. His family's intensity was making him a little uneasy. Out of the corner of his eye, something flickered and moved within the mirror's reflection. But when he looked at it dead on, he just saw his beautiful wife and daughter smiling back at him.

The White Wood
Jude-Marie Green

D*ario the woodsman struggled to dress. Three years since* he lost his hand, all his clothes modified without buttons or ties by his wife, and he still spent too long each morning sliding into his pants and shrugging into his shirt.

His wife, Deirdre, sat on the chest at the end of the bed, only half-dressed herself. She knew better than to offer assistance. He slung the suspenders over his shoulder.

His stomach rumbled. He led his wife downstairs to the kitchen. The hearth was unlit and scrupulously clean. She hadn't even laid up the kindling. He kicked over the log box. Nothing fell out.

"We have no wood," she said.

He grunted and sat at the table.

She put a mug of water in front of him and a dried apple.

He glared.

"The pantry is empty," she said. "I'll dig up some roots today, but there's no wood for fire to cook them."

He stared at her. She met his gaze without flinching. She had once been beautiful, plump, and vivid. Now, she was a pale thin shadow. Only her eyes glowed with vigor and recriminations.

"Bring back some wood to keep your family warm," she said.

He pointed to the master chair, his chair, at the table head. "Burn that."

He stomped out of the house, slamming the heavy door behind him. The dull chunk of wood against wood reverberated, breaking the morning and shocking the birds to stillness, except for a raven high above who shrieked at him.

Five years ago, he'd married the prettiest woman in three counties. She loved him, she said. She smiled a lot and laughed and sang about cheerful maidens and rowdy men. All that had gone with his hand. She still kept the house neat as a pin. She cared for his first wife's children, she cared for him. But she no longer smiled.

His breath plumed white in the frosty air. The change of season caught him by surprise. He was missing the best lumbering time, the best opportunities for work with other lumberjacks. Not that anyone would hire him.

He kicked at a stump. The path outside his house led towards town in one direction and towards the river in the opposite. He set out across the meadow, away from either path, he decided, and away from home.

Most of the wood he passed was owned by the king. Not that the king would ever notice one or two missing trees, or if he did, discover who had taken them. Dario shook his head. He couldn't afford to think like a thief. One minute you're cutting the King's wood, imagining you've gotten away with it. The next minute, you've lost a hand.

It didn't matter how far he had to travel, he decided. Tonight, he'd come home with firewood and stove wood. They'd suffer from the greenness, burning sap smoked terribly, but they'd be warm. And have cooked food.

Movement at his foot startled him out of his day dream. A plump white rabbit hopped past him.

A little extra for the stewpot, he thought. He followed slowly, easing the axe from his shoulder.

It should have been an easy throw. He'd won contests even after losing his hand. But somehow when the blade bit into the earth the rabbit was gone.

He pulled up the ax. A sprinkle of rabbit droppings lay on the ground. Perhaps he'd nicked the creature and it had run off. Or disappeared down a hole.

The disappearance happened at the edge of a copse of woods. Dario examined the dense stand and frowned. No lumberjack signs marked off the wood, no fancy writs declaring this wood forbidden. Still, the white wood was too inviting. Someone must have claimed it before now. His frown deepened. He had never seen such trees before, stark white and leafless, standing in disciplined rows. The trunks looked healthy enough, like stripped pine splashed with whitewash. He decided they would do.

He wiped his forehead and glanced up at the morning sky. A raven spun in the air like a child's toy. The bird arrowed toward the copse of white woods then wheeled in midair, screeching. It dove at Dario. Sharp black wing feathers sliced across his chest.

"Making fun of me, are you?" He brushed his vest, not slashed open after all. "Yes, creatures of the earth and air are safe from me today. I am after wood and only wood will do."

He shouldered his axe again. The pristine wood awaited him. He set foot among the roots.

A spasm of vertigo overtook him. He put out his hand to catch his balance against a tree but touched nothing. His eyes rolled up in his head and he fell in a heap.

With his eyes closed he absorbed the eerie silence. Had a veil fallen over the wood? He opened his eyes.

The stand of trees gleamed white. The grass, which tickled his hand like normal grass when he touched it, showed relentlessly white with no shadings. Nothing sparkled. This was not a winter solstice. The wood appeared as if some malign magic had drained away all of nature's colors. The sky above lowered with close white clouds. He raised his right arm and looked at his remaining hand. His own skin seemed muted and pale. Would he turn white himself if he stayed long enough?

He was a simple man. He didn't allow himself to consider that the wood, clearly unnatural and possibly enchanted, might turn away the bite of his ax, or might respond to the cutting in some horrible manner. He was an honest man, so he had to admit these thoughts lurked at the back of his mind. He pushed the shadows down, hefted his ax, and swung.

The tree felled as if it were a normal tree. True, its descent was almost silent, as if its brothers had stepped aside for it, and true, it bled a green-tinged crystalline sap. Unusual.

Dario trimmed off the tree's crown. Then he lopped off the branches. The trunk lay naked as he rested and drank water. No creatures had made their homes in the tree, he realized. Nothing had scurried away, no sparrows, no squirrels, no snakes or rats, no ants or pill bugs. The white wood was innocent of forest vermin.

He set his water skin aside. One more, he thought. He could drag two logs home.

The sun was gone but the moon not yet risen when he dragged the long trunks into his yard. The curious vertigo had left him when he left the wood. It must be enchanted, he decided. He would not cut there again. But for now, he had warmth and cook fire for his family. Perhaps he could sell one of the trunks, perhaps he could buy his wife a new skirt, his children some toys.

His house was dark. No smoke belched from the chimney. His own fault, he knew, that the load of wood would remedy. But his wife did not come out to greet him. He did not hear his children's voices.

Ingrates, he thought. *They don't appreciate how hard I work.*

He unbound the logs. A few minutes' work with his axe and he chopped enough lengths of wood for the night. *I'll finish tomorrow. A bath with heated water would be a fitting reward for the day's work.*

He opened his door, anticipating the comforts of home.

A candle guttered on the table. Its yellow light illuminated the face of a woman he'd never seen before.

The woman sat in the master chair. A fleeting thought—his wife hadn't burned it—then his attention riveted to the woman. She was not beautiful. She inspired fear in him, and awe. He stood with his hand on the door for a full minute, staring at her. She wore a black dress, richly embroidered with silver, and jewels lined her perfectly-styled hair.

She smiled at him. Her eyes were reddened with tears.

A whimper broke the spell. Deirdre stood near her, her hands clasped under her apron.

He cleared his throat. "Wife, who is our guest?"

His wife whimpered again.

The woman at the table laughed. There was nothing wrong with the sound. In fact, Dario heard brooks burbling in the humor of her laugh. Still, the hairs stood up on the back of his neck.

"Don't bother her with questions she can't answer. Give her those marvelous logs and bid her warm the hearth. I admit to feeling chill."

He gave the bundle of wood to Deirdre. She struggled to set the fire. The logs held no moss and the bark wouldn't strip for kindling. She set a long match to the bare wood then jumped back with a cry.

"Burned me!" she said. "The fire is hungry."

"Feed it wood, not your flesh," he snapped.

She dipped her head. "Yes."

The woman smacked the table to get his attention.

"You need to pay me for those trees you stole."

"I did not know they were your trees," he said. "And I never stole. I did what a woodsman does, cutting wood for a fire."

"I posted boundaries. Those that fly and those that leap knew they could never enter. You ignored the boundary. You entered my wood carelessly and cut my trees."

He stammered. Did she know about his crime? Of course, she did, everybody did. But he was blameless this time. He was certain.

"Do you think to take advantage of me because of my past misfortune? There was no boundary!" He remembered the rabbit that disappeared and the raven that flew at him as if to discourage him. He took a deep breath.

"Do you want the wood? Is that why you're here? Pay me for my work, then. Otherwise, you are welcome to enjoy some warmth with us here, but then you must go."

"You will pay me for those trees. They were mine. They aren't yours until you pay."

"I don't have any money," he said. "I have nothing of interest to you!"

The woman, though seated, grew in size until she overwhelmed the room. Her shadow threatened to snuff out the tiny candle-light.

"You dare much, woodsman. You dare to steal my trees. You dare to guess what might interest me. Few have dared so much and lived to tell it. But you, woodsman, own two things of interest to me. I will have them and your debt to me will be settled."

Dario frowned. He owned so little anymore. He glanced around the barren great room. His family stood near the blazing hearth, silent. No carpet, no mirror. Sold long since. No sturdy lamp or delicate vase. Nothing that she'd want to collect. Unless she meant his livelihood.

He cried out, "My ax? But I only have one."

Her laugh was not kind. "What would I do with that clumsy tool? No, woodsman, you have taken the flesh of my forest. I will take the flesh of your home.

"You have two children. They will do to pay for the wood."

Deirdre shoved the children into a corner and stood in front of them. Dario hefted his axe and loomed over the table.

"Let's say I just cut you into a million pieces of kindling and put paid to the account."

The woman laughed, high and insane like a hyena. "You cannot." She waved her hand, a minor gesture.

All the strength drained from Dario's limbs. He could no longer hold the immense weight of the ax. It slid through his hands and thudded to the floor. He slumped against the table.

The woman leaned towards him.

"Don't try to stop me, woodsman, or you'll lose your other hand. And I'll still have your children."

The woman stood in front of Deirdre.

"Give way, wife," she said. "They never were your children. Now, they are mine."

Deirdre sprang on the woman, fists swinging. The woman stepped aside. Deirdre sprawled full length on the floor. Nonetheless she kicked out with her booted feet. One blow connected with the woman's ankle.

The woman growled.

"You are as pitiful at protecting these children as you were at caring for them. Bethany, Paul, to me."

The children, dazed and silent, put their hands in hers. She turned to leave.

"Don't fret, good wife, woodsman. The white wood you've cut will adequately compensate you for these two.

"But don't try the white woods again. You don't have any more children to trade. Though it's possible your wife could interest me."

Deirdre cringed away.

The woman laughed again. And like that she was gone, along with the children, without even a flicker of a breeze.

Dario crawled to where his wife lay sobbing in front of the hearth. He swept her into his arms. At first, she hit at him, but he didn't feel the blows. She stopped hitting. After a long while, she stopped sobbing.

"She was right, I never liked them. I never wanted them. I did care for them. You never had reason to complain. But how can wood repay us for the loss of the children?"

"I don't know." He stared at the flames dancing in the hearth. Enough wood for a few days' warmth. How was that a fair trade?

Something glinted in the ashes. Puzzled, he leaned close. A crystalline stone reflected the firelight. As he watched, another dropped from the glowing log. He grabbed the blackened fire poker and stirred the ashes. A full dozen stones lay in the hearth.

"Fetch more wood," he said.

The wife struggled to her knees, slow as a grandmother.

"I don't want stones, I want the children!"

"Fetch more wood!" he shouted.

She flinched. In a moment she snatched her woolen shawl from the peg by the door and slipped outside.

They worked all night, stoking the fire in the hearth. Dario cut the trunks into logs, the logs into chunks. Deirdre chipped kindling with her small axe and loaded the wood into the fire. Stones fell silently from the ember-rich wood.

"This is the last of it," Dario said. He gave her a short bit of wood. She tossed it into the hearth. The flames danced.

The house was indecently warm. They both sweated into their loosened clothing. The fire died away as the sun rose. Deirdre sat at the table with the stones piled in front of her.

"We must rescue the children!" she said.

"I didn't think you loved my children so much," he rumbled.

"I love you." She gazed up at him. Her tears glistened more brightly than the emeralds. "And you love them."

He touched her hand, his callused fingers squeezing.

"I have a plan. These are emeralds. I'll give her the emeralds," Dario said. "They're worth more than two scrawny children. They'd buy her a dozen hard-working servants. She'll give them back. Be sure of it."

"I'm sure of nothing," Deirdre said. "You weren't here when she arrived. One moment the children were eating their radishes and I was teaching them the counting song. The next moment she was there. Just standing there. She didn't knock on the door or even yet come through it.

"She is a witch. She must be."

Dario said, "Of course she's a witch. Doesn't mean she won't barter for the return of Bethany and Paul. I'll be back with them."

Deirdre gasped out, "I'm going, too."

"No, you're not. You'll wait until I return with the children. Anyway, you'd be of no use. You can't fight her."

Deirdre stuck out her chin. "I kicked her in the leg and hurt her last night while you lay in a swoon on the table. I can fight her, as much or more than you. Anyway, you might need an extra hand."

His missing hand itched. He almost slapped her. "Insolence! When did you...." He stopped. She was right.

"Eat some bread and some soup," she said. "You need your strength. I'll be right back."

He was amazed that she'd taken time to cook a meal, but then, she'd always taken care of him. The sweet stench of the burning wood had kept the good scents of food from his nose but now he remembered his hunger. He plowed through the food.

Deirdre returned wearing trousers. She had her hand axe stuffed through the belt.

He studied her.

"No," he said. He went to her and knelt on the floor. He pulled up the leg of her trouser and stuffed it into the cuff of her boot. "Wear it like this," he said. "Keeps the burrs and creatures from crawling up your leg." He leaned back on his heels. "Thank you."

She smiled. "Do you have the emeralds?"

He showed her the deerskin bag. "We're ready."

She got the last bit of bread from the table and tucked it into her pocket. "Yes, we are."

He slung his axe over his shoulder and opened the door for her.

"We aren't going to lose," he said.

"We are going to our deaths," she replied. "We are fighting a witch."

He touched her shoulder. She looked up at him. He kissed her.

"Even a witch has weaknesses," he said. "She can't touch iron." He hefted his ax. "Iron can touch her!"

Dario led her onto the path through the meadow. He didn't look around to make sure she kept up. The day was lovely, warm but cool enough that the walk did not exhaust them. Creatures stirred in the forest along the path, birds danced high above, and the sky was blamelessly blue.

Ahead of them was the white wood.

"Here," Dario said, "is where I entered the wood yesterday. But something's different." He pressed against the trunk of the nearest tree. "They weren't this close together!"

The tree shivered against him. He pushed, then turned sideways and shoved through the gap in the trunks. "It's like they're trying to keep me out!"

Deirdre said, "They're her trees, they don't want us in." She pulled her hand axe from her belt and looked at the tree. "Move aside."

The tree stopped moving. Dario watched her from beyond the screen of tree trunks.

She approached the tree and said, "Move aside!" She hacked at the tree with her ax. A small gash spewed green-tinted sap. The trees shrunk away from her.

She joined Dario. "Well?"

"Well." He turned and led her deeper into the wood.

He counted the trees as they passed. Normally he would notch a path, but this was not a normal forest. A count would have to do to find their way back out the other side.

They stumbled over roots. The tree limbs took sly swipes at them. Deirdre threatened another tree with her ax. At one point they fell together in a small pit of crisp white grass.

Yet, they were heartened.

"The trees wouldn't fight so hard if we weren't on the right path," Deirdre said.

"We must be getting close," Dario agreed.

The house, when they found, it was as fantastic and horrible as their imaginations had conjured. The roof was polished green stone, the walls glass and blood-colored wood. The house rested on blocks of white wood. A ramp led to the enormous front door rather than proper stairs.

And brambles grew around the house's foundation, thorny vines that writhed and slithered. They guarded the doorway ramp. They saw Deirdre and Dario and drew up in hissing formation.

"Use your ax," Deirdre said.

Dario stood and pulled his axe to his side. He walked to the ramp and tried his wife's words.

"Stand aside," he said.

The brambles only writhed and shook.

"Have it your way," he shrugged. He swung his ax. The brambles fell before it.

"Get inside!" he panted. "Get the children! I'll be done here very soon."

Deirdre eased behind him on the ramp.

"Cut the roots," she said. "It's the only way to kill vines."

She darted up to the door. Behind her Dario fought the brambles. He leapt from the ramp and chopped into the ground by the house's foundation.

The door was locked. She considered using her ax, but the door looked too solid, the lock too strong. She edged up to the window and peeked in. Nothing moved inside the house's great room. She continued around the outside, peering into windows, until she found the kitchen.

Nothing moved here either, but her children slept on a feather-stuffed mattress inside a wooden cage against the wall. She almost banged on the window to rouse them, then realized she didn't want to alert the witch as well. She crept to the kitchen door.

It was unlocked. In fact, it opened easily when she pushed on it.

She fell on her knees in front of the cage.

"Bethany! Paul! Wake up!" She tried to whisper but excitement raised her voice. "Wake up! I'll take you home." She reached through the bars and shook the children.

Paul roused first. He rubbed his eyes. Then he poked at Bethany. "She's here."

The little girl sat up.

"Go away!"

Deirdre said, "What? I'm here to bring you home." She pulled on the cage's door. It was firmly latched.

"We don't want to go."

"She feeds us."

"She doesn't make us do chores."

"We're warm!"

Deirdre was astonished. "But she keeps you in a cage!"

Bethany took a deep breath. "Mistress! Mistress! Come quick!"

Paul added his shouts to his sister's.

Deirdre swung her axe down on the cage latch. It didn't yield. She put the blade between the cage and the door and pushed, hoping to lever the cage open.

The children screamed.

Dario stormed through the kitchen door, shouting. "What's happening? Are you all right?"

At the same moment, the witch appeared. She laughed, clapping her hands with glee.

"Oh, you're all here! This is wonderful!" She waved a hand at Dario. "Sit!" He fell into a chair. The witch looked at the children. "Peace," she whispered. The children quieted. Then the witch waved at Deirdre who grasped the metal head of her ax. "Sit!" Deirdre sat on the floor.

"I think some hot cider is in order," she said. She plucked a clay kettle from the stove and poured frothy spiced cider into two mugs. The children accepted the drinks and sat in their cage, slurping.

The woman examined the cage door. "Not too much damage. I don't really need to keep them locked up, of course. They won't go back home. But it wouldn't do to have them running around my house like spoiled puppies."

The woman sat at her table across from Dario. "Now. Why have you come to disturb my home? Wasn't our agreement last night satisfactory?"

Dario said, "No, it wasn't. We've come to get our children."

"Truly? And what do you have to bargain with?" The woman's eyes gleamed and a smile played around her lips. As if she knew.

"The emeralds," Deirdre said from her place on the floor.

"The emeralds," Dario said. He pulled out the deerskin bag and flung it onto the table. "You could buy a dozen hard-working servants with what's in that bag!"

"I could," the woman said, "but I want your children. I told you. Your flesh for my flesh." She picked up the bag. Her eyes widened. She pulled it open and upended it.

Nothing came out.

"Did you think to trick me?" she said.

Dario stared in horror. "No! It was stuffed with those stones from your wood." He shook his head. "The bag was full. I swear it."

"It's not full now." The woman poked her finger through a hole in the bottom. "They must have fled. You are not the first to try and bargain with me, but you are the first to fail so badly at it. Now what shall I do about you?"

The woman laughed. "I suppose I could have you cut down more trees. Two more. Yes." She grinned.

"That's been your plan all along," Dario said. "You're a witch, you can't use iron. You'd never be able to get the emeralds. Unless someone helped you, and why would someone help you out of kindness?" He tried to push himself up from the table. His arms were weak but his legs were weaker. He fell back into the chair.

Deirdre spoke up. "You have us to help you get the emeralds. What do you want with the children?"

The woman laughed. "I keep telling you. They're now my flesh. They'll replace the two you stole. They've already begun the process. Two weeks and they'll be ready. Children, show this wife your hands."

Bethany and Paul obediently showed their hands to Deirdre. The fingernails had gone stark white.

"Oh!" Deirdre cried. "Oh, oh, oh! You're turning them into trees?"

The woman nodded. "Flesh of my flesh," she said.

Dario fought the exhaustion that encased his body. He stood up and grabbed his ax.

"Then I shall cut you into kindling, like the wood you are!" he roared.

The witch wove her hands in a gesture larger than any she'd used yet. Dario froze.

Deirdre screamed. She flung her axe at the witch. It sliced into the witch's side. She lurched against the table.

"You dare!" she whispered.

Dario blinked his eyes as if awakening from a spell. He swung his ax.

The woman felled easily, like a tree. Green-tinged crystalline blood flew from her veins. In moments, the woodsman had cut off her crown and trimmed her limbs. Her body was covered with hacked-up clothing, but where her flesh would have shown was only the carved wood of a statue. Dario stood over her, panting.

"The stove," Deirdre said. "Wood burns."

Dario nodded. He filled the stove with bits of the wooden woman. He fumbled one-handed with the matches. Deirdre pushed him aside.

"Let me."

She struck the match and flame leapt onto the wooden woman. Within moments flames blazed.

"Get the children," Dario said.

"I can't; the cage is locked," she said.

He used his axe and the cage opened. The children sat frozen.

"Get them!" he shouted. Flame escaped from the stove and chewed on the table and the chair where he'd sat. They didn't have long.

Deirdre grasped the children and pulled them from the cage. She hauled them to their feet. They stood, eyes unfocused. She grabbed their hands and ran for the door.

The house shook. They fled to the yard, as far away from the house as they could get without entering the white wood. The house burned hot and bright. Red flames consumed the walls. Yellow sparks flew from the roof. The family watched the solid structure turn into char and embers.

They didn't see the white wood disappear.

In the place of the ranks of white trunks stood a normal wood, gnarled trunks and limbs reaching down from pines and oaks and maples. Dario hugged Deirdre with his good arm.

"We're safe," he said.

The children cried. Deirdre hugged them and they hugged her back.

"What happened?" Paul said. "I don't remember anything except that a strange woman took us from you!"

"What happened?" Bethany said. "How did we get here?" She looked at her hands. "I can't feel my fingers!"

Deirdre saw that the child's fingers were still stone white. She shared a dismayed glance with Dario. Then, she lied.

"Don't worry," she said. "They'll be back to normal before you know it!" She hugged the girl again.

"How are we going to get home?" Deirdre said to her husband.

He smiled. "The white woods may have gone, but the emeralds remained. Look!" He pointed to a wide willow tree. An emerald sparkled at its base.

"The children have the best eyesight. Find the path, Bethany. Paul, pick up the emeralds as we go."

They walked into the forest. But they weren't the only ones returning. A flock of ravens watched them and swarmed after them. Before they had gone ten feet, the ravens had descended on the trail and swallowed every emerald. One brave bird even plucked the first emerald from Paul's hand.

"We are going to be lost in the forest." Deirdre didn't want to walk any further.

"Yes," Dario said.

"We still don't have any wood or any money," she said.

"True," Dario replied.

"Our children are permanently marked by that witch," she said.

"Maybe. Unless they grow out of it," Dario said.

"Why are you so happy?" Deirdre stamped her foot into the forest's thick bed of leaves and moss.

He couldn't deny that he smiled. "Because I have my family," he said. "And because I can bring us some meat for the stewpot." He threw his ax. It whirled between the tree limbs and lopped off the heads of five ravens. The birds tumbled to the ground.

"What do you suppose is inside?" And he smiled again.

My Muse Wears Army Boots
Christine Lucas

J*eff Billings loved the dead.*
Having few friends among the living, he found a strange kind of comfort in the cold stillness of the morgue. He had requested to work night shifts just for the opportunity to transport the dead patients of St. Anna's Hospital. In his long experience as an orderly, more people died at night.

The chill of that late November night didn't affect him, even inside the morgue. He took a sip of gin, camouflaged as water in an ordinary plastic bottle, and lifted the sheet covering a corpse still on the gurney.

What a pity, such a pretty girl!

He checked her toe tag. Miss Lucy had died of a brain aneurysm. During her wedding rehearsal, he had heard the ER nurses say. Jeff's head burst with images, as though he had been present. It had started so innocently—just a stress headache. But painkillers failed to ease the pounding in her head, and soon her vision blurred. Her fiancé's voice reached her as if through a haze, her limbs weakened with each heartbeat. In seconds, she collapsed on the floor, her brain swimming in a pool of blood inside her skull.

The vision vanished as fast as it came and left Jeff breathless and bereft. His fingers brushed her pale cheek, traced the outline of her full lips and ended at the small of her neck. Every inch of porcelain skin whispered stories in his mind, memories treasured in her now still heart: the grief over the passing of her first pet cat, the exhilaration of her first kiss, the guilt of flirting with a man other than her betrothed.

Dust to dust. He covered her and placed her in the freezer. Once finished, he took another sip of gin, his blood aflame. So many emotions, so many memories!

Jeff loved the dead and the stories they told him.

§

After his shift ended, Jeff rushed to his apartment and made a pot of strong coffee. He stretched his arms, his shoulders stiff after a busy night. Still, Lucy's presence lingered inside his head, waiting for her story to be told. He opened his notebook and picked up his pen.

And, once more, words failed him.

Lucy's story was there, bouncing inside his head, screaming to be let out, but every line he wrote was worse than the previous one. Flat emotions, colorless scenes, moronic dialogue, like teenagers killing time in chatrooms. He scribbled for an hour, until his waste basket was full of crumbled pages and his vision blurred from frustration and fatigue. His knuckles turned white around his pen, his jaw clenched and he threw the notebook across the room. He might as well go to sleep.

He drifted away with the same persistent thought crushing his chest: *I'll never be a writer.*

§

A week later, Jeff sipped his coffee in the nurses' lounge, browsing the sports section of a day-old paper. It was a slow night for the entire hospital, not just the Stroke Unit of the Geriatrics ward, and he was grateful for the respite. He'd rather avoid a trip to the morgue; enough stories bounced inside his head already, and all his attempts to put them on paper failed miserably.

He had read the paper twice when the door opened and a nurse stuck her head in.

"New patient, Jeff. I need your help."

Jeff followed her down the hall to one of the private rooms. The stench of old age hit him before even crossing the door: urine-soaked diapers, disinfectant, and imminent death. An old man lay on the bed, skeletal under the covers, his face sallow, his eyes shut and sunken. Jeff stopped in his tracks; he had seen this man before. But where?

The unanswered question nudged the back of his mind the whole time he spent there. Alas, the old man was comatose after a stroke and could not enlighten him. He didn't respond to anything— not even when they inserted a catheter into his bladder. Once they were finished, Jeff checked the patient chart and his jaw dropped. That corpse of a man was Gerald Fitzpatrick? The award-winning author, whose works were revered by fans and critics alike?

Jeff's gaze darted from Gerald's face to the chart and back. *What's your secret, old man?*

His fists clenched. One way or another, he'd find out.

§

Gerald died a week later. Jeff was furious. He had spent every free moment of his shifts in the old guy's room, cooling his brow, checking his vitals, arranging his pillows, cleaning him, as though he was his private nurse. But Gerald didn't even moan once. No sign for him, no great revelation of the old man's secrets. Fuming inside, he assisted the night nurse in preparing the corpse for the morgue. Perhaps there Gerald would share a tip or two for an aspiring writer like him.

It was not his lucky night.

In the privacy of the empty morgue, Jeff cupped the old man's forehead, but no images came to him. He pushed harder, his fingers pressing the thin skin on the fragile skull. He pushed with his mind, probing, seeking like he had never done before—he had never needed to. Something cracked beneath his fingers and an electrical surge traveled up his arm and into his head. He tried to break away, but found he could not.

And he *saw*.

Little of it made sense: fragmented images, swirling emotions, impossible plotlines, all imbued with an overwhelming need to *write*. One image dominated all others, the image of a strange girl. Dark-haired, small-framed, she lurked at the corner of each memory, with her goth clothes and strange tattoos. Didn't the old guy have a daughter? But would the daughter of a world-renowned author dress in black, tight tops and army boots?

Something nibbled the edge of his consciousness—literally. Something fanged and clawed, something lurking in the shadows of the old man's mind reached out to him. Persistent, hungry, it sought entrance to his mind. He cried out and jumped back, breaking the contact. He checked his hand. It hurt as though burnt, but he saw no damage.

His heart still raced when he shoved the corpse into the freezer. This time, he fled from the morgue without one glance back.

§

When Jeff returned upstairs, there was a woman waiting for him by the nurses' station. Slim and elegant, in her late thirties, she introduced herself as Suzanne Fitzpatrick, Gerald's daughter. She offered him her hand.

"I'm told you have taken special care for my father during his last week." Her grip was firm and confident. And she looked nothing like the goth girl from his vision.

Jeff avoided her gaze. "Well, Ms. Fitzpatrick, I was a great fan of your father. My deepest sympathy for your loss."

"Thank you." She took a step forward, still holding his hand, her expensive perfume teasing his nostrils. With her free hand she slipped him a folded bank note. "For your trouble."

Jeff's eyes darted sideways, to check if anyone had witnessed the exchange. Taking tips was against hospital regulations and could get him fired. He slipped the money back to her palm.

"Ah, Miss, please, no need for that. I really admired your father." He looked down, his feet the safest spot to focus on. "I only wish one day I'll be half the writer your father was."

"Ah. An aspiring writer." She released his hand. Her gaze lingered on his face, as though seeking something in his stubble or the black circles under his eyes. After an uncomfortable moment that dragged on too long, she reached into her purse. "What's your address? Perhaps a token from my father's study might be more suitable. Unless that too is against regulations?"

He managed a grin. Even if it was atrocious, anything that belonged to Gerald Fitzpatrick would bring him a fortune from the right collector.

"What they don't know can't hurt them."

§

Two days later, a small package arrived in the mail. Jeff tore away the wrapping and found an ornate wooden box in it. Painted black, half the size of an average shoebox, it had silver cast decorations in abstract, flame-like shapes. They seemed to swirl and spiral under his gaze, and the tips of his fingers tingled when he touched them. He placed it on his desk, made some coffee and sat down for a closer examination.

There was no lock and the lid popped open with minimal effort. Inside it lay a doll, roughly the length of Jeff's palm. It was no Barbie doll, though. Clad in tight black clothes and army boots, she had short, spiky hair, along with tattoo-like drawings on her bare arms and exposed stomach. Jeff felt pounding inside his head. Why did that toy look so familiar?

He took a sip of coffee that failed to ease the buzzing in his ears, and rubbed his sore eyes. When he looked at the open box again, the doll had sat up. She stared at him with red, beady eyes. He blinked. Was lack of sleep finally getting at him? She grinned and Jeff pushed his chair back and stifled a scream. That tiny mouth had double rows of piranha teeth. She stood, stretched and looked around.

Jeff wanted to flee, but his legs ignored him. Sweat dripped down his neck and face, stinging his eyes.

"Wh-what are you? What do you want?"

"Write." She licked her lips with a tiny blood-red tongue.

He gasped. "What?"

She climbed out of the box, crouched at the edge of the desk and leaped on his lap with a flea's ease. "Write."

He tried to slap her away. "Ow!" Those teeth were indeed as sharp as they looked.

He sucked his bitten finger while she grasped his sleeve and made her way up to his shoulder. Perched by his neck, her breath chilled his ear. "Write."

Her voice, soft and seductive, fired up his mind. Words exploded inside his skull like stars, words and phrases and scenes, the tales of the dead interwoven in perfect symmetry. Their memories, their hopes and fears were no longer stolen, colorless moments in the cold stillness of the morgue, but songs and hymns. His fingers tingled afresh, seeking a pen. He did not wait for the little creature to urge him again. He pulled the chair close to his desk, picked up his pen and wrote.

The little creature hugged Jeff's neck and oversaw his progress.

§

Jeff called in sick for the next two days, then he requested a month's vacation time. He had to write. Eating, sleeping, personal hygiene had lost importance. Nothing mattered anymore but the stories that flowed effortlessly from his mind. Sustained by unhealthy amounts of caffeine and gin, he filled notebook after notebook, journal after journal, and cursed himself for not having saved enough money for a laptop.

My Muse wears army boots and has piranha teeth.

He glanced at the tiny creature lounging inside the silver-cast box. His free hand traced the bite marks on his neck. Any pause seemed to annoy her. She did allow him short respites to visit the bathroom, drive to the shop for coffee, gin and writing supplies, even sleep a couple of hours per day. But watch a ball game or a movie over dinner? No chance in hell. "*Not yet,*" she'd whisper in his ear. "*You haven't earned it.*"

He once dared to ask: "What *are* you?"

"I'm your Muse, silly. Now, write." She giggled, and his skin crawled. He never asked her again.

So, Jeff wrote. Story after story, the tales of the dead stopped bouncing inside his head and found their way into words. Into *good* words, he admitted to himself, allowing his face to relax to a thin grin of pride.

"Hey!" The creature's bite made his grin vanish. When had she climbed back on his shoulder?

"Write." Tiny claws traced his carotid artery.

"I'm writing, okay? Stop that!"

"Write. And, tomorrow, send that off?"

His hand froze mid-phrase. "What?"

She leapt on the desk and shuffled through the notebooks. She turned the pages and pointed at a story. "This one. Send it off for publication."

He scoffed. "Right. As if I stand a chance."

Her tiny eyes narrowed and chilled his blood.

"Fine," he mumbled and rubbed his exposed neck. "What do I have to lose?"

§

Jeff polished and mailed that story to one of his favorite magazines, then resigned from work. The creature wouldn't let him leave his desk for a whole shift at a time anyway. He spent his days writing. Sometimes he shaved, sometimes he ate, sometimes he slept, his past life a distant memory.

The days turned to weeks, the weeks to months and one day the reply from the magazine came. That particular week had been a muddled mist in Jeff's mind. He recalled driving to the store at some point for gin, chips and notebooks but, for the life of him, he couldn't recall where he had parked his car when he came back. And why were his face and hands scratched and bruised? Had the little demon started beating him as well?

But none of that mattered now. The reply had come. He placed the unopened letter on his desk and stared at it for a long time. He got up and paced the length of his apartment a dozen times. He lit a cigarette, checked both sides of the envelope, weighed it in his hand, and put it down again. Then he paced the length of his apartment another dozen times, sweaty and agitated. Surprisingly, the creature in the army boots sat quietly in her box all this time, watching him.

In the end, he made coffee, lit a second cigarette and tore the letter open.

"Dear Mr. Billings,

We are pleased to accept your short story "A Dead Man's Tale" for publication in…."

Jeff choked on his coffee. He put out his cigarette and held the letter with both hands. It couldn't be. Could it? His gaze darted from the letter to the creature and back. She was grinning, content for the first time. She licked her lips, her eyes glowing as though his success tasted like sweet wine.

"They'll publish it." He wanted to call someone, tell the world about it. Too bad he had no friends, no one who'd care for his success. Not among the living, at least.

"Of course, they will."

He looked away. "Th-thank you."

"You're welcome. Now write." She climbed up to his shoulder.

Jeff sighed and reached for the pen. He had barely written half a sentence when his doorbell rang. He blinked. Who could that be? He pushed his chair back to get to the door, when the creature hissed and hid inside his shirt, little claws digging into his flesh. He grimaced, but knew better than try to shake her off.

"Who's here?" Behind the closed door, Jeff wiped his sweaty palms on the seat of his pants.

"Police, Mr. Billings. Please open the door."

His knees weakened. "Got some identification?"

The short, stocky police officer at the other side of the door held his badge close to the peephole.

Jeff wiped his brow. "What's this about?"

"Please, open the door, Mr. Billings." The moment stretched in silence. "Unless you have something to hide and I should return with a warrant."

The urge to bang his head against the wall made his vision blur. *This can't be happening. Not now. Not today.* He drew in a deep breath and opened the door. "I have nothing to hide, officer." He managed a nervous grin. "Except for a messy apartment."

The officer glanced around, at the empty gin bottles piling by his desk, the used tissues and empty soda cans littering the floor. "There has been a hit and run accident, sir. A car registered to you has been found near the scene. I'd like you to follow me to the precinct to answer some questions."

"Uhm, sure. Just let me get my jacket." His throat burned, his mouth was dry and he hoped that he didn't look guilty. One look at the officer's frown told him otherwise.

As he closed the door behind him, the little creature inside his shirt dug her claws deeper.

§

All alone in the holding cell, Jeff cursed his bad luck. Apparently, his car had been abandoned close to the accident site, with the victim's blood on it, and his own blood inside. He rubbed his temples. Why couldn't he remember anything? Good God, had he really killed that poor guy?

"Damned booze!"

Jeff clutched the edge of the cell bench so hard his knuckles turned white. He'd have to spend the night in there and appear to court tomorrow for his arraignment. And his Public Defense lawyer had seemed a total jerk.

Great timing, Universe. Having me arrested the day I get my first acceptance.

He tapped his fingers on the bench. At least it was quiet—*too quiet*. He shifted on his seat, agitated. If only he had thought of bringing a notebook along…

The little creature crawled out of his shirt, glanced around the empty room and climbed up his shoulder. "Write."

"Shut up. It's not a good time."

"Write." Her voice dropped several degrees in temperature.

"Don't be ridiculous. Not here. I'll write when I get back home." *If I ever get back there.*

"Write. *Now.*" Tiny claws traced his exposed jugular.

"I have no pen or paper." They had taken away his pen, his belt, even his shoelaces. And they had left the little demon. How had they missed her? Was she invisible to them? Short of breath, he rubbed his temples, struggling to fend off the flood of thoughts and words. Scenes and plotlines cramped inside his head, fighting for release. What was she doing to him? He walked to the door and called through the bars, "Can I get some paper here?"

No one answered him. No one heard him, most likely, everyone too busy with a triple homicide. Located in the back of the building, the area of the holding cells was pretty much deserted, save for a drunk in the first cell.

"Stop procrastinating and write!" The lash of her command added fiery pain to the cacophony inside his skull.

"Fine, I'll write!"

Half-blinded from the waxing pain, he bit the tips of his fingers and started writing in blood on the bench surface. His fingertips hurt, but after a while Jeff hardly noticed it. Funny how effortlessly the words flowed in this unfamiliar environment, filled with threatening sounds. Inch by inch, he scribbled his best story ever. The tale of a man wrongly accused of murder took shape, a complex tale of intrigue and mystery.

When the upper surface had been covered with words cramped close together, Jeff crawled under the bench and started writing there. When that filled too, he moved to the walls. Halfway through the first wall, he felt lightheaded. He closed his eyes and drew deep breaths. Was the blood loss getting to him? Perhaps he should ask again for pen and paper. He walked to the door and waved his arms through the bars, trying to get someone's attention.

"Hey, can I have a pen and some paper here?"

No response.

Jeff tried again. "Hello? Anyone?"

"Shut up," yelled the drunk. "People are trying to sleep here!"

Jeff's shoulders slumped. He sat down. "I'm done writing for today. I'm getting dizzy."

"Write." The creature's hiss chilled his ear.

"Hey, give me a break! What more do you want from me?"

"Write."

Sharp fangs closed around his collar bone, and he yelled. He grasped the creature, squeezed it with all the strength he could muster, and threw it against the wall.

"Leave me alone!"

Before he could blink, she jumped on him and bit his shoulder. He threw her off again, and his eyes watered at the sharp jolt of pain from his shoulder into his chest. The little demon still had his flesh in her fangs. She chewed it with wicked delight, licked her lips and claws and crouched, ready to jump on him again. Jeff cowered against the wall.

"Okay, okay, I'll write! Just leave me alone," he whimpered.

She sat cross-legged on the floor and licked a droplet of blood from her alabaster arm. "Write, then."

Tearful and shaking, Jeff touched the wound on his shoulder. He stared at his blood for a moment that stretched on.

Certain that he would not live to see morning, he continued his unfinished story.

§

"Good heavens, what happened in here?"

CSI officer Derek Evans had seen a good deal of gruesome crime scenes in his career. This certainly qualified for the top five. There was blood everywhere: the walls, the floor, even the ceiling. He tilted his head sideways, focusing at the mangled body of the thin man sprawled on the floor. How could that slender body hold that much blood? It certainly seemed more than five liters.

He approached the body, each step slow and cautious. The dead man lay naked, every inch of his skin torn and scratched. On closer examination, the scratches seemed like…words? Derek glanced around. Words were everywhere. The poor guy had written on every free surface with his own blood.

Beside the corpse lay a doll. A weird doll, Derek decided, but very life-like. Was it some sort of fetish, with that ugly goth look? He shrugged, bagged it and placed it in his case. He had hardly left it when his fingers tingled. Instead of collecting blood samples from the carnage, Derek took out his notebook.

All of a sudden, he had the pressing urge to write.

When Phakack Came to Steal Papa
A Ti Jean Story
Ace Jordyn

*O*nce *upon a time, not that long ago, and maybe even* yesterday, a young boy named Ti Jean lived in the wilds of northern Canada with Mama Marie and Papa Pierre, and two older brothers. One day in late fall, when the ice was forming on the rivers and lakes, Papa Pierre left to work the trap lines.

Everyone helped with the fall chores, knowing that Papa Pierre would return in two weeks with a bundle of furs. They'd trade those for flour and clothes. Papa would then hunt a moose so they'd have enough meat for the long cold winter. Two weeks later, Papa Pierre didn't return as expected and with winter quickly approaching, they were worried indeed.

"Papa can take care of himself," the eldest brother said. "But as he is late, I'll shoot a moose." So, he shot a moose and brought it back home. They skinned the moose, cut the meat in strips, and dried it. Some of it they kept for jerky, and the rest they crisped over a fire, pounded into powder, mixed it with dried berries and melted fat to make pemmican.

"Papa likes his fried bread and bannock," said the second brother. "Without his furs, we can't buy flour." So, he set off in the direction of Papa's trap line and found a pile of pelts. He tied a strap around the pelts, and after hefting the pile onto his back, he secured the band across his hairline, leaned forward, and carried the bundle to the trading post. He bought flour to make fried bread and bannock for Papa.

They were now set for the winter except that Papa still hadn't returned. Without him, there would be no one to play the fiddle to protect them from Phakack, the skeleton who stole souls and gnawed on dead people's bones through the winter.

Their mother wrung her hands with worry so much that she nearly wore out her wrists. Ti Jean told his brothers they needed to find Papa or poor Mama would die of grief and Phakack would feast on her bones. His brothers said not to worry, because Papa Pierre always came back.

But, Ti Jean did worry. He hopped from one foot to the other as he fretted. His brothers teased him that he'd wear out his moccasins and the floor, too, if he wasn't careful. Ti Jean knew that unlike his older brother, he wasn't big enough to hunt a moose. He couldn't carry the bundle of furs like his second brother could. He couldn't even play the fiddle to keep Phakack from stealing their souls and gnawing on their bones. All he could do was dance.

The next morning, while everyone still slept, Ti Jean put on his moccasins and dressed in his warmest wool sweater and leather coat. He spied the corner where Papa Pierre kept his fiddle. It was empty and he vowed to bring Papa and the fiddle home to keep Phakack away. Outside, Ti Jean felt the cold of the night sweep over him as it sprinkled its shiny seeds for the coming snow. A branch rattled. Phakack! Ti Jean bolted into the wilderness.

Ti Jean ran to escape Phakack. He ran to find Papa. He ran right to Old Grandmother's tipi.

"Ti Jean, my son," she said. "I heard you running from far away. What problem have you when the seeds of snow fall?"

"Papa Pierre is missing," he said, "and I must find him."

Old Grandmother nodded. "I am one hundred years old," she said. "Come, let me feed you and rest you for the night."

Ti Jean did as he was told, and on a pile of furs, he slept well.

The next morning, Old Grandmother fed him breakfast and gave him a gift.

"Thank you," he said as he took a beaded leather pouch from her and slid it into a coat pocket.

"This pouch will feed you for as long as you need. But beware, if you come across the black wolf, remember he is *rougarou*, half man, half wolf. If he tricks you, say once to the wolf-man, *do not eat me*."

Ti Jean ran all day. As night fell, he came across another tipi. Inside, Older Grandmother waited for him.

"Ti Jean, my son," Older Grandmother said. "I heard you running from Old Grandmother's house. What problem have you that worries you so?"

"Papa Pierre is missing," he said, "and I must find him."

Older Grandmother nodded. "I am three hundred years old," she said. "Come, let me feed you and rest you for the night."

Ti Jean did as he was told, and atop a pile of furs, he slept well.

The next morning, Older Grandmother fed him breakfast and gave him a gift.

"Thank you," he said as he accepted a sash woven in the browns, reds, and greens of autumn. and tied it around his waist.

"Two eyes have you to see. If Raven tricks you, say you to him, *my eyes you cannot pick, my eyes you cannot pick*. Wrap then, this cloth twice around your head—once above your eyes and the other below leaving the tiniest slits through which to see. Then, Raven will let you be."

Again, Ti Jean ran all day. As night fell, he came across a third tipi. Oldest Grandmother waited inside for him.

"Ti Jean, my son," she said. "I heard you running from Older Grandmother's house. What problem have you that you run to the wilderness where old Phakack lives?"

"Papa Pierre is missing," he said, "and I must find him."

Oldest Grandmother nodded. "I am six hundred years old," she said. "Come, let me feed you and rest you for the night."

Ti Jean did as he was told, and on a pile of furs, he slept well.

The next morning, Oldest Grandmother fed him and gave him a gift of beaded moccasins.

"Thank you," he said, "but I have moccasins."

Oldest Grandmother held up his moccasins. The bottoms were worn to the felt.

"Mend these, I could not," she said. "Your feet you need to find Papa Pierre. Hurry, my son."

Ti Jean slipped on the new moccasins and tied them tight. Outside, everything was covered in brilliant white snow. Unwilling to wear their fresh white blankets, tree branches shook and rattled like dry bones. Phakack searched for him! Ti Jean ran from Oldest Grandmother's tipi as hard and as fast as he could.

But then, he tripped over a big heaping mound and felt the cold sting of fresh snow when his face hit the ground.

The mound howled and sprang into the air so quickly that Ti Jean found himself on his back, staring into the face of a big black wolf. A *rougarou!* A man who had changed into a wolf!

Rougarou towered over Ti-Jean; its front paws pinned his shoulders to the ground. The wolf's red eyes burned into his, but fear kept Ti Jean's eyes wide and round. Drool dripped from Rougarou's mouth and onto Ti Jean's face. He wanted to scream, but Rougarou's bad breath choked him. Never again would he argue with Mama about chewing on mint and using reeds to clean his teeth. That is, if the wolf-man didn't eat him first.

Rougarou bared his teeth and snarled. Ti Jean almost peed himself. The wolf-man's nose almost touched his.

"I smell Old Grandmother's food," Rougarou said. "Give it to me or I'll eat you instead."

"How?" Ti Jean yelped. "I can't move!"

"I'll let you go," Rougarou growled, "but remember, I'm faster than you."

Ti Jean wasn't certain of that, not with Oldest Grandmother's moccasins. Rougarou took his paw off one shoulder.

"Give it to me!"

"I would," Ti Jean said, "but it's in a pocket on the other side."

Rougarou pinned his free shoulder and released the other. Now, Ti Jean's other hand was free but he still couldn't run.

"Give it to me!" Rougarou snarled, his eyes as red as blood. His teeth glistened with drool. He opened his mouth wide and leaned in.

"Please," Ti Jean said, "don't eat me!"

Rougarou jumped off and sat beside Ti Jean. He didn't growl or snarl or drool. It was then that Ti Jean remembered—Old Grandmother had told him to say *please don't eat me.*

The wolf-man sniffed at Ti Jean's pocket.

"Hungry, aren't you?" Ti Jean said.

He shared the pemmican and Rougarou snapped it down. Then something strange happened—Rougarou changed from wolf to man. He still smelled bad and his clothes were tattered, but he was a man. A scared man whose eyes were no longer red but blue.

"I was lost," the man said. "Hungry and I…"

"Take this." Ti Jean filled the man's pockets with pemmican.

"But how?" the man looked from his pockets to Ti Jean.

Old Grandmother's gift was sacred, so Ti Jean simply pointed and said, "If you go that way, you'll find your way back."

"But you?" the tattered man asked.

"I'm not lost, just searching."

Bones rattled deep in the forest. Phakack! He'd beaten Rougarou and he wasn't going to let Phakack catch him now. He ran.

The day was bright and it got brighter as the sun went higher and bounced off the snow, stabbing Ti Jean's eyes until they began to hurt. He saw black spots and they grew bigger and bigger. He was going blind! The black spots flapped, and landed beside him. Ravens!

"Why don't you lay down," the first raven said, "and rest your eyes?"

"Please do," croaked the second. "We'll guard you."

"Make sure no one bothers you," added the first.

Ti Jean sat on a fallen log and closed his sore eyes. These ravens, with their constant croaking, made his head ache.

"Leave me be!" Ti Jean snapped. "My head hurts and my eyes are sore."

"I'll guard one eye," said the first.

"And I the other," croaked the second.

"Aye we will!" they cawed.

"You know," said the first raven, "if you give us your eyes, we'll stop the light from hurting them."

"And they won't pain you anymore," said the second.

"We brought the light to the world," said the first.

"And we can take it away," croaked the second.

They wanted to trick him into thinking they were helping him and then they'd peck out his eyes. The tricksters!

"You cannot eat me," Ti Jean said hoping it would stop them as it had Rougarou.

Still, the ravens cackled for his eyes. He threw them pemmican, but they still pestered him for his eyes.

When Ti Jean covered his burning eyes with his hands, he peeked at the ravens through his fingers. Now, he remembered Older Grandmother's gift. He whipped the sash from his waist and wrapped it around his eyes just as Older Grandmother had told him to. He could squint between the wrapped sash just enough to see without the brightness stabbing his aching head.

"My eyes you cannot pick. My eyes you cannot pick," he said.

"In this world his eyes still be," the first raven said.

"No darkness to ease your pain can we bring," cawed the second.

The ravens flew in the same direction he'd been running. Papa Pierre! If they had wanted to eat his eyes, what would they want from Papa? What if Papa was sick and couldn't save himself? Running as hard as he could, Ti Jean followed the disappearing dots.

The ravens circled over a trapper's hut. It was a small wooden building, just big enough for one man to sleep in and to hold his pelts and store his food. The hut was as cold and still as a frozen cattail in the winter ice. Frozen pelts hung on drying racks outside. There were no footprints in the snow; no sign that papa was here. This was not good.

Ti Jean rushed to the hut, flung open the door and tore the sash off his head. The hut was dark despite the door being open. The place smelled horrible, like someone had been sick over and over again. The little potbelly stove was silent and cold. Fur pelts were piled in a corner by the door. Papa's fiddle sat on a shelf. His bear-skin coat was thrown over the lone chair in the room. The cot was a rumpled mess of blankets and a fur which had nearly slid off it.

The rumple moved. Papa!

Ti Jean ran to the cot and nearly slipped on the frozen mess of sickness on the floor. Papa was cold and sweaty, and he barely breathed. Ti Jean gently shook Papa's shoulders.

"Papa!" Ti Jean shouted. "It's me!"

"Nooooo, Phakack! Noooo!" Papa coughed and Ti Jean heard the distant sound of Phakack's rattling bones.

What should he do? Papa was too sick to eat Old Grandmother's pemmican. Older Grandmother's sash wasn't big enough to keep Papa warm. But Oldest Grandmother's moccasins—he'd run back to Oldest Grandmother for help.

Phakack's bones rattled through the forest. Phakack was coming! Ti Jean couldn't leave Papa alone.

Papa moaned. Ti Jean touched his forehead. It was hot. That was bad. Ti Jean grabbed fur pelts and fur side down, he covered Papa. He gathered wood for the potbelly stove and lit a fire. Bucket in hand, he ran to the river, broke through the shell of ice and scooped water. He cut willow branches and brought them in with the water. After filling the kettle, he put it on the stove to heat. Ti Jean peeled the bark off the willow branches and scraped the insides into a tall tin teapot to which he added dried Labrador Tea leaves, and hot water. Then, he held Papa's head and made him drink. Papa coughed and his chest rattled. Phakack! What to do now? Ti Jean hopped from one foot to the other with worry.

The fiddle! He plucked a string. The twang hurt his ears. Again, Papa's chest rattled. Ti Jean plucked all the strings. They sounded horrible. Another coughing fit rattled Papa's chest. The hut shook. The door shuddered and door blew open. Phakack had come!

Tall, white and bony, Phakack's skeleton filled the doorway.

"For Papa Pierre, I have come," Phakack said. His bones rattled as he stepped into the hut.

Sweat rolled off Ti Jean's brow. What to do? How to stop him? He plucked a string on the fiddle.

"The wind ruffling the hair of the dead, that is the tune," Phakack rattled closer to Papa.

The pemmican in Old Grandmother's pouch wouldn't feed Phakack, but…

"Please, don't eat Papa!" he yelled.

"A wild cat's last yowls, is your voice!" Phakack rattled a step closer. "Eat him, I will!"

Older Grandmother's sash had kept the ravens from stealing the light from Ti Jean's eyes. He wrapped it around Phakack's skull.

Phakack laughed. "Think you that now I cannot see? The eyes of your world I have not, but the eyes of the dark I do." Phakack flung the sash off its head.

Older Grandmother's words had stopped the ravens. "His bones you cannot pick! His bones you cannot pick!" Ti Jean yelled but Phakack still moved. Ti Jean drew the bow across the fiddle.

"Play, you cannot," Phakack whistled through his empty skull. "Papa Pierre I will have."

"Play I cannot, but dance I can," Ti Jean said. "Dance I can, dance I can, dance I can!" All night, Ti Jean danced around Phakack, never letting the creature get close to Papa Pierre. Sometimes he danced to his singing, sometimes he danced to the fiddle's screeches, but always, he danced. The more Ti Jean danced, the less and less Phakack moved and soon, Phakack was just a stack of swaying bones.

Ti Jean danced into the early hours when those brave enough to wake swallow the sun's first rays with their morning yawns.

"Ti Jean," Papa rasped. "Stop that racket!"

Phakack disappeared and Ti Jean collapsed into the chair.

The next day, Ti Jean snared a rabbit to make a stew to which he added chopped cattail roots, buffalo berries and hazelnuts. He was sad because he didn't have any flour to make bannock for Papa. The second night they ate Old Grandmother's pemmican. On the third day, when Ti Jean was deciding if he should catch a fish or a grouse for their dinner, the door to the hut opened.

A man stood in the doorway. Tall, and in a heavy fur coat.

"Rou—" Ti Jean began, and then caught himself.

"Henri Devreaux," the man said and held out his hand.

To Papa he said, "Your son saved my life. When I got back to camp, I told my men about him. We decided that if he was searching for something, we needed to help him."

And so it was that Henri and his friends had come with two dog sleds. In one they loaded Papa Pierre under a pile of furs. The other they filled with furs. Two men walked behind the sleds while Ti Jean danced to keep Phakack away.

When they arrived home, Mama Marie and his brothers were overjoyed to see them all. Mama fussed the way mamas do, and once Papa was comfortable, his brothers told him everything they'd done.

"I hunted a moose!" the oldest brother bragged.

"I found your pelts six hills away from the river on Rocky Creek and I traded them for flour at the trading post," bragged the second.

"You," Papa said to the oldest brother, "hunted a moose alone!"

The oldest brother beamed.

"Don't ever do that again without me," Papa said. "Moose are dangerous this time of year. We are lucky to have the meat but foolish you were."

To the second brother he said, "Those pelts you took, they were not mine. You were on the Kennedy's trap line. You must carry those furs to them." Papa pointed to his pile of furs.

"And you," he said to the oldest, "must go with him because the way to the Kennedys is far."

Ti Jean gave his brothers Old Grandmother's pouch that always had pemmican so they wouldn't be hungry on their journey. He gave them Older Grandmother's sash in case the ravens wanted to peck their eyes. When his brothers laughed and said they didn't need these things because they were older, stronger and knew what to do, Papa Pierre said, "Unlike you, Ti Jean accepted help. He not only survived, but he saved me, too."

After his brothers left, papa played the fiddle while Mama clapped and sang. Ti Jean danced in the moccasins Oldest Grandmother had made just for him. He loved them for it was their magic that had helped him dance all night to save Papa.

And that is the story of a young boy named Ti Jean who lived in the wilds of northern Canada who was clever enough to ask for help, and to do what he did best, so he could save Papa Pierre.

Stone Gift
Robert N. Stephenson

***M**yulli gazed awe-struck at the distant Kyjihm mountain* range. Her young eyes were wide and glistening as she stared at the craggy peaks. The great, black walls frowned under the weight of the billowing, dark sky. "It brings Gallerra," whispered Myulli.

"It will bring nothing but much needed rain," growled Fiali, Myulli's uncle. He wore orange robes, was tall, lean, and cantankerous. "But the message on the stone of coming? Gallerra prophesied…"

"You know nothing about the stone, child," growled her uncle. "Every storm brings with it the prophecy of Gallerra and the Waiters' usual claims to have seen it foretold in the stone." Fiali looked down on the girl. "The Waiters are fools, Myulli, and the sooner you see them for what they are the better." Storm clouds embraced the mountains, cutting off their tops. They swallowed the sky like a growing, angry mouth. The range was shrouded with dread. A vibrant contrast against the black-and-gray cliffs were the Pellin tree forests, their brilliant red foliage spread out like a fluorescing fan at the foot of the ranges. It was through this forest that Gallerra had fled during the Great Expulsion.

Fiali turned to look down into the girl's face. "Not since the Great Storm sixty years ago has anything come from such prophecies." The memory of the time eased back like a drop of water over parched earth. He knew these clouds. He shook his head and looked down at the girl. "All the sky has ever brought is rain." He offered a faint smile. "Today, will be a wet day, let us go inside and throw some bones to pass the hours."

"No!" Myulli stamped her bare foot. "Jashm showed me what to look for, Uncle, she knows things about Gallerra." Myulli's eyes sparkled with wonder and excitement at the mere mention of the ancient oracle. "As a Waiter, she knows the signs, she knows…"

"Enough of this foolishness, child. Your sister has filled your head with her misty truths and bleary-eyed visions. If this is Gallerra's return, where is she? Where is your all-knowing sister?" Fiali scowled at her. *Myulli looks more like her father each day,* he thought. The tightness of the girl's square face and the liveliness of her green eyes, even the subtle wave in her shoulder-length hair resembled her father's dark locks. "Jashm knows!" Myulli stamped her foot again. She winced as her bare foot scraped against the raised edge of a paving stone. "You'll see it is so, Uncle. You will see." Fiali turned from the girl, shrugging off her childish indignation and started back towards the house. He knew the truth about the Great Storm, he knew the truth behind Gallerra, and he also knew it was best kept secret.

The family dwelling stood barren amongst the orchard of blood fruit trees. Its windowless walls of ochre stone and mud mortar deepened in color and texture under the fading light. Fiali watched as the matted leaves of the thatched roof shivered under the caress of the increasing bluster. "Come now, child, before it rains."

"But…"

"I said enough!" Fiali stood, his back towards Myulli, facing the heavy slatted wood door. He waited for the following steps of his niece, but all he heard was the strengthening breeze brushing against the wide leaves of the blood fruit trees. *Foolish child,* he thought to himself as he headed to the door.

§

Beneath the dim light of an oil lamp, Jashm wove the thick strands of spun balla ox hair. A small loom, held deftly in her thin, slight hands, held a good day's work. Jashm hoped to finish the hat before the next harvest gathering so that her father would not suffer under the parching heat of the sun. From beyond the door she heard her Uncle's voice bellow. *What has Myulli done now?* she wondered. With haste she stowed the half-finished hat under her thick woolen clothing. Maybe her father's early return from the fields had hastened Uncle Fiali's coming inside. Jashm turned on her stool to face the door. "Jaja," called Fiali, opening the door and pulling back the draft curtain.

"Yes, Uncle," she answered. Her voice was soft, so as not to disturb the peacefulness of the room. Jashm's bald head shone under the flickering yellow lamplight and her blue eyes sparkled, reflecting the small flame.

"What have you filled that girl's head with?" Fiali growled, crashing through what she had tried in vain to preserve. "She's standing waiting for the rain again."

"I don't know what you mean, Uncle. I have told her nothing other than truths."

"Truths! Do you call the prophecy of Gallerra truth? Myulli is at this moment standing out in the courtyard waiting for the approaching storm to bring a legend to life." Fiali rubbed his arms with vigor. "It grows colder by the moment," he huffed. "That girl will catch the sniffing death if she does not come inside."

Jashm stood from her stool and handed her uncle a blanket.

"What storm?" she asked. Jashm fought her excitement. *Can it be?* "Why didn't you tell me a storm was coming. You know the signs, you know…"

"I know nothing, Jaja." Fiali snatched the blanket from her and wrapped it around his shoulders. The old man sagged and his aged grey eyes closed. "There is a storm approaching from over the mountains," he said. He opened his eyes and stared into Jashm's face. "It is just a seasonal rain storm, nothing more."

"Is it as black as the night?" Jashm asked, as she pulled a small cloth sack from inside her vest. "Do the clouds swallow the sky?"

"Yes, as do all storm clouds," he sighed. "Why do you Waiters persist in your quest?" Fiali scowled. "Gallerra will not return."

Jashm stiffened in defense. "You forget, Uncle, that Gallerra was a great teacher, a diviner. He brought us prosperity from out of the fires of despair."

"He was a fraud who stole the village's wealth," Fiali scoffed.

"He is the promise of the future," Jashm cried. "When he left he gave us his promise and left a stone engraved with the scene of his return."

"Gallerra was a thief and the stone is loot he could not carry," grunted Fiali. "It is only coincidence that his leaving saw the arrival of the rains again."

"And the rains still come on time each year," Jashm felt angry with her uncle. He would never believe in the prophecy and this saddened her.

"You worship a thief!"

"Lies!" Jashm felt her face reddened with rage. "You disbelievers spread lies about Gallerra and all have failed to stop us Waiters. Gallerra will come back to us and he will bring with him great wealth to share with his people, as he has promised." She clenched her fists. "He will come, and the stone does not lie."

Fiali looked long and hard into her eyes before he broke contact. "Go," he breathed, "Myulli waits for you."

Jashm nodded once at her Uncle, sidestepped him, pulled back the curtain, and slipped out the door. The stiffening wind that swept down the courtyard to the house halted her. A smile spread across her face. The sky overhead was a rich blue, but the coming darkness was consuming its color with its rolling, thick clouds. Leaves, dancing together, filled the air with hissing. It was the singing of nature's song, as was prophesied.

"Is it the sign?" called Myulli standing at the edge of the courtyard, one hand holding a branch of an old blood fruit tree.

"Can you see the path?" Jashm called, as she braced herself against one of the stone pots that dotted the courtyard. She leaned forward against the wind, her slight body trembling with the embracing cold. The Waiters had taught her the signs over the last five years and they were now clear in the heavens and the earth. She patted the offering she'd collected from the secret place. The place in the mountains the Waiters said couldn't be found.

"Faith," Jashm laughed softly to herself. Her faith in the secret place had driven her to search, and the voice of Gallerra from the sky made it possible. The voice guided her through the mountain forests to a white stoned clearing barely three paces across. Here she found her offering, and now she would be the one to greet Gallerra.

"Yes, I see it." Myulli's small voice, picked up by the wind, was thrust into Jashm's ears. She was facing the shadows at the base of the mountains. Myulli shielded her eyes from the dust filled air with her hand.

Jashm pushed against the wind to stand beside her sister. Both took shelter behind the thick trunk of the tree. They looked towards the base of the mountain. Jashm recalled her return from the mountain forest only yesterday and she was disappointed at not being there now. The crooked line of a path lay out in the distant tight foliage of the Pellin trees. It glowed white within the shadows. Jashm dropped to her knees and began chanting the song of welcome, casting out each word like a ship on a rolling sea.

From beyond the walls
of yesterday's promise
You bring to us a new dawn.
From beyond the walls
that imprison our hearts
You bring freshness to our lands.
Gallerra we wait.
For the spirit of re-birth.

Gallerra we chant.

For we are the Waiters.

The keepers of your stone.

"Is it Gallerra?" Myulli called.

"Yes, little sister, it is." Embracing her, Jashm's eyes filled with tears of joy.

§

Fiali scooped another ladle of soup into his bowl and sat on one of the stools arranged around the central stone table. The walls of the room were cluttered with shelves, filled with pots, bowls, boxes, furs, clothing, everything that its four occupants owned—it pressed against him with the warmth of memory. This place, of all places, always calmed his heart, eased his mind's wanderings into the past. The only other place he gained comfort from was the other room, the place where they all slept. During the bitterly cold nights they would all huddle around its central pit furnace. Dank smoke rose through an iron flue in the middle of the ceiling to stain the crisp night sky. It was in this room that they would whisper secrets to each other until sleep claimed them. Fiali longed for the return of those nights. *Perhaps today's weather will bring a shard of it back this evening,* he pondered as he sipped his soup.

On the second mouthful of the rich spicy soup Fiali felt a tingling in his mind. The storm was awakening something deep within his guts, the familiarity of the clouds. The secret he was forced to keep by his father and the curse promised by his grandfather. He remembered the night his father had come down from the Kyjihm Mountains. His face bright with the excitement of discovery, and Grandfather. *Yes!* Grandfather had cried, and cursed his father for his foolishness. He remembered the truth behind the Great Storm.

Fiali could see the scene as if it had happened this morning.

It was the day of the Great Storm. Grandfather thought he was sleeping, but he heard his tale of the ancient mountaintop clearing, of Basstel and the mysteries of the past. He spoke of the secrets of the Kyjihm Mountains. He admonished his father. Fiali paused. His spoon hovered above the bowl. The thick brown soup trickled over its edge to fall on the table in soft splashes. He could see Grandfather snatch a cloth bag from his father's hand and shake a gnarled fist in his face.

"You fool! May the bells of the night riders steal your dreams." He shook the bag in front of father's face. *"These are Basstel's chattels. A sacrifice must now be paid and, damn it, I'll let it be you."* Grandfather stormed from the room. Father fell to his knees.

Fiali thought about the long-forgotten legend of Basstel, the butcher priest of the virgin sacrifice. He was so evil that everyone banished even the thought of him from their minds. He was the bringer of the darkness, the infertility of the land. His temple now lay in ruins, hidden somewhere in the mountains, but his curse still haunts the land. 'Move one stone and I will seek sacrifice.' It was his father who brought the Great Storm on the land and it was his grandfather who paid the sacrifice to Basstel.

The Temple of Basstel! Fiali recalled. *Jashm's journey yesterday. Her triumphant return from the mountains. Her wide-eyed smile.* His mind grasped onto the meaning like a callused hand on a hot fire poker. *The storm?*

Fiali leapt up from the table, tore the curtain from the doorway and rushed out into the courtyard screaming.

"Jashm, no!" he screamed into the fierce wind.

§

Jashm held up the small bag to the blackening sky. "My gift, Gallerra, my offering to your return."

"Jashm! Myulli! It is not a storm. Quick children, get inside. It is not a storm!" Fiali pushed against the wind. He faltered under its strength.

"It is Gallerra," Myulli smiled.

Fiali was almost to Jashm when the wind turned into a gale and blew him from his feet. Myulli, standing a few paces from the tree, stumbled and slid several arm lengths to be caught by Fiali who had managed to grab hold of one of the heavy flowerpots. Jashm stood facing into the wind, one arm tightly embracing the tree's trunk, the other holding up her gift. Her wet cloths slapped about her, as the light rain began to fall harder.

"Myulli!" yelled Fiali into the girl's face. "Get inside, this is not a storm, it is Basstel coming for its sacrifice."

"It is Gallerra," Myulli cried, her eyes still wild with excitement.

"Get inside, girl! Gallerra is a lie," Fiali cried out. "Watch through the cracks in the door if you must, but get inside." Fiali released the girl and pushed her hard in the back towards the house, the gale tumbled her until she connected with its hard, stone walls. Myulli pushed against the wind and crawled inside. Fiali watched the girl struggle to close the door. Once it was closed, Fiali turned to Jashm.

The rain fell heavily, sleeting into his eyes. The clear blue of the sky was now night black, it was hard to see in the deepening gloom. Jashm stood less than five arm lengths from him but the wind was too strong. He saw with horror the bag Jashm held up to the sky.

"Jashm!" His words were snatched from his lips by the wind. "What…is…in…the…bag?" He could feel his Grandfather's fear growing deep in his own belly.

Jashm turned her cold face towards her Uncle, a smile fixed in place and her eyes crazed with wild expectation.

"The…bag, Jashm. What is in the bag?" He yelled again, trying to make signs she could understand.

She looked at the bag and smiled wider. "Stones, Uncle. I found the secret place." Her words flew past him like wet leaves flapping against a rock.

"NO!" Fiali bellowed in terror. "Throw the bag away," he cried, tears competing with the rain in his eyes. "It is Basstel, the bringer of death." The wind was now a howl and he struggled to hear his own voice.

"They are a gift to Gallerra," Jashm continued, not hearing her Uncle's warning.

"They are the remains of the Temple of Basstel," he yelled again. "Throw away the bag." Jashm heard nothing over the howl of the wind. Fiali was frantic; his heart ached with despair. Calling on his deeper strength he forced himself from the ground and began to crawl towards his niece, gripping the raised edges of the stone paving to pull himself forward.

A great flash of light lit up the valley and mountain face as the heavens exploded in thunder. The sky roared its anger down upon them, as the lashes of Basstel struck out for their victim. Great cloud fingers appeared through the billowing blackness. They clawed at the earth sending trees and soil into the air. The screaming wind and rain assaulted the land.

"Jashm!" sobbed Fiali, touching the heel of her bare foot with his outstretched hand. "Give me the bag. Please, Jashm, give me the bag."

The clouds erupted again with light and bellowing. Rain dropped like ponds, threatening to drown Fiali as he lay gripping the edge of a stone. Another flash scorched and exploded the pot Fiali had been holding onto just moments before and his ears rang with the clapping percussion that filled the air. A great finger from the sky struck the ground and rent through the courtyard between him and the house. Stone paving danced into the wind like leaves. Fiali clawed his way to his knees, finding minimal shelter from the tree, and pulled at Jashm's wet, flapping dress.

Jashm turned her head, anger erupting from her eyes. "Let go, Uncle. Gallerra comes, I must receive him." She was screaming at him.

In turning, Jashm dropped her arm to within reach of Fiali. Releasing his grip on her he grabbed at the bag, his thick fingers gripped hard against the coarse cloth. Fiali, no longer holding on, was picked up by the wind like a child's cloth doll and flung into the stone walls of the house. Jashm, feeling her Uncle's hand rip the bag from her grasp, turned her back to the wind in time to see his body smash into the house and see the thatched roof rip from its walls to join the wind in its destructive dance.

"Uncle!" she screamed, as another flash of light flung him into the air and into the teeth of the wind. The cloth bag was swept up into the sky with him; both disappeared into its enveloping blackness. Jashm wailed, as she fell to her knees. The wind dropped, then died. Tears flowed from her eyes. Despair sucked her anguish out into the leaving storm. The storm had left. Nothing remained but the cold slap of silence and the trickle of water over stone.

Standing beside the stripped tree, Jashm felt weak, drained of energy. The storm had ended, as if the sky had run out of tears and the wind out of breath. Silence fell like the ash from a funeral pyre, a cold, eerie silence. The darkness lifted, a brilliant sun burnt high in the blue sky. She heard the whimper of a child. Feeling the weight of foreboding grace her shoulders, Jashm cried.

Myulli emerged from the ruins of the house, shaken and scared. She scampered over the deep rent in the earth to fall into the arms of her sister, wet and crying. "Jashm," she whispered, fearful of the quiet. "Jashm, what happened?"

Jashm looked at her sister and touched her smooth cheeks with a trembling hand, and cried again. "Gallerra was displeased."

§

The wind was cold, the sky darkening. Jashm murmured praise to Gallerra while Myulli walked around the small clearing collecting smooth, white stones. It had been a hard walk to the mountain for Myulli, but she had wanted to come.

"Will Gallerra be pleased with our offering?" Myulli said, interrupting Jashm's prayers.

She looked up at her little sister and saw the wonder in her eyes. "Yes, Gallerra will be pleased, and so, too, will Uncle Fiali." Jashm eased herself from the ground and checked in Myulli's cloth bag. "I see you have gathered fine stones."

"They should look pretty around Uncle Fiali's grave," Myulli smiled as she took back the bag. "I still need some more."

"Save some for Gallerra," Jashm laughed. "Uncle isn't the only one we are doing this for."

The voice from the sky that had led them to the clearing had stopped when the cool wind had arrived, but like before, Jashm could remember her way back. The Waiter's wouldn't believe her when she told them Gallerra spoke to her on the mountain, but now she didn't care. Gallerra would come again and she would be ready.

"Come now, Myulli," she called. "We must get to Uncle's grave before the rains come and make the path muddy."

Myulli ran to stand beside her bigger, wiser sister, the bag held tight to her breast. "He will be pleased." Her eyes glittered with childish glee. They left the clearing and headed back down the mountain. On the horizon a black cloud began to swallow the sky.

Color
Alma Alexander

H*e had come to give back what he had once begged for.* To return the gift. To plead and grovel, if that was what it took, because it would mean a return to innocence.

"I cannot," she had said. "What I have given…cannot be taken away." She had reached out, traced a finger down the curve of his cheek, and then showed it to him, the fingertip damp with the tears that had streaked down his face when he had come into her presence. "This," she said. "I gave you this. You cannot unlearn to weep."

He remembered coming to this house—it wasn't as long ago as it now seemed to him, his days had been lengthened by his anguish. But the thing that had led him here, that had been building, for a while; it was as though he had been living on the edge of something for what seemed like several lifetimes, seeing something out of the corner of his eye, feeling a yearning he could not quite understand, overhearing conversations he could not make sense of.

Mahoud and Lila, it had been—the two human changelings—who had pushed him into it at last.

The humans stayed the age at which they had been taken, never growing older in the woods of Fae. Sometimes the reason why was obvious—the King or the Queen had a sudden hankering for nubile mortal flesh and they would turn up, the young knights or the girls barely stepping into the full flower of their womanhood, doomed to smile and to dance forever in the courts of the Fae, never to return to their homes and their families again even after the ones who had plucked them away from it all had long lost interest in them and had moved on to new favorites. But Fae could be random, or simply curious, or acting on geas, or occasionally just plain malicious. Sometimes, the humans taken were older people, grandmothers snatched from hearthsides and condemned to an eternity of the aches and pains of old age or old men who hobbled through the woodland paths of the Fae kingdom with canes and walking sticks and used them, when taking a moment to rest from their exertions, to swat the nodding flower heads off their stems or to swipe at a passing doe, or dove, or butterfly.

And sometimes, they were younger—much younger—than the ones chosen for reasons of physical infatuation alone. If they were babies, then the Fae allowed them to grow up—to a point—and then get stuck at whatever age the whim of the Fae had decreed. But if they were older than a handful of years—if taken at age five, or six, or seven—they would stay children of that age. The Fae didn't seem interested in allowing these to grow up and into young adults. After all, if the Fae wanted more young men and women there were more in the human kingdoms that were ripe for the taking, without waiting for the inconvenient years to pass until the children already underfoot grew up enough to become interesting.

Lila had been six years old when the Fae had stolen her away. She was a fragile pale child of sunny disposition and endless curiosity, and most of the Fae had time for her, to smile at her, to answer a question or two, to offer her the magic of a bird landing on her small wrist or a mushroom that tasted like gingerbread. But there were times when she was left to fend for herself, alone and lonely, and it was the other changelings who cared for her then.

Mahoud was thirteen human years old, but he had been living in the world of Fae for longer than anyone cared to remember. He was a thin, wiry, brown-skinned boy with skinny limbs and calloused bare feet; in his face, his dark eyes burned like twin coals. He was old enough to remember his world and what it was like and what it had meant—he had been a pauper born into a family of paupers who made their living thieving in the bazaars. Before Mahoud was seven he had been an accomplished cutpurse, contributing to the kitty of his large and tumbling family—his wizened father who was old before his time, worn down by a life of unrelenting hardship; his regretfully fecund mother, who could be counted on to produce a new baby almost every year; his tribe of brothers and sisters, nine of them by the time he had been snatched, ranging in age from babes in arms to grown men and to full-bodied women capable of bearing children of their own, and another in his mother's belly already on the way.

Mahoud had been payment for an ill-conceived debt his father had been conned into owing one of the Jinni. That was pretty much all he knew of the matter—that, and the fact that one night he had gone to sleep as usual surrounded by people and noise and the smells of the dregs of the bazaar and the places where the poor people slept…and woken up here, in the woods of the Fae, in a place that was strange and foreign to him, stranger than anything he could have ever imagined. He had been frightened, in the beginning, and for a little while he had been cosseted by a number of the Fae who found him intriguing. If the Jinni who held his father's debt was one of these, Mahoud never knew it. But in time they drifted away, as Fae do, to other entertainments—and Mahoud had appointed himself the protector of the younger and more bewildered of the changeling children, as lost and adrift as he himself had once been.

Mahoud was Lila's guardian shadow, protecting her fiercely from harm or even a harsh word. The pair of them were always together, Mahoud's dark curly head bent down to her pale ringlets as they walked the woods or shared their meals by the brookside or on the beach of the long lake where the water lapped gently at the shore. And he would keep her entertained, and stave off her sadness, by telling her stories, things he remembered from his own mortal days, things Lila had never seen or could barely imagine.

It was these that had drawn the attention—and eventually kindled an obsession—in the mind of a Fae who once overheard

Mahoud's stories purely by accident, and then found he could not stay away from that hypnotic voice and the images it conjured up.

"…busy paved courtyard," Mahoud would say, in his singsong voice and the exotic accent he had never lost, lying back against a piece of driftwood with Lila's small hand in his own and her head pillowed on his chest. "They sold herbs and potions and spices and incense over in the far corner, and you could tell, because the scents rose and mingled like spirits, and you could smell rose, cinnamon, patchouli, and cardamom and nutmeg, and sesame. And there would be honey sold in the stalls beside those, rich, fragrant, and golden, and sesame cakes, and a man who roasted green berries right there in the market place filling the air with a heady aroma."

But Lila was a girl. "And the clothes?"

"Oh, the clothes," Mahoud said. "Over in the eastern quarter, they sold silks—scarlet silks, and sky blue, and golden, and even the most expensive of all, the purple, although it was supposed to be reserved for those in whose veins the blood ran royal… but you could buy it if you had enough gold, or you knew somebody, or you knew the right questions to ask. And next to that an old woman sold sheer veils in jewel hues, and next to her, the cobbler sat out in the streets and you could see how he made the shoes—the simple leather sandals for the poor folk, and the elaborate ones with long curved toes for the highborn ones in their halls of pale marble and porphyry and soft carpets."

"And the carpets?"

"You could buy them, too, not far away, and behind them there were stalls which sold the skeins from which they were woven—the silk and the wool, dyed all the colors of the world."

"And what did the rich people buy?"

"They bought the best—they bought the carpets which they believed could fly, little girl—the most expensive ones of all, the ones woven from the finest wools, with intricate patterns of dark blue, gold, and rose madder. And they bought hats and turbans out of golden silk, and jeweled hat pins with gems like blood—red rubies and sapphires, blue like a summer sky or the dark ones the color of midnight with bright stars swimming in their depths, jewels as big as your fist. And ropes of pearls, white like the teeth of maidens or flushed with a faint tinge of pink, like a dawn across the ocean, or pale blue, like the birds' eggs that they sold over in the part of the *souk* where the animals flapped and squawked and screamed and roared all together…"

"And what kind of animals?"

"Oh, all kinds! They sold monkeys with scarlet leather collars and leashes, and tawny lions captured far to the south, and blooded horses, midnight black or pure white or roan with four white socks. And also peacocks, with their magnificent tails and the plumes winking purple and green in the fall of blue feathers. And birds of paradise, red, white, golden, green, and blue, and the lyre birds with the strange tails, and then also…"

"The tigers?" Lila would murmured, growing sleepy, her long-lashed eyes fluttering closed against the silk of his vest.

"The tigers," Mahoud said, his voice slipping into a whisper that was a lullaby. "The great tigers with their black-and-orange striped fur, and their glowing jeweled eyes…"

Other times, Lila would be the one telling the story—describing in vivid and childlike detail the gardens she remembered from her days in the human world, where she had been left to kick her heels on the green lawns of her mother's garden, watched over by a yawning nursemaid drifting off into a quiet nap on a summer afternoon…a nap which had allowed Lila to be snatched away…and that was the point in the story where she would always falter, and look sad, and then speak no more until Mahoud cajoled her into a smile many hours later. But until she got there, she would describe the flowers that grew in that garden as though they were still growing in ghostly profusion all around her.

"Mama told me all the names, but I could never remember which was which," she explained earnestly to Mahoud. "There were foxgloves, hollyhocks, daisies, poppies, bluebells and things that smelled good, like hyacinth and lily of the valley. Lily of the valley was always white, but the others, there was blue, dark blue, like nanny's stockings—and there was pink—and there was yellow—oh, those were my favorites, the yellow!—and there were red ones, too. And she grew roses, I remember those, and they could be any color at all, white like the lily of the valley…and they could be yellow, too…or dark, dark, dark red…"

"Like the Queen's rubies," Mahoud said.

"Redder," Lila said staunchly.

Such were their conversations, and their memories. They would talk of silks or flowers, and it would all come back to color and hue. Or Mahoud would start talking about the sky and the sea and how the color of the sky could change the color of the sea—or Lila would start asking him if where he came from the sky was a different color in spring and in summer and he would explain patiently that what she would call *spring* was not a season in his own country, and no snow fell in what she would call *winter*. And the one who lingered in the woods just out of their sight would listen, and he found himself fiercely missing…something that he had never, before that moment, realized that he had lacked.

The Fae never noticed color. They never saw it. They saw shape, and form, and light; to them, the adornments they wore, the jewels that gleamed on their clothes or in their hair, were chosen not by virtue of their color but by how bright they were, and how the internal facets in their depths where the light was caught and broken and reflected back changed the quality of that light.

The one who listened to the two human children talk of color would rise from his place of hiding, and walk out on his own, and stare hard at the sky above his head or at the waters of the lake to see if he could glimpse what the children had been talking about. He began to spend his time painfully trying to compare the quality and—yes—the color of the light which broke into a summer's day, or wound down a winter twilight; he would sense that the quality of the light was different at different seasons or at different times of day or in the depths of the wood as compared to out in the middle of the lake, but he could only begin to glimpse it, to realize that there was something different, that it might have something to do with all that color that the children always talked about, the color of jewels and of living things and of the earth and the sky. But if he turned his head and took his focus away he saw again as the Fae saw, no more than that, no less—and no vivid colors to put hue and nuance into his world.

It was *not* his world.

But he could not let it go.

He even cornered Mahoud once, demanding that he explain the way he saw things, but only succeeded in frightening the boy and frustrating himself even further.

"It's no use," he said, throwing his hands up in resignation. "I don't understand."

"The witch in the garden of statues does," Mahoud said, after a small pause.

"What was that? How do you know?"

"Because I talked to her, and told her of things I had seen, and she could see it," Mahoud said.

"Why do you call her the witch?" The question was almost an afterthought, but the tone of Mahoud's voice had been one of respect, and awe, and not a little fear.

"They told me…when I first got here…that she had powers," Mahoud said, almost unwillingly, as though he was betraying a secret. "That she had walked in the human world. That she might be able to return a human child to the place from where he had been taken."

"I listened to your stories," the Fae said slowly, staring at the human boy. "Your life was not easy. But here, you are not hungry and you do not need to steal for your food. Here, you have a place to sleep and no vermin nibble on you in the night. Here, you have the freedom to go where you please and do what you wish."

"And here, nobody loves me," Mahoud said softly.

The words fell into a silence. And then, after a long pause, after it became obvious that Mahoud had said everything that he had wanted to say, the Fae sighed.

"And could she help you?" he asked.

"She said that for those like me the road leads only in one direction," Mahoud said. "When I spoke to her she told me that most of the people I had known and loved would already be dust and ashes. She could not take me back, not to the moment in which the Jinni took me in place of my father's debt, not to the warmth of my mother's love, or my sisters' affection—and those were the things I wanted to go back *to.*"

"Human emotion," the Fae said. "Ephemeral and passing."

"And eternal," Mahoud said. "*She* understands."

§

He had never thought of the one who dwelled in the garden of statues as a witch of any sort. She was Fae, like himself, and that was enough. But Mahoud's words lingered with him, and finally he found himself loitering on the path that led to her garden, the blind stone eyes of two of her statues staring unseeingly at him from either side of the carved wooden gate which stood ajar. If Lila had been there, she might have explained where all the flowers were supposed to go—but there were no flowers here, that the visitor could see, even though he glimpsed what might have been rose bushes allowed to go to twisted briar and tangling against the side of the house that stood there in the middle of the garden. The garden itself was a maze of paths, laid out in crumbled white stone or perhaps shell, winding their way like a labyrinth between green hedges, and statue after statue after statue brooding where the paths crossed and recrossed.

She had been waiting for him on her doorstep, the one he had come to see, leaning against the doorjamb, watching him approach slowly, almost unwillingly, but drawn to this place by something he could no longer hold down.

"I know why you have come," she had told him.

"I want to see," he said. "Never in my existence in this place have I thought of myself as blind—but I am, I *am*, and those children with their mortal eyes see the world far better and far brighter than me. I want to see the way they do. Just *once*, I want to see the way they do. To feel the colors on my skin."

"I can do this for you," she said. "Are you certain?"

"More certain than I have ever been of anything," he said, and he meant it. Then.

She lifted a small crystal phial, dangling it by the narrow neck between two fingers of her left hand. "This will open your eyes," she said. "A drop in each eye, that will be enough. I ask you again, are you sure?"

"I am," he said.

"Three times I must ask, and three times you must affirm it. Do you truly wish this to be done?"

"Yes," he said. "I wish it done."

"Kneel," she said, "and look up, and do not blink or close your eyes until I tell you to."

He did as he was bid, kneeling on the white path at her feet, feeling the sharp shards of whatever had been strewn upon it cut into his legs. She opened the phial and carefully allowed a single drop of the liquid within to fall into each eye. It burned, like acid, like fire, but she had told him to keep his eyes open and so he did it, concentrating on the points of pain on his knees and shins rather than on what his eyes had to endure. Only one small gasp of pain was permitted to escape.

It was she who reached out at last to fold his eyelids closed over the thing she had put into his eyes.

"It is done," she said. "Go, then, and see the things you wanted to see."

"And the price…?" he asked, after a moment, opening his eyes to stare at her.

"Oh, you will pay it," she said softly. "But not, perhaps, to me…"

He wandered for a while in the Fae woods, afterwards, feeling a little lost, a little afraid—but the obsession was upon him in full strength and power now, and he physically ached to experience that human sight that he had bought…for a price he still did not know the nature of.

And so he crossed the boundary, through the Shadowlands, into the world where the humans teemed and laughed and ran and loved and dreamed.

And for a little while, everything took his breath away. Everything was richer and brighter and more vivid than even Mahoud had managed to paint with his stories. He wandered the world that was open to him, from the *souks* and bazaars which still existed in the place where Mahoud's family had once walked, quite probably not greatly changed from his day—to the cottage gardens that little Lila had brought the memory of into the woods of the Fae—to rivers where light scintillated on the muddy brown waters and fishermen pulled out writhing fish from the deeps, impaled on cruel hooks and twisting iridescent in the sunshine—to the spread of wings of the scarab beetle, and the ladybird, and a kingfisher—to a bruise-colored sky brooding over a field of golden grain studded with scarlet heads of poppies—to the flower markets of the old cities, where tier upon tier of vibrant hues cascaded one upon another until his eyes hurt from the blaze of glory…

And then, slowly, he began to realize what he had done.

The colors were not just on the surface of things. They had roots deeper than that, sunk into the minds and souls of the creatures that his gaze touched, and he could see it all now. There was no hiding from any of it now. The veils had all been torn away, and the world was naked to him, and raw, and the colors had edges like sharp knives.

For every mysterious or serene blue, there was also a curling tendril of the blue of pain—of bruising, of enduring loss and sadness.

For every warm shade of yellow or gold, there was an amber-hued shadow lying on people's faces, huddling in the depths of their eyes—shadows of cowardice, or of malice.

For every green of leaf and bough that rested the eyes and healed the soul, there was a green wraith of envy, jealousy, and possessive greed that lurked in the deep shadows of people's homes.

For every vivid scarlet and ruby red, there was an explosion of fury somewhere, tongues of flame—of anger, terror, and cruelty, the fires that burned heretics, the fire that came out of the mouth of a gun, delivering death.

For every color, there was a dark twin, a shadow, and it came to him in hues and nuances, just as he had dreamed, but he could not close his eyes to any of this, could not unsee, and when he tried…his eyes leaked, and burned with the same burning that he had felt when the witch from the garden of stone statues had put a drop from her phial into each of his trusting eyes.

He recoiled from it all, in the end—and ran back, to the things that he knew, to the quiet woods of the Fae. But the colors followed him there, the memory of it all, and it was as if they had lodged deep inside of him, a slow poison in his soul, and were never going to let him turn away again.

He endured—but before long they noticed, the others. He was the only one with eyes that ran water, and sometimes they would do that at a mere memory of something that he now carried within him. He began to avoid the other Fae, avoided the changelings altogether, drifted alone and wretched through the woods for a little while until he could take it no longer and made his unwilling way back to the garden of the statues and the witch who dwelled within.

To beg for it to be taken away.

Believing that it would be. Might be. Could be.

Right until the moment she shook her head and told him no.

§

"Mahoud said you understood—that you can see—if he speaks the truth then how do you bear it?"

"I ripped my own heart out and ate it dressed with saffron and cinnamon…but I would not do that to another…and it's already far too late for that, with you," she said. "I could have offered you the same bargain, right at the beginning of it all, but, like all those who came here before you begging for the thing that you wanted, you would not have taken it, you would never have accepted the simple truth that the clarity of vision you demanded would shatter your own heart in your breast. For you… I only have three choices. I can take your eyes and leave you in darkness forever more; I can take your memory and send you back into the world a drooling idiot who will spend his days wrestling with a regret and a sorrow that he knows no reason for; or I can turn you to stone and take it all, so you have neither soul nor memory and will feel nothing more ever again."

"What was in that phial?" he asked at last, his hands twisted into fists of fear, of fury, of shame.

"Tears," she said softly. "Human tears. And once you've seen through human tears, you can never unsee that world again, gift and curse, yours to bear, now and until the end of time. Now, choose— your eyes, your memory, or the stone."

In the end, it was no choice at all. His eyes, brimming with the human tears which she had put there, followed where she pointed— into her garden where all the paths led, where brooding statues lined the labyrinth. There was a place out there, waiting for another.

Any Kiss Would Do
Kelly A. Harmon

2018, Menorca, Spain

Greg would follow Neva anywhere—but *hells bells,* it was hot out here.

Sweat rolled down his back in itchy torrents. He lowered the mattock—so similar to his pickaxe—and pulled a handkerchief out of his back pocket. Wiping his sweaty brow, he surveyed the camp with a critical eye.

Archaeological digs were cleaner than mining, but he missed the cool, dry mines and the brotherhood built with each stroke of the pick. At the dig, there was no whistling while one worked, and it seemed every man was out for himself. Except him. He wasn't here for the glory of making the next big find.

He was here for Neva. Another name that meant *Snow.*

He would follow her anywhere, through all of their lifetimes— until she realized *he* was her one true love.

Damn, that sounded stalkerish, even to him. But it wasn't like that. He'd loved her for eternity—and he knew in his miner's heart that she loved him. So why couldn't they be together?

And why couldn't she ever seem to find a job that didn't leave calluses on his hands? He wished she would find a better vocation, because he seemed doomed for eternity to dig in the dirt for his living.

An hour later the noon bell rang.

Greg joined Neva in the lunch tent. She was quivering with excitement. Even the pixie ends of her black hair seemed to vibrate. "Discover anything new in the crypt?" he asked.

Neva's eyes were dancing, and she put a finger to her red lips. "I'm not supposed to tell." She leaned in close, her lips brushing his cheek, then whispered in his ear. "I found a hidden room. We're going to wait for the inspection this afternoon to explore it."

Greg's heart sank. The inspection. The financier of the dig would be arriving—and with him, Greg's last hope of winning Neva. "Marry me," he begged.

She sobered. "You know I can't."

And with those words, she'd doomed them to another lifetime of friendship.

2241, Meekatharra, Australia

Another mining town. This time it was the bite of a brown snake that laid her low.

Mud on his boots and dirt ground into the seams of his hands, Greg had rushed to the hospital after the ambulance. He'd arrived too late, finding *Livvy* awake—groggy, yes—but *awake* and laughing quietly with the doctor about how close she had come to dying.

"Greg—" With apologies in her voice and in her eyes, she reached out to him.

But he'd seen the triumphant look on the doctor's face.

A doctor. How did the prince always come out smelling like a rose, time after time, life after life? How did he always manage to show up at the exact right moment?

Greg turned on his heel and left, driving back to Meekatharra and quitting the mines. It was the first time he'd spent the remainder of his life without her.

2561, Edinburgh, Scotland

As soon as he realized who he was, and who *she* was, he'd quit his job in the newly re-opened Upper Hirst mines and moved to the city. Robots did the digging these days, but one couldn't escape the dust anywhere near the quarry. Never again would he dirty his hands in pursuit of her.

But that didn't mean he didn't love her—and wouldn't keep trying. Only his tactics were changing.

Enter technology. And college. What were a few years of his time in the given scheme of things? As a librarian at the National Library, he had access to a thousand databases. For a small fee he had real-time alerts on a number of subjects delivered directly to his implant, guaranteed to inform him whenever there was a change in her status.

This was stalking, and he knew it was wrong. *But I love her!* he'd tell himself when he was feeling particularly defensive, when his conscience really bothered him. *And I know she loves me.* It never sat right with him, but he couldn't face the possibility of unrequited love *again*.

When the flood occurred, she shouldn't have been in the mines—it wasn't her job—but he knew she was somehow involved. The curse again: Tragedy followed her, of course.

He was at the corner transfer pad before he could whistle *hi-ho*. Nearly three hundred miles traveled in the blink of an eye, but he still wasn't fast enough.

Even the prince had been thwarted, this time.

It was the eighty-six-year-old retired doctor in town who'd re-awakened her, brought her back to life with mouth-to-mouth resuscitation.

Greg knew for certain then what he'd long suspected: Any kiss would have awakened her. Any. Kiss.

True love's kiss? They should have called it for what it was: true love's curse.

He was glad he hadn't stuck around.

2736, Baltimore, United States

Greg lit the candle in the tiny shoebox alcove of his habitat on Bond Street and said a quick prayer to the flame goddess that he would be successful this time. Candles were not allowed in the tiny one room shelter he called home, but it seemed blasphemous—even in this day and age—to offer up a flickering, digital flame at the end of a mock taper. The gods still expected sacrifice, and there was no sacrifice in the flick of a switch.

The idea seemed ludicrous. Who believed in gods anymore?

But he had suffered through a dozen reincarnated lives in the last thousand years or so. Lifetime after lifetime after lifetime. Except for the curse, magic didn't exist anymore, so the only explanation he could find for his and Snow's continued existence was the capricious will of the gods. Perhaps *this* god in particular, a goddess of reincarnation.

Tatarama—born in fire, forged in flame. Ancient icons show her sitting in the midst of a furnace, a cyclical inferno spiraling behind and around her, flames roiling in her outstretched hands. More gentle portrayals showed her seated in the heart of an aged, evergreen oak, with its many, many branches of life forming a canopy around her.

Greg preferred the flames. They were closer to his miner's heart and more like the passion burning in his breast.

It had taken him more than a hundred years in this lifetime to learn Tatarama's name. Once he did, things began to make sense. But he was so weary of living without Snow.

He remembered the curse—any kiss would awaken his love and doom them to an eternity of life. The truest love, his love, would end the curse, once and for all. He'd awaken her, and they'd spend the rest of their days—their final days—together at last.

This time, he would get it right by the tools of his current trade or by the will of his god. Perhaps both.

He would earn his rest, but not until after a single lifetime with her. *Snow—though she was going by Gwen these days. A different name in every lifetime, all meaning the same thing: white as snow.*

He'd once thought being a librarian would enable him to reach her before the prince did, but data mining was better. There was a vast difference between standing on the shore, waiting for the information to arrive and being a part of the stream itself. He could find Gwen's whereabouts, and then he could hide her from the prince until he could arrive and awaken her.

The news was barely a blip on his implant about the accident in Sparrows Point, Baltimore. A woman, said the report, was struck and thrown by a swinging crane at Bethlehem Steel—the mill revived from the long-cold ashes of the old company. It seemed fitting somehow. He and Snow were back to coal—if not mining, at least smelting.

She was lucky she hadn't been dragged into the steel rollers or there would have been nothing left of her to revive. Medical 'bots on the scene lacked the ability to kiss. He was in luck.

As soon as the notification flew across his implants, Greg began monitoring hospitals. Once found, it was easy to hack in and change her name and room number. The prince would have a hard time finding her this time.

Greg was in her room within minutes of her arrival.

She lay on the hospital bed, her face whiter than the sheets.

He bent and kissed her.

Her eyes fluttered open. "I love you, Snow."

"Oh, my grumpy love, I knew it was only a matter of time. You've finally done it."

A single tear rolled down her face. Then another. She was crying, but it didn't look like tears of joy.

His heart thudded in his chest. "We can be together now."

She smiled sadly, her words were a whisper. "We've always been together. Time after time after time."

"Together, yes, but always apart."

"Apart, because I love you, too." She gasped. Her face began to grow sallow, it wrinkled and grayed. Her skin was shrinking, pulling tight across her bones, wrinkling elsewhere. Greg reached for her hand, clasping it firmly in his own. It felt dry and papery to his touch. He felt an echoing pain in his chest, as if his heart were giving out. Then, his face burned, the skin tight as though he'd stepped too close to a fire—*Tatarama's?*

"Snow!" He bent, touching his forehead to hers. "What's happening, Snow?"

"True love's kiss." She gasped again and patted the bed beside her with her free hand. "Join me here." She made room, turning onto her side, tugging him toward her.

Greg joined her in bed, his chest to her back, their knees and feet entwined. It was the closest he'd ever been to her. He wrapped his arms around her, breathing softly into the dark hair at her nape, and pulled her closer. The pain was growing worse. He'd never been so happy. "I have loved you since the day we met. And I know you love me, too, Snow. Of course it was True Love's Kiss." Pain clutched his waist, his knees, his ankles—and he couldn't move them anymore. "What's happening?" he asked again.

She wriggled closer, then stiffened against him. "One lifetime was never ever enough for me."

She was hard to his touch now, like stone, wherever they touched. Her body felt cool. She was dying.

One lifetime was never enough? Greg thought about all the miserable lifetimes he'd spent waiting to get the jump on the prince. He and Snow had held hands, they'd embraced a few times, and then shared only an abiding friendship while he sat by and watched her *current love* win her over again and again and again.

Had Snow been as miserable as he? Had she *sacrificed* herself lifetime after lifetime, so they could have these stolen moments through time, never voicing their deepest feelings for one another? Had she fostered a deep abiding friendship—so they could have it for *eternity?*

He'd always thought his love had been the stronger one. "Oh, gods—what have I done?"

"You have loved me," she whispered, as her heart stopped beating, "as I have loved you."

"I do," Greg said, breathing his last.

And then Eternity—held at bay by True Love's Curse—swept across their clasped bodies like a maelstrom. Shriveling, drying, peeling, wearing—until only their bones remained. Then those crumbled into dust.

Justice
Vonnie Winslow Crist

A *lessa heard the baby crying before she saw the child* strapped in its car seat. The vehicle's windows were cracked, but she knew that small amount of ventilation would not save the child's life on a hot, sunny day. She scanned the parking lot and nearby picnic tables for a parent. Saw no one. The frightened eyes of the baby followed her as she tried without success to open each of the automobile's doors. The black sedan was locked tighter than a snapping turtle's jaws, so Alessa chose to act.

Knowing her baton would be inadequate, she picked up one of the nearby boulders. Had there been a human about, they would have been shocked to see a slender woman in a deputy's uniform lift the huge rock. Heavy enough to require a bulldozer to set in place, the boulders were used to keep people from driving their cars and trucks off the asphalt parking lot and onto the path that led down to the river.

Alessa tried to reassure the trapped baby that all would be well as she made certain she had a firm grip on the boulder. Next, using only as much force as necessary, she slammed the rounded hunk of granite into the driver's side window. The glass shattered upon impact. And as planned, none of the shards ended up in the backseat.

The baby stopped crying. Perhaps it was the rush of cooler air into the car. Perhaps it was the loud crash of stone into glass. Perhaps it was the wave of love that emanated from Alessa. Whatever the reason for the infant's silence, Alessa was grateful. Once they'd chosen to save a child, secrecy became an important part of an aguane's plan.

She reached inside the automobile and unlocked the doors. Swift as a riptide, Alessa unlatched the restraints and plucked the little girl from the car seat.

"Hush, sweet one," crooned Alessa as she cradled the baby in her arms, careful not to scratch the tender skin of the child's face with her badge. Again, she surveyed the parking area. Satisfied that no humans were close at hand, she strode towards a nearby oak grove.

So lighted-footed was she, that even with her leather boots on, Alessa made little noise when she crossed a gravel path and slipped into the forest. The tangle of raspberry branches and Virginia creepers beyond the oaks parted for the aguane in deputy garb and the human baby she carried. Then, swifter than a minnow, the plants returned to their normal positions the instant the pair had passed. After hiking for about five minutes, Alessa and her charge finally reached a thick swatch of cattails growing alongside a still-water finger of the river.

"Hand her to us. Hand her to us," whispered female voices from the boggy beginnings of the river's edge.

Alessa nuzzled the baby's fine hair. "Show yourselves. I can't hand her over to thin air."

Alessa's three younger siblings removed their red caps and popped into view. Though the shades varied, Pia, Elena, and Calida each wore a red gown. The filmy fabric of their garb clung to their human-like upper bodies, but ended above their feet. Alessa saw her sisters had wisely chosen deer legs and hooves instead of human feet when they'd climbed onto land. If someone bothered to search this part of the river's edge, it would appear that a trio of deer had come to the water for a drink.

"Another careless person has gifted us with a child," she said as her sisters leaned closer.

She noted that Pia, her youngest sister, held an earthen substitute for the rescued child. Unlike some changelings, the replicas used by Alessa and her kin were not truly living. A golem of sorts, the aguanes' changeling was little more than a mud-baby. But with a bit of glamour, a dash of DNA, and a professional visit from Deputy Alessa Delfiume to the morgue, the autopsy would confirm the death of a human child.

This human child, thought Alessa as she gave the squirming youngster a kiss.

"Take her to Faerie, and tend to her," she said and handed the baby to her second youngest sister, Elena. Alessa took the earthen changeling from Pia. "The child will get along fine with the others as she grows."

"Her name?" queried Elena.

"I found no identification. So let us call her Seraphine—for she truly is angelic," responded Alessa. She caressed the little girl's cheek.

The sisters nodded and sighed. Each of them seemed to glow with mother-love as Elena stripped the clothing from Seraphine and handed it to Alessa.

"I am sorry, my pet," whispered Elena to Seraphine as she pricked her with a long thorn. "We need three drops of blood to complete the transformation."

The baby flinched, but did not cry. Instead, she watched her new guardians with a wrinkled brow and wide eyes. Pia squeezed the little girl's blood onto the changeling's forehead. The four sisters each placed a hand on the changeling, and together they chanted a glamour spell. The mud-baby morphed into an uncanny replica of Seraphine.

"The first step is complete," said Alessa as she held the changeling against her shoulder.

"Calida, be ready," she told her oldest younger sister. "If I can get the mother to go for a swim, we end this here. If not—we will get word to the goblins and they can finish things in a jail cell."

Calida pursed her lips. "Just get her into deep water, point her out, and I will do the rest," she promised.

"It was the mother who left her in the car?" asked Pia crushing her cap in her hands.

"There was make-up, female clothing, a pair of plastic earrings, and other womanly odds and ends in the car. No sign of a man this time."

"Then, she deserves as much kindness as she showed Seraphine," snapped Calida as she withdrew a small red cap from a pocket hidden in the side-seam of her gown and handed it to Elena.

Elena slipped the cap onto Seraphine's head. The girl child seemed to vanish. Seconds later, Pia, Elena, and Calida put on their caps and disappeared.

Alessa snorted, shook her head, turned, and now satisfied Seraphine was safe, lugged the changeling back to the black sedan.

Once the changeling was dressed in the human child's clothing and strapped in the car seat, Alessa strode to her patrol car. She opened the door, grabbed the radio mic, and called in to report a dead baby found locked in a black sedan. After relaying the location and license tag of the automobile where the deceased could be found, she told the dispatcher to send the coroner. Lastly, she informed the dispatcher that she was going down to the river-side beach to try and locate the owner of the vehicle in which the child had been left unattended.

Modern times have made an aguane's life more difficult, mused Alessa as she walked. In the olden days, less science and more superstition made the changeling for child switch easier and an aguane's search for and seizure of abused children less noticed. Now, with DNA testing, surveillance cameras mounted everywhere, phones at the ready for quick photographs, not to mention drones, Alessa and her sisters had to be more cunning than ever.

§

The path to the river wound about a thousand yards through the woods. As Alessa neared the actual beach area, the trail became wider and sandier. With her sensitive aguane ears, she could not only hear kids squealing and splashing in the water and the barking of a large dog, but also every word spoken by the two hundred or more people lounging on the shore.

She stood at the edge of the sand, deputy hat under one arm, and filtered out one conversation after another. Within minutes, Alessa had located the careless mother. From her position far from the woman and her two male companions, she eavesdropped:

"Liz, shouldn't you go back and check on her?" said a man with sunglasses and thinning hair.

"Nah. She was sleeping. Besides, I left the windows down part way," replied a skinny woman with a cigarette in one hand and a drink can in the other."

The man with a mustache sitting on the other side of Liz rubbed his chin. "You've been here for a while. Maybe..."

"If I want your advice, I'll ask for it." Liz took a drag on her cigarette, exhaled, then crushed the butt in the sand. "You ain't the father, so you have no say."

"I can go up to check if you'd..."

"Didn't you hear me?" said Liz as she stood, tugged on her bikini bottoms, then ran her fingers through her bleached blond locks. "Stay out of things that don't concern you, Tony."

Tony shrugged his shoulders and returned to ogling a group of teenage girls a few yards to his right.

"Take it easy." The man with sunglasses pulled another drink from a nearby cooler.

"I take it any way I can," responded Liz with a smirk as she sashayed across the sand to the water.

And that's when Alessa began to walk towards Tony and Mr. Sunglasses. As she neared the pair, she contemplated the deep river waters beyond the swimmers. She easily spotted Calida's head bobbing in the darker blue current.

Decision time. Drowning or an unfortunate accident while in custody?

Personally, Alessa believed speed was the bedrock of Faerie justice. She tapped her forehead with her fingers in a mock salute.

Calida saluted back. With little pity for Seraphine's human mother, Alessa turned her attention to the two men who had been chatting with Liz.

"Do you gentlemen know whose baby was left in a car at the parking lot?" she asked as the men gazed up at her.

"No ma'am," said Mr. Sunglasses.

"Donnie! What the..." Tony gaped at his friend, then stood. "It's her kid." He pointed to the scrawny blond who was now swimming in water at least seven feet deep. "She said it was fine, and to mind..."

Donnie got up out of his chair. He was shaking his head. "Listen, Deputy..." Donnie studied her badge. "Deputy Delfiume. Liz was taking one last dip, and then, she was going to go get the baby and bring her..."

"A little late for that," replied Alessa as she pulled out her notepad and pen. "Your names?"

Donnie and Tony relayed their names, addresses, and phone numbers. Alessa jotted down the information. But she also examined the surface of the river behind the two men.

She witnessed Liz disappear with a jerk. She glanced at the solitary lifeguard struggling to monitor too many swimmers. He had missed Calida's embrace of Seraphine's mother. In her head, Alessa began to count the seconds.

When she was certain enough time had passed, she stopped taking notes and said, "Now, if you two would be so kind as to point out the child's mother again..."

Donnie and Tony faced the river and searched for their friend.

"Actually, I don't see her." Tony rubbed his chin. "I mean, I'm pretty sure she was right there a few minutes ago..."

"Maybe she snuck out," suggested Donnie. "She's left other people to clean up her messes before."

"Donnie! She is your girlfriend. How could you..."

"We ain't married or nothing like that. If she's in trouble it's her own doing."

"Gentlemen!" Alessa re-established her authority. "I would like you to accompany me up to the car where the baby is, and we can sort this out there."

Donnie and Tony gathered their towels, chairs, and cooler. Alessa followed them as they climbed back to the parking lot.

She was relieved to see three patrol cars carrying two deputies, and the sheriff had arrived on the scene along with the crime investigation tech in her van. Alessa quickly filled her coworkers in on how she'd discovered the baby, tried to rescue it by breaking in the window, and had then gone down to the beach to locate the child's mother. She also let her fellow deputies and the sheriff know that the only links to the missing mother were Donnie and Tony.

The sheriff barked instructions at Alessa and the other two deputies, loaded Donnie and Tony into his vehicle, and headed back to the station for questioning. As ordered, Deputy Wu hiked to the beach to try to locate Liz, while Deputy Dupree and Alessa stood near the black sedan and waited for the crime investigation tech to take her photos and samples.

As Alessa waited, she slapped her notepad against her thigh. She suspected by now Liz's body was floating downstream. The newspaper would speculate whether it was suicide, swimmer's cramps, or swift currents that caused the drowning when her bloated, fish-mutilated carcass was discovered in a day or two or ten. Aguanes would never be mentioned. Not this time, and not the many times before when Alessa, Pia, Elena, and Calida had meted out punishment in the miles and miles of river that wound their way from source to sea.

She closed her eyes and recalled the hundreds, maybe thousands of times over the centuries her sisters and she had swum through the murky waters of this river and other rivers seeing to it that justice was done. Her mouth curled as she recollected the feel of a human ankle in her grasp. Though the swimmers kicked and struggled to break their handhold, Alessa and her sisters always won. And then, there was the pleasure of observing the handiwork of the fishes and crabs. Bottom-feeders knew how to pick a body clean.

The sound of a sneeze brought Alessa back to the present. The tech, who had finished gathering evidence from the sedan, blew her nose, then slipped the used tissue in her pants' pocket. She finished packing her evidence-gathering equipment into her van, and was about to depart when the elderly coroner and his assistant arrived.

Alessa looked down at her muddy boots and smiled. Her plan was going smooth as seal skin.

The coroner nodded at Alessa and Deputy Dupree, approached the sedan, and adjusted his glasses. His assistant stood slightly behind him relaying statistics about baseball players from the local triple A team. For the entire time it took the coroner to pull on his plastic gloves, check for a pulse, and poke and prod the changeling, his assistant continued to blather.

Hurry up, old man, thought Alessa. *Before I curse your idiot assistant.*

Finally, the coroner pronounced the changeling Seraphine dead.

The tow truck had arrived, and the driver was preparing to hook up the black sedan under the watchful gaze of Deputy Dupree. As soon as the car was secured, Dupree would follow the tow truck and sedan to the impound lot.

"I will meet you back to the morgue and finish up the paperwork," Alessa called to the coroner as she climbed into her patrol car.

The coroner nodded, took off his gloves, tossed them in a plastic bag, sealed the bag, gathered his gear, and with the help of his assistant, bagged and loaded the dead changeling. Both men climbed into their vehicle, and moments later the wagon pulled onto the road.

Alessa followed the wagon to the morgue, then strolled behind the coroner and his sidekick, still blathering about baseball, as they entered the building. With a wave of her hand, she made sure the changeling's glamour held and bewitched the balding coroner and his simple assistant so they would see what Alessa and her sisters wanted them to believe. Per usual, the autopsy forms for the mud-baby Seraphine were bland as codfish.

After Alessa exited the morgue, she made a note to return for the changeling's release to Seraphine's next of kin. She would have to make sure the glamour held. *If* next of kin showed up before a fish-nibbled Liz floated to a dock or was hooked by a fisherman out for a day on the river.

An open casket was unlikely for Liz or the changeling, but even in the case of cremation, there would be a mortician with whom she'd have to deal. She was certain with a sprinkle of magic, all would go well.

Her shift over, Alessa pressed down on the accelerator and headed back to the station to turn in her report on today's tragedy.

§

From the porch of her house along the riverbank, Alessa watched the sun sink in a bloody display of color. She loved warm summer nights filled with stars. They brought people out to the water.

She thought back to a long-ago night when Pia, Elena, Calida, and she had breast-stroked through the ocean. Fish had been afraid to come close. Even the sharks and rays avoided the quartet of aguane. Only the seals swam to the sisters. Some were just seals, others, selkies.

The selkies had begged for justice. They told of a cruel fisherman who'd come across a young selkie playing on the beach. Laughing at his luck and the girl's misfortune, the man had stolen her skin. The child, for she was only thirteen, was held captive. Now the fisherman's slave, the girl cried every night and called for her mother. Unable to secure the girl's release themselves, they pleaded for the aguanes' help.

It had only taken a few hours to reach the beach in front of the house where the selkie was held against her will. Pia, Elena, and Calida shape-shifted into womanly form with horse's hooves instead of feet since wild ponies wandered these shores. Alessa had chosen human feet, as she would be the one to knock upon the door.

169

When the man answered, Alessa held his gaze with her eyes and cast a spell which caused him to reveal where he'd hidden the selkie's skin. Quick as a piranha's strike, she'd grabbed the pelt and child and taken them to her waiting sisters. Upon her return, she'd grasped the hand of the ensorcelled fisherman and led him into the sea. The simpleton smile had remained on his lips as he waded into the surf. It was only after Alessa had released him from the enchantment, that he'd realized his plight. Despite his efforts to swim to safety, he'd been pulled underwater by the strong hands of the aguane sisters.

Such lovely memories... It was a pleasure to add one more, thought Alessa as she surveyed the river's surface. She sighed as she spotted Pia, Elena, and Calida.

"At last, it's time to go for a swim," she whispered as she raced across the beach. "And search the waters for others who need a little justice."

The Wild Swans

Hans Christian Andersen

*F*ar away, *in the land to which the swallows fly when it is* winter, there dwelt a king who had eleven sons, and one daughter, named Eliza.

The eleven brothers were princes, and each went to school with a star on his breast and a sword by his side. They wrote with diamond pencils on golden slates and learned their lessons so quickly and read so easily that everyone knew they were princes. Their sister Eliza sat on a little stool of plate-glass and had a book full of pictures, which had cost as much as half a kingdom.

Happy, indeed, were these children; but they were not long to remain so, for their father, the king, married a queen who did not love the children, and who proved to be a wicked sorceress.

The queen began to show her unkindness the very first day. While the great festivities were taking place in the palace, the children played at receiving company. The queen, instead of sending them the cakes and apples that were left over from the feast, as was customary, gave them some sand in a teacup and told them to pretend it was something good. The next week she sent little Eliza into the country to live with a peasant and his wife. Then she told the king so many untrue things about the young princes that he gave himself no more trouble about them.

"Go out into the world and look after yourselves," said the queen. "Fly like great birds without a voice." But she could not make it so bad for them as she would have liked, for they were turned into eleven beautiful wild swans.

With a strange cry, they flew through the windows of the palace, over the park, to the forest beyond. It was yet early morning when they passed the peasant's cottage where their sister lay asleep in her room. They hovered over the roof, twisting their long necks and flapping their wings, but no one heard them or saw them, so they flew away, high up in the clouds, and over the wide world they sped till they came to a thick, dark wood, which stretched far away to the seashore.

Poor little Eliza was alone in the peasant's hovel, playing with a green leaf, for she had no other playthings. She pierced a hole in the leaf, and when she looked through it at the sun she seemed to see her brothers' clear eyes, and when the warm sun shone on her cheeks she thought of all the kisses they had given her.

One day passed just like another. Sometimes the winds rustled through the leaves of the rosebush and whispered to the roses, "Who can be more beautiful than you?" And the roses would shake their heads and say, "Eliza is." And when the old woman sat at the cottage door on Sunday and read her hymn book, the wind would flutter the leaves and say to the book, "Who can be more pious than you?" And then the hymn book would answer, "Eliza." And the roses and the hymn book told the truth.

When she was fifteen, Eliza returned home, but because she was so beautiful the witch-queen became full of spite and hatred toward her. The queen would have turned her into a swan like her brothers, but she did not dare to do so for fear of the king.

Early one morning, the queen went into the bathroom; it was built of marble and had soft cushions trimmed with the most beautiful tapestry. She took three toads with her, and kissed them, saying to the first, "When Eliza comes to bathe, seat yourself upon her head, that she may become as stupid as you are." To the second toad she said, "Place yourself on her forehead, that she may become as ugly as you are, and her friends not recognize her." "Rest on her heart," she whispered to the third; "then she will have evil inclinations and suffer because of them."

So, she put the toads into the clear water, which at once turned green. She next called Eliza and helped her undress and get into the bath.

As Eliza dipped her head under the water one of the toads sat on her hair, a second on her forehead, and a third on her breast. But she did not seem to notice them, and when she rose from the water there were three red poppies floating upon it. Had not the creatures been venomous or had they not been kissed by the witch, they would have become red roses. In any event, they became flowers, because they had rested on Eliza's head and on her heart. She was too good and too innocent for sorcery to have any power over her.

When the wicked queen saw this, she rubbed Eliza's face with walnut juice, so that she was quite brown, then she tangled her beautiful hair and smeared it with disgusting ointment until it was quite impossible to recognize her.

The king was shocked, and declared she was not his daughter. No one but the watchdog and the swallows knew her, and they were only animals and could say nothing. Then poor Eliza wept and thought of her eleven brothers who were far away. Sorrowfully, she left the palace and walked the whole day over fields and moors, till she came to the great forest. She knew not in what direction to go, but she was so unhappy and longed so for her brothers, who, like herself, had been driven out into the world, that she was determined to seek them.

§

Eliza had been in the wood only a short time when night came on and she quite lost the path; so, she laid herself down on the soft moss, offered up her evening prayer, and leaned her head against the stump of a tree. All nature was silent, and the soft, mild air fanned her forehead. The light of hundreds of glowworms shone amidst the grass and the moss like green fire, and if she touched a twig with her hand, ever so lightly, the brilliant insects fell down around her like shooting stars.

All night long she dreamed of her brothers. She thought they were children again, playing together. She saw them writing with their diamond pencils on golden slates, while she looked at the beautiful picture book which had cost half a kingdom. They were not writing lines and letters, as they used to do, but descriptions of the noble deeds they had performed and of all that they had discovered and seen. In the picture book, everything was living. The birds sang, and the people came out of the book and spoke to Eliza and her brothers; but as the leaves were turned over they darted back again to their places, that all might be in order. When Eliza awoke, the sun was high in the heavens. She could not see it, for the lofty trees spread their branches thickly overhead, but its gleams here and there shone through the leaves like a gauzy golden mist. There was a sweet fragrance from the fresh verdure, and the birds came near and almost perched on her shoulders. She heard water rippling from a number of springs, all flowing into a lake with golden sands. Bushes grew thickly round the lake, and at one spot, where an opening had been made by a deer, Eliza went down to the water.

The lake was so clear that had not the wind rustled the branches of the trees and the bushes so that they moved, they would have seemed painted in the depths of the lake; for every leaf, whether in the shade or in the sunshine, was reflected in the water.

When Eliza saw her own face she was quite terrified at finding it so dirty, but after she had wet her little hand and rubbed her eyes and forehead, her skin gleamed forth once more. And when she had undressed and dipped herself in the fresh water, a more beautiful king's daughter could not have been found anywhere in the wide world.

As soon as Eliza had dressed herself again and braided her long hair, she went to the bubbling spring and drank some water out of the hollow of her hand.

It was so still that she could hear the sound of her own footsteps, as well as the rustling of every withered leaf which she crushed under her feet. Not a bird was to be seen, not a sunbeam could penetrate the large, dark boughs of the trees. The lofty trunks stood so close together that when she looked before her it seemed as if she were enclosed within trelliswork. Here was such solitude as she had never known before!

§

The next night was very dark. Not a glowworm glittered in the moss. Sorrowfully, Eliza laid herself down to sleep. After a while it seemed to her as if the branches of the trees parted over her head and the mild eyes of angels looked down upon her from heaven.

In the morning, when she awoke, she knew not whether this had really been so or whether she had dreamed it. She continued her wandering, but she had not gone far when she met an old woman who had berries in her basket and who gave her a few to eat. Eliza asked her if she had not seen eleven princes riding through the forest.

"No," replied the old woman, "but yesterday I saw eleven swans with gold crowns on their heads, swimming in the river close by." Then she led Eliza a little distance to a sloping bank, at the foot of which ran a little river. The trees on its banks stretched their long leafy branches across the water toward each other, and where they did not meet naturally the roots had torn themselves away from the ground, so that the branches might mingle their foliage as they hung over the water.

Eliza bade the old woman farewell and walked by the flowing river till she reached the shore of the open sea. And there, before her eyes, lay the glorious ocean, but not a sail appeared on its surface. Not even a boat could be seen. How was she to go farther? She noticed how the countless pebbles on the shore had been smoothed and rounded by the action of the water. Glass, iron, stones, everything that lay there mingled together, had been shaped by the same power until they were as smooth as her own delicate hand.

"The water rolls on without weariness," she said, "till all that is hard becomes smooth; so, will I be unwearied in my task. Thanks for your lesson, bright rolling waves. My heart tells me you will one day lead me to my dear brothers."

On the foam-covered seaweeds lay eleven white swan feathers, which she gathered and carried with her. Drops of water lay upon them. Whether they were dewdrops or tears no one could say.

It was lonely on the seashore, but Eliza did not know it, for the ever-moving sea showed more changes in a few hours than the most varying lake could produce in a whole year. When a black, heavy cloud arose, it was as if the sea said, "I can look dark and angry, too," and then the wind blew, and the waves turned to white foam as they rolled. When the wind slept and the clouds glowed with the red sunset, the sea looked like a rose leaf. Sometimes it became green and sometimes white. But, however quietly it lay, the waves were always restless on the shore and rose and fell like the breast of a sleeping child.

When the sun was about to set, Eliza saw eleven white swans, with golden crowns on their heads, flying toward the land, one behind the other, like a long white ribbon. She went down the slope from the shore and hid herself behind the bushes. The swans alighted quite close to her, flapping their great white wings. As soon as the sun had disappeared under the water, the feathers of the swans fell off and eleven beautiful princes, Eliza's brothers, stood near her.

She uttered a loud cry, for, although they were very much changed, she knew them immediately. She sprang into their arms and called them each by name. Very happy the princes were to see their little sister again—they knew her, even though she had grown so tall and beautiful. They laughed and wept and told each other how cruelly they had been treated by their stepmother.

"We brothers," said the eldest, "fly about as wild swans while the sun is in the sky, but as soon as it sinks behind the hills we recover our human shape. Therefore, we must always be near a resting place before sunset; for if we were flying toward the clouds when we recovered our human form, we would plummet to the earth.

"We do not dwell here, but in a land just as fair that lies far across the ocean. The way is long, and there is no island upon which we can pass the night—nothing but a little rock rising out of the sea, upon which, even crowded together, we can scarcely stand with safety.

If the sea is rough, the foam dashes over us; yet we thank God for this rock. We have passed whole nights upon it, or we should never have reached our beloved fatherland, for our flight across the sea occupies two of the longest days in the year.

"We have permission to visit our home once every year and to remain eleven days. Then we fly across the forest to look once more at the palace where our father dwells and where we were born, and at the church beneath whose shade our mother lies buried. The very trees and bushes here seem related to us. The wild horses leap over the plains as we have seen them in our childhood. The charcoal burners sing the old songs to which we have danced as children. This is our fatherland, to which we are drawn by loving ties; and here we have found you, our dear little sister. Two days longer we can remain, and then we must fly away to the beautiful land which is not our home. How can we take you with us? We have neither ship nor boat."

"How can I break this spell?" asked the sister. And they talked about it nearly the whole night, slumbering only a few hours.

Eliza was awakened by the rustling of the wings of swans soaring above her. Her brothers were again changed to swans. They flew in circles, wider and wider, till they were far away. But one of them, the youngest, remained behind and laid his head in his sister's lap, while she stroked his wings. They remained together the whole day.

Towards evening the rest came back, and as the sun went down they resumed their natural forms. "Tomorrow," said one, "we shall fly away, not to return again till a whole year has passed. But we cannot leave you here. Have you courage to go with us? My arm is strong enough to carry you through the wood, and will not all our wings be strong enough to bear you over the sea?"

"Yes, take me with you," said Eliza.

They spent the whole night in weaving a large, strong net of the pliant willow and rushes. On this Eliza laid herself down to sleep, and when the sun rose and her brothers again became wild swans, they took up the net with their beaks, and flew up to the clouds with their dear sister, who still slept. When the sunbeams fell on her face, one of the swans soared over her head so that his broad wings might shade her.

They were far from the land when Eliza awoke. She thought she must still be dreaming, it seemed so strange to feel herself being carried high in the air over the sea. By her side lay a branch full of beautiful ripe berries and a bundle of sweet-tasting roots. The youngest of her brothers had gathered them and placed them there. She smiled her thanks to him. She knew it was the one that was hovering over her to shade her with his wings.

They were now so high that a large ship beneath them looked like a white sea gull skimming the waves. A great cloud floating behind them appeared like a vast mountain, and upon it Eliza saw her own shadow and those of the eleven swans, like gigantic flying things. Altogether it formed a more beautiful picture than she had ever before seen; but as the sun rose higher and the clouds were left behind, the picture vanished.

Onward, the whole day, they flew through the air like winged arrows, yet more slowly than usual, for they had their sister to carry. The weather grew threatening, and Eliza watched the sinking sun with great anxiety, for the little rock in the ocean was not yet in sight. It seemed to her as if the swans were exerting themselves to the utmost. Alas! She was the cause of their not advancing more quickly. When the sun set they would change to men, fall into the sea, and be drowned.

Then, she offered a prayer from her inmost heart, but still no rock appeared. Dark clouds came nearer, the gusts of wind told of the coming storm, while from a thick, heavy mass of clouds the lightning burst forth, flash after flash. The sun had reached the edge of the sea, when the swans darted down so swiftly that Eliza's heart trembled. She believed they were falling, but they again soared onward.

Presently, and by this time the sun was half hidden by the waves, she caught sight of the rock just below them. It did not look larger than a seal's head thrust out of the water. The sun sank so rapidly that at the moment their feet touched the rock it shone only like a star, and at last disappeared like the dying spark in a piece of burnt paper. Her brothers stood close around her with arms linked together, for there was not the smallest space to spare. The sea dashed against the rock and covered them with spray. The heavens were lighted up with continual flashes, and thunder rolled from the clouds. But the sister and brothers stood holding each other's hands, and singing hymns.

In the early dawn the air became calm and still, and at sunrise the swans flew away from the rock, bearing their sister with them. The sea was still rough, and from their great height the white foam on the dark-green waves looked like millions of swans swimming on the water. As the sun rose higher, Eliza saw before her, floating in the air, a range of mountains with shining masses of ice on their summits. In the center rose a castle that seemed a mile long, with rows of columns rising one above another, while around it palm trees waved and flowers as large as mill wheels bloomed. She asked if this was the land to which they were hastening. The swans shook their heads, for what she beheld were the beautiful, ever-changing cloud-palaces of the Fata Morgana, into which no mortal can enter.

Eliza was still gazing at the scene, when mountains, forests, and castles melted away, and twenty stately churches rose in their stead, with high towers and pointed Gothic windows. She even fancied she could hear the tones of the organ, but it was the music of the murmuring sea. As they drew nearer to the churches, these too were changed and became a fleet of ships, which seemed to be sailing beneath her. But when she looked again she saw only a sea mist gliding over the ocean.

One scene melted into another, until at last she saw the real land to which they were bound, with its blue mountains, its cedar forests, and its cities and palaces. Long before the sun went down she was sitting on a rock in front of a large cave, the floor of which was overgrown with delicate green creeping plants, like an embroidered carpet.

"Now we shall expect to hear what you dream of tonight," said the youngest brother, as he showed his sister her bedroom.

"Heaven grant that I may dream how to release you!" she replied. And this thought took such hold upon her mind that she prayed earnestly to God for help, and even in her sleep she continued to pray. Then it seemed to her that she was flying high in the air toward the cloudy palace of the Fata Morgana, and that a fairy came out to meet her, radiant and beautiful, yet much like the old woman who had given her berries in the wood, and who had told her of the swans with golden crowns on their heads.

"Your brothers can be released," said she, "if you only have courage and perseverance. Water is softer than your own delicate hands, and yet it polishes and shapes stones. But it feels no pain such as your fingers will feel; it has no soul and cannot suffer such agony and torment as you will have to endure. Do you see the stinging nettle which I hold in my hand? Quantities of the same sort grow round the cave in which you sleep, but only these, and those that grow on the graves of a churchyard, will be of any use to you. These you must gather, even while they burn blisters on your hands. Break them to pieces with your hands and feet, and they will become flax, from which you must spin and weave eleven coats with long sleeves. If these are then thrown over the eleven swans, the spell will be broken. But remember well, that from the moment you commence your task until it is finished, even though it occupy years of your life, you must not speak. The first word you utter will pierce the hearts of your brothers like a deadly dagger. Their lives hang upon your tongue. Remember all that I have told you."

And as she finished speaking, she touched Eliza's hand lightly with the nettle, and a pain as of burning fire awoke her.

It was broad daylight, and near Eliza lay a nettle like the one she had seen in her dream. She fell on her knees and offered thanks to God. Then she went forth from the cave to begin work with her delicate hands. She groped in amongst the ugly nettles, which burned great blisters on her hands and arms, but she determined to bear the pain gladly if she could only release her dear brothers. So, she bruised the nettles with her bare feet and spun the flax.

At sunset her brothers returned, and were much frightened when she did not speak. They believed her to be under the spell of some new sorcery, but when they saw her hands they understood what she was doing in their behalf. The youngest brother wept, and where his tears touched her the pain ceased and the burning blisters vanished. Eliza kept to her work all night, for she could not rest till she had released her brothers. During the whole of the following day, while her brothers were absent, she sat in solitude, but never before had the time flown so quickly.

One coat was already finished and she had begun the second, when she heard a huntsman's horn and was struck with fear. As the sound came nearer and nearer, she also heard dogs barking, and fled with terror into the cave. She hastily bound together the nettles she had gathered, and sat upon them. In a moment there came bounding toward her out of the ravine a great dog, and then another and another. They ran back and forth, barking furiously, until in a few minutes all the huntsmen stood before the cave. The handsomest of them was the king of the country, who, when he saw the beautiful maiden, advanced toward her, saying, "How did you come here, my sweet child?"

Eliza shook her head. She dared not speak, for it would cost her brothers their deliverance and their lives. And she hid her hands under her apron, so that the king might not see how she was suffering.

"Come with me," he said. "You cannot remain here. If you are as good as you are beautiful, I will dress you in silk and velvet. I will place a golden crown on your head, and you shall rule and make your home in my richest castle." Then, he lifted her onto his horse. She wept and wrung her hands, but the king said, "I wish only your happiness. A time will come when you will thank me for this."

He galloped away over the mountains, holding her before him on his horse, and the hunters followed behind them. As the sun went down they approached a fair, royal city, with churches and cupolas. On arriving at the castle, the king led her into marble halls, where large fountains played and where the walls and the ceilings were covered with rich paintings. But Eliza had no eyes for all these glorious sights; she could only mourn and weep. Patiently she allowed the women to array her in royal robes, to weave pearls in her hair, and to draw soft gloves over her blistered fingers. As she stood arrayed in her rich dress, she looked so dazzlingly beautiful that the court bowed low in her presence.

Then the king declared his intention of making her his bride, but the archbishop shook his head and whispered that the fair young maiden was only a witch, who had blinded the king's eyes and ensnared his heart. The king would not listen to him, however, and ordered the music to sound, the daintiest dishes to be served, and the loveliest maidens to dance before them.

Afterwards, the king led her through fragrant gardens and lofty halls, but not a smile appeared on her lips or sparkled in her eyes. She looked the very picture of grief. Then, the king opened the door of a little chamber in which she was to sleep. It was adorned with rich green tapestry and resembled the cave in which he had found her. On the floor lay the bundle of flax which she had spun from the nettles, and under the ceiling hung the coat she had made. These things had been brought away from the cave as curiosities, by one of the huntsmen.

"Here you can dream yourself back again in the old home in the cave," said the king. "Here is the work with which you employed yourself. It may amuse you now, in the midst of all this splendor, to think of that time."

When Eliza saw all these things which lay so near her heart, a smile played around her mouth, and the crimson blood rushed to her cheeks. The thought of her brothers and their release made her so joyful that she kissed the king's hand. Then, he pressed her to his heart.

Very soon, the joyous church bells announced the marriage feast; the beautiful dumb girl of the woods was to be made queen of the country. A single word would cost her brothers their lives, but she loved the kind, handsome king, who did everything to make her happy, more and more each day. She loved him with her whole heart, and her eyes beamed with the love she dared not speak. Oh! If she could only confide in him and tell him of her grief. But dumb she must remain till her task was finished.

Therefore, at night she crept away into her little chamber which had been decked out to look like the cave, and quickly wove one coat after another. But when she began the seventh, she found she had no more flax. She knew that the nettles she wanted to use grew in the churchyard and that she must pluck them herself. How should she get out there? *Oh, what is the pain in my fingers to the torment which my heart endures?* thought she. *I must venture. I shall not be denied help from heaven.*

With a trembling heart, as if she were about to perform a wicked deed, Eliza crept into the garden in the broad moonlight, and passed through the narrow walks and the deserted streets till she reached the churchyard. She prayed silently, gathered the burning nettles, and carried them home with her to the castle.

One person had seen her, and that was the archbishop. He was awake while others slept. Now, he felt sure that his suspicions were correct. All was not right with the queen—she was a witch and had bewitched the king and all the people. Secretly, he told the king what he had seen and what he feared, and as the hard words came from his tongue, the carved images of the saints shook their heads as if they would say, "It is not so; Eliza is innocent."

But the archbishop interpreted it in another way; he believed that they witnessed against her and were shaking their heads at her wickedness.

Two tears rolled down the king's cheeks. He went home with doubt in his heart, and at night he pretended to sleep. But no real sleep came to his eyes, for every night he saw Eliza get up and disappear from her chamber. Day by day his brow became darker, and Eliza saw it, and although she did not understand the reason, it alarmed her and made her heart tremble for her brothers. Her hot tears glittered like pearls on the regal velvet and diamonds, while all who saw her were wishing they could be queen.

In the meantime, Eliza had almost finished her task. Only one of her brothers' coats needed to be made, but she had no flax left and not a single nettle. Once more only, and for the last time, must she venture to the churchyard and pluck a few handfuls. She went, and the king and the archbishop followed her. The king turned away his head and said, "The people must condemn her." Quickly, she was condemned to suffer death by fire.

Away from the gorgeous regal halls she was led to a dark, dreary cell, where the wind whistled through the iron bars. Instead of the velvet and silk dresses, they gave her the ten coats she had woven to cover herself, and the bundle of nettles for a pillow. But they could have given her nothing that would have pleased her more. She continued her task with joy and prayed for help, while the street boys sang jeering songs about her. Not a soul comforted her with a kind word.

Toward evening she heard at the grating the flutter of a swan's wing. It was her youngest brother. He had found his sister, and she sobbed for joy, although she knew that probably this was the last night she had to live. Still, she had hope, for her task was almost finished and her brothers had come.

Then, the archbishop arrived to be with her during her last hours, as he had promised the king. She shook her head and begged him, by looks and gestures, not to stay; for in this night she knew she must finish her task, otherwise all her pain and tears and sleepless nights would have been suffered in vain. The archbishop withdrew, uttering bitter words against her, but she knew that she was innocent and diligently continued her work.

Little mice ran about the floor, dragging the nettles to her feet, to help as much as they could; and a thrush, sitting outside the grating of the window, sang to her the whole night long as sweetly as possible, to keep up her spirits.

It was still twilight, and at least an hour before sunrise, when the eleven brothers stood at the castle gate and demanded to be brought before the king. They were told it could not be. It was yet night—the king slept and could not be disturbed. They threatened, they entreated, until the guard appeared, and even the king himself, inquiring what all the noise meant. At this moment the sun rose, and the eleven brothers were seen no more, but eleven wild swans flew away over the castle.

Now, all the people came streaming forth from the gates of the city to see the witch burned. An old horse drew the cart on which she sat. They had dressed her in a garment of coarse sackcloth. Her lovely hair hung loose on her shoulders, her cheeks were deadly pale, her lips moved silently while her fingers still worked at the green flax. Even on the way to death, she would not give up her task. The ten finished coats lay at her feet. She was working hard at the eleventh, while the mob jeered her and said, "See the witch—how she mutters! She has no hymn book in her hand. She sits with her ugly sorcery. Let us tear it into a thousand pieces."

They pressed toward her, and doubtless would have destroyed the coats had not, at that moment, eleven wild swans flown over her and alighted on the cart. They flapped their large wings, and the crowd drew back in alarm.

"It is a sign from Heaven that she is innocent," whispered many of them, but they did not venture to say it aloud.

As the executioner seized her by the hand to lift her out of the cart, she hastily threw the eleven coats over the eleven swans, and they immediately became eleven handsome princes. But the youngest had a swan's wing instead of an arm, for she had not been able to finish the last sleeve of the coat.

"Now I may speak," she exclaimed. "I am innocent."

Then the people, who saw what had happened, bowed to her as before a saint. But she sank unconscious in her brothers' arms, overcome with exhaustion, anguish, and pain.

"Yes, she is innocent," said the eldest brother, and related all that had taken place. While he spoke, there rose in the air a fragrance as from millions of roses. Every piece of kindling in the pile made to burn her had taken root, and threw out branches until the whole appeared like a thick hedge, large and high, covered with roses, while above all bloomed a white, shining flower that glittered like a star. This flower the king plucked, and when he placed it in Eliza's bosom she awoke from her swoon with peace and happiness in her heart. Then all the church bells rang of themselves, and the birds came in great flocks. And a marriage procession, such as no king had ever before seen, returned to the castle.

The Way of Sisters
April Steenburgh

*S**he used to stand out there and caw at the crows, you know."*
Nana sat with me at the kitchen table. Every now and then she
casually tapped me on the knees as my little legs felt the need to fidget
and kick against the table legs and set the hanging leaf clanging. "She
would be out there in the morning, early as anything, waking her father
up, hollering at them, trying to send messages to her dead grandmother."

Ma had been a skinny girl, sticks for limbs and straw for hair. I
had seen pictures on Nana's wall, sitting on display in various corners
of the house. I loved to imagine her out back, shouting back at the
crows as they gathered and gossiped along the branches of the old
butternut tree—her posture assertive, just this side of aggressive, as
she added her gossip and gab to theirs.

Nana loved to tell stories of how crows could be coaxed into
carrying messages from our world to that of the spirits, stories that
seemed unreal as soon as we were back home in the city. Nights
visiting Nana were nights riddled with cricket song and the huffling
snore of my sister in the cot beside my bed. They were nights rich
with thoughts of crows moving between one world and the next with
messages strung on their wings. Something as mundane as a crow
gained a mysterious, mystical air up in the mountains, and they were
always present—settled atop trees and phone poles, poking about in
the grass. As my sister and I tussled like a pair of puppies in the front

lawn over our favorite blue ball, I could always hear the crows cackling right along with us.

I always felt the crows were laughing at me as they sat up in the old butternut tree, talking to each other about things I did not know, could not know, and mocking me for my lack of knowledge. I would stand out there, waiting as Grandpa gathered butternuts for us to shell on the front porch, listening to the chuckles of crows.

Maybe they knew I was the daughter of the brazen girl who used to get up each morning to join in their conversation. But I was never brave enough myself to glare up at them, puff out my chest, and let out a harsh 'caw' of my own. I was always afraid of messing it up. I was concerned I would only manage a hideous garbled message. I would end up insulting where I meant to praise the gleam of morning light on particularly well-preened feathers. In my own way, I was as strange a child as my mother—my attention and interest fixated on the crows.

If I was a strange child, my sister was unfathomable. From her first tumble from the lowest branches of the butternut tree as she tried to climb up after the crows to the time she showed me the battered old cigar box she had started to fill with feathers, my sister was some sort of sprite that had wafted out of the forest. I teased and taunted her by stealing feathers to tangle in my hair, chasing her around pretending to be a fierce Indian. My sister would run from me only until her temper snapped and her hands pulled, little fingers like talons, liberating just as much hair as feathers in her fury.

"Those are mine!" Face flushed, eyes bright and fierce, my sister was the brave one who should be out with the dawn challenging the crows.

"Fine. Keep them." We would go our separate ways. Our stiff scrawny legs, sharp eyes, and small scowls were an amusing mockery of the crows stalking around the yard, but we never noticed the humor of the situation.

But as soon as Nana's blueberry muffins came out of the oven, we crept close, drawn by warmth and familiarity and family. Butter still on lips slightly purpled with blueberry juice, we would curl up in our room and whisper our secrets to each other.

I don't know exactly when Ma's attitude toward the crows changed. In a city setting, far removed from Nana's stories and the rhythmic creak of Grandpa's rocking chair, the crows were easier to ignore. I would catch them carefully observing our comings and goings from atop power lines and the walnut trees out in front of our suburban home. I tried to laugh at the gooseflesh that felt the need to march up and down my arms, at the way I felt a flush creep across my face. There was nothing malicious or malevolent about a bird.

They just were.

"Maybe they want to be us," my sister mused one morning as she lay on her belly in the living room, watching the crows out the cathedral window that let in enough light to have us sunning like cats, only half lucid in our laziness. "Maybe they want earrings and necklaces and fancy hats." She rolled onto her back, stretching with a scowl. "But that's stupid. I'd rather fly."

I bared my teeth in a slow sneer, wrinkling my nose in the disdain of the older and wiser in the face of a silly suggestion. But she never saw it, her attention caught and held by the trio of crows holding court in the yard.

One morning, sometime later when my britches got shorter as my legs got longer, after a sleepover with a middle school friend that involved very little sleeping and quite a few movies and giggled secrets, I scrambled from her parent's car and stopped. I saw the crows that were waiting for me. Seven of them. Sitting on and around the stump of a lightning-struck walnut tree. Staring at me. My whole body went shivery and nauseous. I blinked. For a moment it had not been birds standing there but tiny, bony women wearing feathers, talons for feet, staring out from masks made of bird skull and beak with something far too close to anticipation. Suddenly insecure in my own skin, I slunk from car to garage and let myself into the house as swiftly as possible.

I no longer imagined having conversations with the crows. The image of my Ma, wind pulling at her straw-blond hair as she shouted and laughed with the crows, was forever darkened into something far more forbidding. She was no longer a gangly, gawky child entertaining herself as best she could in the morning; she was no longer my beautiful and whimsical mother trying to shout messages to ancestors long gone. She was a warrior warding the spirit world away from her family.

But I grew up and moved out and into college dorms. The crows faded into nothing more than something to study in biology lectures, a bit of lore to examine in literature workshops. Animal people belonged in the stories I wrote in class, in the books I read—they had no place on my front lawn. They were added to the mythology of my youth, sequestered somewhere between a belief about the wind blowing leaves in-side-out signaling thunder and that to squish a spider would bring rain. I clung to my mundanity almost out of spite. Some sort of anachronistic sense of duty pulled me to numbers and other nonsense that entangled adult life. I needed to be the stable one, the solid one.

My sister grew to be a fey and unfathomable woman—bright-eyed and dazzling in an array of jewelry and fabrics that caught every eye she passed before, a pair of wings tattooed on her shoulder blades. She was an artist of small, glittering things with eyes always looking somewhere none of us could see, hearing voices too quiet for the rest of us to notice with her head cocked ever so slightly to the side as her lips curled into a smile.

We grew apart, as sisters often do as they grow into young women. I would watch with a fascinated lack of comprehension as she made her way through life, and reality tried its best to fumble along after her. She was as strange to me as the crows that called out to the morning, their voices heavy with secrets.

I came home for holidays, and always the crows were waiting for me, smiling and hopping—my own little court of the impossible and macabre. My sister seemed unaware of anything odd about what I had always assumed to be proper birds, seemed untouched by the apprehension that hung around me like a miasma. She was a peal of laughter, a glitter of silver, and whisper of bells as she wandered barefoot room from room. I found her out in the front yard after a casual Independence Day dinner, sitting in the lawn swing, bare toes wiggling through grass green with a mild summer.

"They're beautiful."

I assumed she was talking about Ma's flowers, a mix of lilies, black-eyed susans, and bachelor's buttons, the butterflies and bumblebees making their way from blossom to blossom in a quiet bit of last-minute industry as the day wound down. "I wish I had been here to see the lilacs blooming."

"Not the flowers. The crows."

The words, the wistful bit of worship in her voice, startled me into taking a step back, dropping out of comfortable camaraderie as I cast about for the dark spots I should have known would manage to mar the quiet evening.

I blinked again, and saw two tiny women, dragging feathers through thick grass as they hopped and laughed, heads cocked to the side, peering at us from one glittering eye, then the other. The sun gleamed on plumage that glistened with the same sickly mix of colors as oil—blues and greens with shades of yellow and purple stretching between.

Words, I could almost hear words in their chattering chuckles, their rough and rasping exhalations. Their chests heaved with a passion that had no place in a pleasant summer evening, was too feral to be familiar. And my sister tilted her head in an unconscious mimic of the crows and smiled.

The crows took to flight with pleased shouts, pulling their feather cloaks tight and jumping, flapping. My sister bent to pick up a feather that had fallen, preened it absently with her fingers.

There was something musty mucking up the mulch and mowed grass smell of the evening—an old smell, dry, not altogether unpleasant. It overpowered the flowery perfume of the garden, of my sister.

My sister.

How does one explain that slow ambling descent into something just this side of madness? It was in the tilt to my sister's head, the way she was slower to click back to the here and now, lingering in her own thoughts, caressing a silky black feather. Not madness, not really. More of an untethering from everything solid and simple. Holding her hand, it felt like trying to hold onto early morning fog—beautiful, visible, but ultimately intangible but for a ghost of sensation across the palms. A moistness, a coolness, a slight hint of *other*. She was still here, my sister, but not looking at me, never looking at us. Her eyes were on the crow-women and their glittering stares.

We snarled and spat at times, for such is the way of sisters. I grumbled at her lack of concern with the way the world goes. She hackled at my lack of understanding, but always in the end our fingers curled together and, for a few heartbeats, everything was alright and understandable until time deigned notice us once more and life carried us back into our individual concerns. She drifted back to her apartment and her cats and her art. I walked into my own home, with its coffee prepped and meals packed for work the next morning.

§

And, suddenly, everything changed. There was a hole where my sister had been settled for as long as I could remember. Her presence was missing and what remained in her place was an ache so bone-deep it left me gasping. No clue, no hint, not reason why—my sister was just gone. It left me scrabbling for reason and rational thought, trying to sort out just what had happened and why I was suddenly on my own.

It was suicide, they whispered, never quite far enough that I could not hear them, the disappointment and accusation in their voices. They gave voice to a thick and often inadvertently malicious insinuation that something had been wrong with my sister, it hung heavy in their tone. The insidious idea that the death was her fault and intention slipped through every aspect of interaction, pulled at expressions, and added a surly weight to conversation.

My sister with the eyes that could see things no one else could, who made magic out of everything small and smiles out of silence—I could not believe she was gone. There must have been a reason, a catalyst or instigator no one had noticed. We were blind to the things my sister had seemed to see. We were blind to her as well. Perhaps it was me who went mad, who had something wrong with them, as my eyes and accusations fixated on the crows. They observed our muted walk into the small church where we held funeral services, eyes bright and interested, voices raucous in the quiet afternoon. They settled into the trees over the newly turned dirt of a fresh grave. Everywhere I looked, I was met with the cruel laughter and crooked beaky grins of the crows. They were a bitter constant and I was done ignoring them.

Nana had said the crows could carry messages to the dead. I wanted them to carry me. I needed them to carry me to my sister.

§

It was ever so strange, to be standing out there in the early dawn, doing things I had never been brave enough to do, not even as a child. I didn't know what to say, so I said it all.

"I know you can hear me—I know you are there. I want my sister back. You took her from me, and I want her back. I can see you, bird women, I know you, I know what you are. Take me to her."

"Claiming so much knowledge, for someone squawking about like a fledgling who wants back into the nest."

Was this the voice my sister had heard, head tilted to the side and a smile on her face? Had this throaty speech been familiar to her as my own? I wanted to be terrified but my heart was too busy with aggression to worry with fear. I wanted their voices to be harsh, a crass cackle, not be rough in all the right places like a grandparent's admonishment, and soft at the end to remind you were still loved.

But most of all I didn't want to understand them, as they settled down in the branches before me—gaunt little women pulling wings about them like shawls against the morning chill. I hadn't wanted two-way communication, not truly. But I wanted my sister, a want that was so heavy, so thick, that it hung about in my stomach like a sickness and stuck me with a ferocity that put any migraine I had ever experienced to shame.

"Please. I want her back."

"We are messengers, fledgling. We are both here and there, but we cannot give what is not ours for the taking." The beak of her mask gaped open in a grisly smile. "But that is not what you want to hear, with your sharp eyes and harsh words. What reason have you to trust the nurses who have ever been at your cradle." The beak shut with a clack, bony mask rattled.

"We can carry you, little fledgling."

"If you are brave enough."

"If you are bold enough."

"If you love enough."

"You can fly with us."

"Find your feathers."

"Yes, find your feathers!"

"Feathers!"

It was a breathless cacophony, voices demanding and daring and my first instinct was to cover my head and duck, just in case they all took to flight and sharp beaks and claws were aimed at me. But the chant, *feathers feathers feathers*, caught my attention and I scrambled from the back yard back into the house, to the spare room where my sister's things were being kept as the family tried to process what had happened.

Feathers. My sister's beloved collection, still in its battered old cigar box. It had to be in here somewhere—childish fancy hidden amidst the finery of young womanhood. Beneath a parasol and beside a pair of black boots with silver buckles sat that familiar box, a bit of red on it from that time we had stolen Ma's polish and propped our hands on it to paint our nails. It smelled of old wood and the musky vanilla of my sister's favorite hand lotion as I gripped it close, blindly navigating through a house that had never seemed so unfamiliar and back out to the yard.

"Feathers."

It was a hiss, a rattle of bone and a dying breath. The trees were filled with them, crow women hunched in their masks, claws clutching the branches, eyes glittering with anticipation.

In the stories there is always a sacrifice, but I had always assumed it would be something tangible. A token, a treasure, a life. But as I felt a precious bit of sanity slip away, the comforting and sane replaced by the shifty and surreal, I knew I had paid my dues.

No more the normal life of nine-to-five for me. My eyes were opened as I opened that cigar box and offered my sister's feathers to the crows. Offered myself to the crows and asked for wings.

A mob, a murder, they descended from the trees to crowd me with their wings and their laughter. They smelled of old places, old secrets—books that had been left on dark shelves and rooms shuttered with stale air and last breaths. I wanted to cough, to push the smell of them away from me, but they clustered close, brushed me with their fingers and feathers, and I inhaled.

I inhaled as they gathered up feathers from finches, sparrows, and parrots from the pet store. I inhaled as they wove bits of a cardinal's wing into my hair, pushed turkey feathers into my hands. I inhaled with a mourning dove's feather behind my ear at a jaunty angle.

I exhaled and the world streamed away with my breath.

Feathers rustled, crows called and cackled in the darkness, and I tried to feel distressed at being neither here nor there. Guided by the wings of crows, carried on wings borrowed from my sister, I was drifting from the place of the living and into the place of the dead.

The dead have no use for light and color, but the living find comfort in such things. I sought out solid ground for my feet once I grew anxious with the seemingly endless drifting and dancing along currents of air that had no source and no destination. I stood, feathers settling around me, illicit flashes of color in the light from the moon I dreamed up above me. A single point of stability in a fluid bit of nothing. No, it was something, just lacking in definition as it drifted. Half thoughts, bits of now and then, here and there, you and me. I could hear the crows, the susurration of their wings in the darkness. Gentler here, even their voices seemed smoother, natural.

Or I was merely growing more accustomed to their presence.

The dead have no need for color and light, but that does not mean they do not want it. They were drawn to me, the little moon I pulled along above me like a luminescent balloon as I walked. I could see them, flickering shyly at the corner of my eye, vanishing if I looked too hard or moved too fast. They were not used to attention, not used to motion, would pop like a soap bubble if startled.

I looked down, curious, and saw the conjured ground in the light of the little moon through my arm. "Am I dead, crows?" Impressed at my lack of inflection, holding my panic close, smothered beneath the drive to find my sister.

"How can you be alive?" They laughed and clacked, swooping around me in the darkness. "What is there for the living here?"

"Hope," I answered.

Hope, the ghosts around me sighed without breath. "Hope!" The crows repeated, tasting the word and all of its flavors as inflections.

Hope, and I felt more solid than before. I tugged my moon behind me and set out in search of my sister.

Solidity was not the benefit I had imagined. With being more defined, more alive, I became more appealing to those who had been dead the longest, those who had forgotten, perhaps, what it was to be human, or who never were to begin with. They were the hungry ones— the things you feel staring at night when you walk between rooms in the dark. They are the shadows that twist just out of sight, reach towards your back and cause gooseflesh to skitter across your skin.

The only warnings I got were the changes in the wing beats of the crows, the harsh coughs of alarm, before claws swiped close. The first one pulled something of me away—something warm that reminded me of hot cocoa on a cold night. They wanted the good parts of me, the comfortable parts that were used to being loved. The tastiest parts.

I had a small moon to give me a bit of light to huddle in, but nothing else that could be considered a weapon.

Nothing apart from my own temperament and temper. I had always been afraid of things lurking under my bed, skulking about the shadows of my home. Walking through endless, shapeless dark was the last straw.

"No."

The word wobbled at first, shivering and awkward and not at all as fierce as I had intended it to be. It was the voice of a child scared of the night and wanting their mother.

"No."

It was stronger, the voice of a girl pushing as far off the bed as possible when getting up at night to get a drink. Braver, but still anxious enough to lack power. Another swipe, and the smell of blueberries drifted away into the wavering dark.

"No." They were not allowed to have those parts, the parts warm with my sister curled around me. Those were mine. I bared my teeth, straightened my back and strode forward, pulling my moon and my murder of crows with me. Shadows and lurking things had no power over someone that failed to look over their shoulder and be frightened of them. Yes, I was solid, but I was solidly determined and the shadowy things would have to look for their meals elsewhere. I had a sister to search for.

How does one search within a place that has no here, and has never determined a there? Location was a whim—the idea of looking for something, an impossible concept. Locations would not do, so I sought for impressions.

My sister was the sound of bells—the ones around her ankles on bits of string, even her laugh danced down the spine like a light chime. Her smile sparkled like a little bell, her temper rolled like a tubular bell. She was the smell of vanilla and musk—essential oils placed carefully so, shampoos sniffed before being selected. She was distracted, she was distraction.

She was a little ghost gazing up at my moon with all the joy in every world reflected in her eyes.

That was my sister. Looking ever to the bright things in the world and utterly missing the dark.

"So why?"

I didn't mean to ask that question. I meant to hug her, gather her up and take her home. Keep her in a little cigar box with a bunch of old, beloved feathers perhaps. I had not thought that part through, the care and keeping of a ghost. But I had not intended to come and inquire, my tone bordering on accusation. I did not intend on letting the bitterness of those left behind out into the not-air of the land of the dead, tainting its nonchalance with something sour.

I stood there, in the light of a moon that did not exist, the intentionally dead staring down the intentionally dead.

She looked at me, my little sister, and for the first time I allowed myself to realize I did not know her at all. I saw her, perceived her, but I had nothing to call her, not in this place where a birth name seemed so trite. Her eyes were sad in the light of the moon, an expression I seemed to remember, but could not remember acknowledging.

So, I gathered her up, holding a memory of what she felt and smelt like, loving every inch of her. Remembered her snuffling snores, blueberry breath. I had flown along the wings of crows, carried like a message to the land of the dead, and I had a message to give, though I hadn't really thought of it that way.

"I love you." I whispered. Love was a bright word in the darkness. It chimed like the little bells my sister had favored, it pealed with our laughter. It danced along remembered nerve endings until I was crowded with crows, crowded away from my sister.

My sister who was left holding the invisible tether to a moon I had brought her and smiling. Really smiling. I could see it in her eyes.

I had delivered my message and the crows were taking me home.

Being again hurt. The sun was too bright, the ground too hard, the air too rough on lungs that had only been thinking about breathing. There were crows on my shoulders, preening my hair with bony fingers, soothing, crows at my feet, pulling at pant legs, begging for attention. I stood in the middle of my murder, a babe to a world that suddenly had far too many things in it, and one thing too few.

But it hurt less now, that lack. I remembered her smile.

"Feathers!" The crows chortled, gathering them up as they fell from my hair, from behind my ears, placing them carefully in the old cigar box left open from before.

My sister had found them beautiful, these bony juxtapositions of bird and woman. And I suppose they were—feathers iridescent in the light, eyes glittering with avian joy and manic avarice. There was such a liveliness to them…

They probably would not tussle in the grass with me for possession of a favorite ball, but they could be company just the same. They reminded me of her—tilt of a head, broad gaping grin, hopping dance at the pure exuberance of being.

The world was different now. Bigger.

Stranger. It was my turn to be the mad one, the one who saw the spirits sitting in corners, whistling in the wind. I had traded my life for the chance to fly a message on the wings of crows to my sister in the land of the dead, and had made it back. And I would do it again. For such is the way of sisters.

A Lantern Maker of Ai Hanlo

Darrell Schweitzer

*I*n Zabortash, all men are magicians. The air is so thick with magic that you can catch a spirit or a spell with a net on any street corner. Women wear their hair short, lest they find ghosts tangled in it. Still, they find them in their hats.

In Zabortash, even the lantern makers work wonders: the present moon is not the first to shine upon the Earth. The old one went out when the Goddess died, but a Zabortashi lantern maker consulted with a magus, and was directed to that hidden stairway which leads into the sky. He hung his finest lantern in the darkness, in the night, that the stars might not grow over-proud of their brilliance, that men might know the duration of the month again.

In Zabortash, a land far to the south and filled with sluggish rivers, with swamps and steaming jungles, the air is so thick that in the darkness, in the night, the face of the moon ripples.

So it is said.

In Zabortash, further, for all that the folk are magicians, there are men who love their wives, who look on their children with pride when they are young and wistfulness when they are old enough to remind the parents what they were like in their youth.

In Zabortash, people know beauty and feel joy, and know and feel also hurt and hunger and sorrow.

So it is said.

§

In the time of the death of the Goddess, there dwelt a lantern maker in Zabortash named Talnaco Ramat who was skilled in his art. He was a young man, and wholly in love with the maiden Mirithemne, but she would not have him, being of a higher caste than he, and he would not be satisfied with any other. Therefore, he labored long on a lantern of special design. He cut intricate shapes into the shell of it, making holes for light to shine through. The lantern was like a metal box, as tall as an outstretched hand, rectangular with a domed top and a metal ring hinged onto the dome to serve as a handle. At the outset, it was like any other lantern Talnaco Ramat might make, but he inlaid it with precious stones and plated it with gold. He carved schools of fish into it, swimming around the base, and those winged lizards called *kwisi*, which hop from branch to branch and are supposed to bring constancy and long life. He carved hills and villages, the winding river which is called Endless, and he fashioned the top half of the lantern into the shape of Ai Hanlo, the holiest of cities and center of the world, where the bones of the Goddess lie in blessed splendor. That city is built on a mountain; at the summit stands a golden dome, beneath which the Guardian of the Bones of the Goddess holds court. In this likeness was the dome of the lantern made, complete with tiny windows and ringed with battlements and towers.

Finally, Talnaco Ramat carved his own image and that of his beloved into the metal. He depicted the two of them walking hand in hand along the bank of the river, going up to the city.

Then he lit a candle inside the lantern and carried it into a darkened loft. Light streamed through the carven metal, and all his creations were outlined by it. As he watched, the river seemed to flow. The images were projected onto the walls and roof of the loft. Then he was not in the loft at all, but beside Mirithemne. All around them lizards hopped from branch to branch, wings buzzing, fleshy tails dangling.

§

Mirithemne smiled. The day was bright and dear. Rivermen sang as they poled a barge along. A great *drontha*, a warship of the Holy Empire, crawled against the current like a centipede on its banks of oars.

They came to the holy city, entering through the Sunrise Gate, mingling with the crowds. They passed through the square where mendicants waited below the wall that shut them out of the Guardian's palace. Once a week, he explained to Mirithemne, priests came to the top of that wall, and, holding aloft reliquaries containing splinters of the bones of the Goddess, blessed the people below. Miraculous cures still happened, but they were not as common as they had once been. The power of the Goddess was fading.

He led Mirithemne to a house at the end of a narrow lane. A wooden sign with a lantern painted on it hung over the door. He got out a key.

"This will be our home," he said.

He unlocked the door and went in, only to find himself alone in the loft, with the candle of the lantern sputtering out.

He was satisfied. The lantern was adequate.

That night, in the darkness, after the moon had set, he spoke a spell into the open door of the lantern and it filled with a light softer than candle flame, with vapors excited by the ardor of his love.

He climbed onto the roof of his shop and set the lantern down on a ledge. He spoke the name of his beloved three times, and he spoke other words. Then he gently pushed the lantern off the ledge.

It hung suspended in air, and drifted off like a lazy, glowing moth on a gentle breeze. He sat for a time, watching it disappear over the rooftops of the town.

But the next morning he found the lantern on his doorstep. Its light had gone out and its shell was tarnished. He knew then for a certainty that his suit was hopeless. A sorrow lodged in his heart, which never left him.

The sign was very clear.

§

So Talnaco Ramat transported himself to Ai Hanlo by some means which comes as easily to a Zaborman as breathing. The great distance was traversed, the tangled way made straight, dangers avoided, and the lantern maker come to the Sunrise Gate, dragging a two-wheeled cart filled with his belongings.

For a moment he had the idea that he would become rich here in Ai Hanlo, since the folk there had surely never seen anything as wondrous as a finely-wrought Zabortashi lantern.

He was wrong. There was no novelty. In fact, there are so many magicians in Zabortash that many of them go abroad in search of work. A number of them had settled in Ai Hanlo. Some of those made lanterns. He had to join a guild and pay a share of his earnings, but it was a comfort to be surrounded by men and women who spoke his own language. They found a place for him to live and work.

It was a house at the end of a narrow lane, with a wooden sign over the door.

He prospered in his new life and seemed to forget his old. In time, he married a woman of the city called Kachelle, and she bore him three daughters, and, later, a son, whom he named Venda. His life passed peacefully as his family grew. He made lanterns of great complexity and beauty and sold them to nobles of the city, even to the Guardian himself. For all that, he was never too proud to turn out a simple oil lamp, or even to mold candlesticks.

So his years were filled. Then, his daughters married, and went to live with their husbands. Later, his wife Kachelle died, and he had only Venda, his youngest, for company. He taught the boy every facet of his craft, all the secrets of magic that he knew. He knew only little spells and shallow magic—he was not a magus who could make the world tremble at his gaze—but to Venda it was impressive.

In time, Venda married, and brought his wife to live with his father. As his sisters had done before him, he made his father a grandfather, and the house was filled with the shouts of children, and the sounds of their running feet, not to mention the clangor and crash when one of them blundered into a pile of lanterns.

All these children were of the city. They spoke without the accent of Zabortash, as did Venda's wife, who never seemed quite convinced that Zabortash was a real place, and that the stories about it were other than fables. Venda himself had never been there.

So Talnaco Ramat began to feel alone, a stranger once more in a strange country. For the first time in decades he began to long for his homeland and the places of his youth.

One day, while rummaging in the loft above his shop, he found something wrapped in an oily rag. He unwrapped it, and beheld the tarnished lantern he had made for Mirithemne, so long ago. He had forgotten about it all these years. Now, memories flooded back.

Once again he saw himself on the rooftop, watching the lantern float above the town. He remembered the songs he had composed for Mirithemne, and the letters he had labored over with uncertain penmanship. He remembered the great fairs of Zabortash, where grand magi and lesser magicians and craftsmen of all sorts came together to conjoin their magic, that the Earth might continue to follow the sun through the universe, now that the Goddess was dead, and not be lost in the darkness, in the night. There were wares displayed, feats performed. The high-born women of the land were in attendance, among them Mirithemne. He smiled at her, and waved, and even spoke with her when she mingled with the crowd of common folk. She smiled back—was it out of politeness, or something more?

Talnaco Ramat remembered what it is like to be young.

Therefore, he took up the lantern and carefully polished it, until it shone as it had on the day of its completion. He oiled the hinges of its door.

He waited for evening with barely controlled excitement, speaking to his son and his son's family about trifling things, his mind far removed in time and space.

High up Ai Hanlo Mountain, a soldier blew a curving horn that hung from an arch, announcing that the sun had set.

Talnaco Ramat went out into the cool evening air, bearing the lantern. The dome of the Guardian's palace still glowed with the last light of day. He came to a courtyard he knew, which was filled with trees. It was the autumn of the year, and dead leaves rustled underfoot. He sat down on a stone bench and looked up at the dome, waiting for it to grow dark.

He was alone. The night was quiet, but for occasional distant noises of the city.

When the time came, he did not hesitate. He lit a candle and placed it inside the lantern with a steady hand, speaking as he did the most powerful spells he knew. The candle burned more brightly than it would have with mere flame. He closed the door of the lantern and at once the intricate carvings in the metal shell were outlined in fire. He set the lantern down on the bench and knelt before it, entranced by the shifting shapes. The glowing fishes swam in the air before his eyes. The Endless River flowed around him, its fiery waters splashing over the walls of the courtyard, swirling between the tree trunks. Everywhere, spirits of the air were suddenly visible in the magic light: glowing, stick-legged things wading in the earth like impossible herons; an immense serpent beneath the ground, engirdling the world, its gold and silver scales polished bright as mirrors. He saw turning at the world's core that great rose, half of fire, half of darkness, where dwell the Bright and Dark Powers, the fragments of the godhead.

He turned away from all this, drawing his awareness back into himself, into the courtyard. He concentrated on the lantern before him. It seemed to float in the air. The light grew brighter, brighter; the door opened and he was blinded.

When he could see again, he was by the side of the river called Endless, at a spot he knew well. Mirithemne was with him. He could not see her; but he sensed her presence. She was just beyond the periphery of his vision. He spoke; she did not answer; but he knew she heard.

He was still kneeling, as he had been in the courtyard. He got to his feet, expecting every joint to ache with the strain, but he found that, although he still wore the clothes he had as an old man, and his tools were still in the pockets of his apron, he was young again. He got up easily. He looked at his beard and saw that it was no longer white.

When he walked, he heard Mirithemne's footsteps beside him, but when he turned, she was not there. He continued walking. The sky was clear and the day warm.

He came to the mouth of a cave in the side of a hill which sloped down to meet the river. From within he heard a voice crying, "I am burning!"

He rushed inside and there found an anchorite writhing on the floor of the cave. The man was dressed in rags. His beard and hair were matted with dirt. His skin was brown and wrinkled, like old leather, but there was no fire.

"I prayed for it. Long I prayed for it. Now I have it, and I am burning," the anchorite said, his voice frenzied.

"What have you prayed for? You don't seem to be burning," Talnaco said, puzzled. He turned to Mirithemne, sure that she would understand, but she was not there.

"I prayed," said the anchorite. "I prayed that a fragment of the Goddess would settle on me, that I might be made as holy as she. Oh, it was an arrogant wish! But now it is fulfilled, and I am burning with the spirit. Soon I will be completely consumed."

Before the lantern maker could reply, the other began to babble. He prophesied in tongues, but there was no one to understand his prophecies, except perhaps Mirithemne. He spoke the thousand names of the Goddess, first the common ones, then those known to sages, then those which only the greatest of Guardians may apprehend but dimly, and finally, all the rest, which never before had been spoken.

Talnaco waited patiently while he was doing all this.

At last the holy man sat up, and stared at the lantern maker in a distracted way.

"You, too, are burning," he said. "No, it's not like that at all."

The holy man fell down once more, writhing. He babbled. Then he was calm and lay with his eyes closed, as if he were sleeping. Slowly, with apparent deliberation, he spoke the name of Mirithemne.

Talnaco fled. For a time, he lost his way in a dark forest, but still his beloved seemed to be with him. For days and nights he travelled, resting little. When he finally emerged from the forest, the river was before him again. Once more an imperial *drontha* crawled against the current on the legs of its oars. Once more the rivermen sang as they poled their barge.

He made his way to Ai Hanlo, entering through the Sunrise Gate. He followed streets he knew until he stood before his own door.

The key was in the pocket of his apron. He went inside. The place was filled with dust and cobwebs. At once he set to work cleaning it, making it ready for the practice of his craft.

So again, a young Zabortashi lantern maker established himself in Ai Hanlo, He labored long and hard, selling excellent lanterns to the best clients. In each lantern, somewhere among the intricacies of the design, he carved the image of Mirithemne, all the while sensing her nearness. She became more evident every day. He found his bed rumpled when he had not slept in it. His cupboard was left open when he had closed it. He heard footsteps. He heard shutters and doors opening and closing, but when he went to see, no one was there.

One day, he found a woman's comb on a chair. There were long, yellow hairs in it. Mirithemne's hair was like that. Then, he found her mirror, and when he looked into it, he saw someone staring over his shoulder.

He turned. The carpet on the floor moved slightly, but he was alone in the room.

At last, as he sat in his workshop in the upper room of the house, just below the loft, there were gentle footsteps on the stairway outside, followed by a light rapping at the door.

"Enter," he said.

The door opened slowly, but no one entered: He got up, and found Mirithemne's lantern on the threshold.

The sign was very clear.

Therefore, Talnaco Ramat bore the lantern into a courtyard he knew. It was sunset, in the autumn of the year. High above the city, a soldier blew on a curving horn. The light of the golden dome faded, while the light of the lantern grew brighter.

The door of the lantern opened. His eyes were dazzled. He fell to his knees.

And when he could see again, Mirithemne stood before him, holding the lantern, as graceful and as beautiful as he had remembered her. She smiled at him, and, reaching down, took his hand in hers and lifted him to his feet. Then she danced to music he could not hear, her long dress whirling, the leaves whirling, the golden shapes projected by the lantern whirling over the walls, the trees, the ground, over Talnaco himself as she danced, the lantern in hand.

He could never imagine her more perfect than she was at that moment.

Later, she was in his arms and they spoke words of love. Later still, he sat with his memories, and it seemed he had lived out his life with her, in the shop at the end of the narrow lane, in the city, and that he had grown old. Still, Mirithemne was with him. He vaguely remembered how it had been otherwise, but he was not sure of it, and this troubled him.

He vaguely remembered that he had a son called Venda. He was old. He was getting confused. He would ask Mirithemne.

§

In the darkness, in the night, Venda made his way up a narrow, sloping street that ended in a stairway, climbed the stairway, and came to the wall which separates the lower, or outer part of Ai Hanlo from the inner city, where dwell the Guardian of the Bones of the Goddess, his priests, his courtiers, and his soldiers. Venda could not go beyond the wall, but he could open a certain door, and slide into an unlighted room no larger than a closet, closing the door behind him.

He dropped a coin into a bowl and rang a bell. A window slid open in front of him. He could see nothing, but he heard a priest breathing.

"The power of the Goddess fades like an echo in a cave," the priest said, "but perhaps enough lingers to comfort you."

"I don't come for myself," Venda said, and he explained how he had watched his father go into a courtyard with an old lantern and vanish in a flash of light.

The priest came out and went with him. He saw that the priest was very young, little more than a boy, and he wondered if he would be able to do anything. But he said nothing, out of respect. Then he realized that this was a certain Tamliade, something of a prodigy, already renowned for his visions.

They came to the courtyard and found the lantern, still glowing brightly. The priest opened its door. The light was dazzling. For a time, Venda could see nothing. For a time, they seemed to walk on pathways of light, through forests of frozen fire.

They found Talnaco Ramat sitting in the mouth of a cave, with the lantern before him, its door open, the light from within brilliant.

"Father, return with us," Venda said.

"Go away. I am with my beloved."

Venda saw no one but himself, his father, and the priest, but before he could say anything, his father reached out and snapped the door of the lantern shut.

The scene vanished, like a reflection in a pool shattered by a stone.

§

They found themselves in the courtyard, standing before the lantern, which rested on the bench. Again, the priest opened the little door, and the light was blinding. The priest led Venda by the hand. When he could see again, they were walking after his father, up the road to the Sunrise Gate of Ai Hanlo. His father hurried with long strides, bearing the lantern. Its door was open. The light was less brilliant than before.

"Father—"

"Sir," said the boy priest. "Come away."

Talnaco stopped suddenly and turned to the priest. "What do you know of the ways of love, young man?"

"Why— Why, nothing."

"Then you will not understand why I won't go with you."

"Father," said Venda softly.

Talnaco snapped the door of the lantern shut.

"If you want to get another priest, do so, but it won't do any good," the boy Tamliade said.

They stood in the courtyard, in the darkness, in the night. "It's not that," Venda said. "What do we do now?"

"We merely follow him to where he is going. He has gone far already."

The priest opened the door of the lantern. The light was dim. It seemed to flow out, like the waters of the river, splashing over the ground and between the trees.

Again, they stood by the riverbank. An imperial *drontha* went by. Boatmen poled a barge.

Venda followed the priest. They came to a cave, where lay the blackened, shriveled corpse of an anchorite. They passed through the dark forest and eventually into Ai Hanlo, along a narrow street, until they came to the shop with the wooden sign over its door.

The door was unlocked. The two of them went quietly inside, then up the stairs until they stood before the door to Talnaco Ramat's workroom.

Venda rapped gently.

"Enter," came the voice from within. They entered, and saw Talnaco seated at his workbench, polishing a lantern. He looked older and more tired than Venda had ever seen him before.

"Father, you are in a dream."

His father smiled and said gently, "You are a true son. I am glad that you care about me."

"None of this is real," the priest said, gesturing with a sweep of his hand.

"Do you think I don't know that? I have lived out my life suspended in a single, golden moment of time. It doesn't make any difference. Mirithemne is with me."

He glanced at the empty air as if he were looking at someone.

"This thing you think is your beloved," the priest said, "is in truth some spirit or Power, some fragment of the Goddess which has entered your mind through the lantern, like a moth drawn to a random flame. It is without form or intelligence. Your longing gives it a certain semblance of a shape, but it loves you no more than do the wind and the rain."

"Perhaps I am in love with the mere memory of being in love. Perhaps…in my memory now, I remember two lives. In one my wife was called Kachelle, in the other Mirithemne. In both, I had a son, Venda. Both are in my memory now. How shall I weigh them and know which is the more true?"

Venda looked helplessly at the priest, whose face was expressionless.

"I am tired," said Talnaco Ramat. He rose, taking the lantern, and walked slowly out of the room. The light was very faint now. They followed him to the courtyard. By the time he set the lantern down on the bench, the light had gone out.

The priest snapped the metal door shut. Then he and Venda led Talnaco home. He was delirious with fever.

"He is burned by the spirit," the priest said. "There is little we can do."

They sat by Talnaco's bedside, as he lay dying. Venda wept. Toward the very end, the old man was lucid.

"Do not weep, son," he said. "I have known great happiness in both of my lives."

"Father, was there ever someone called Mirithemne, or did you imagine her?"

"She is real enough. She's probably old and ugly now. I don't think she ever knew my name."

Venda wept.

At the very end, his father said, "I have found the greatest treasure. It was worth the struggle."

Venda did not answer, but the priest leaned forward, and whispered, "What is it?"

"A smile. A touch. Whirling leaves. A single moment frozen in time."

Black Angel
Nancy Springer

*T*imes *were tough for the Jersey Devil. Hoof-prints on the* housetops, which were enough to win his South Devon granddaddy uproar and a place in the history books back in 1855, went all but unnoticed in the Garden State in the days since the New Jersey Turnpike had replaced the supernatural as most Jerseyites' personal experience of hell. When something screamed like a woman in the pine barrens, Jersey dwellers assumed it was a woman, presumably a New Yorker, screaming in the pine barrens. Few humans, even young humans, bother to stray into the ever-shrinking sand-and-scrub wilds of south Jersey anymore; for adventure, they preferred video games. What was a weird manifestation to do for attention? Not to speak of food. Few people kept chickens in their backyards anymore. What was a meat-eating equine to do for blood? Hooves were not meant for hunting.

What a bite. Skulking in the moonlit scrub along a secondary highway, searching for a nice fresh roadkill but affronted by the odor of rancid possum, the Jersey Devil indulged in despondent and rebellious thoughts. *Why do I even bother with the rules anymore? There's no respect for monsters left in the world. Life has lost all meaning, all mystery. How can I compete with TV? I might as well start showing myself in daylight and be done with it.*

"A horse!" whispered a breathy, youthful female voice.

In the shadow of a scrub pine the Jersey Devil froze, outraged to be caught by surprise but even more outraged to be mistaken for a common horse. *Can you not see the red fire of my eyes in the darkness? Can you not see how blackly I loom?*

What are you doing out here?

The pine barrens, or what pitiful remnants were left of the pine barrens, belonged to creature denizens at night. By the rules, the human had to be frightened away. Lifting a head worthy of an equine gargoyle, stretching his heavy, muscular neck and working his bulky chest like a bellows, the Jersey Devil shrilled forth his distinctive scream, a warning as chilling as a panther's screech.

"What's the matter, horsie?" The girl pattered forward from the shadows. "I love horses," she said in soft, exalted tones. "What's the matter? Are you caught in that bush?"

The nincompoop seemed to have taken his challenge as a squall for help. From exactly what form of brain damage was this human suffering?

"Oh!" She stopped where she stood, a pre-adolescent wraith in the moonlight. "Oh!" she breathed in tones yet more hushed, more rapt, "oh, wings! You're a Pegasus! Oh!"

Poised to scream again, the Jersey Devil gave an undignified grunt of surprise instead. Surprise and sneaking gratification. He had always felt, although never daring to express the thought, that he was at least as worth of immortalization as Pegasus. Why should a beautiful, white, grass-eating horse with wings be considered a major-league mythological creature while a not-so-beautiful black meat-eating horse with wings—bat wings—was considered a monster, and a minor one at that? It was unfair. It was discrimination.

Obviously, this girl was exceptionally intelligent among humans. The Jersey Devil lowered his rawboned head to regard her with unwonted interest. There she stood, fearless, a skinny child in owlish glasses, her clothing skimpy and cottony and undistinguished, her bare feet curled in protest against the pine needles—he noticed the pallor of her feet in the moonlight, small fish-like surfaces even whiter than the south Jersey sand. Why did humans have such soft and inadequate feet? Dependent upon shoes. How pitiful.

"I must be hungrier than I thought," the girl murmured. "I'm seeing things." She stepped forward until she stood directly by the Jersey Devil's shoulder, her soft feet inches from his hooves, her scrawny hand reaching for him. He shuddered at her touch yet was so fascinated by her lack of fear that he did not move either to escape or resist that fumbling contact. "No, they're real," she whispered, stroking the leather of his wings.

Her touch was as weak as her voice. Her lack of fear was perhaps due to—what? Had something driven her out here, to the darkness, the wilderness? Out of her home and out of her mind? Some extremity?

"I guess somebody heard me after all," she said. "They sent me a horse angel."

Oh, sure. Give me a break.

"What are you doing stuck in this bush?" she asked the Jersey Devil. "Are you okay?" She limped around his head to scout the other side of him, running her hand down his neck. Muscles tensed to fight or flee, crouching, taut, and more than a trifle discombobulated, he had pressed into the shelter of a pine scrub as if it could hide him from her. "Are you caught by your mane or something?" Her spidery fingers groped, trying to ascertain that he was not. "I don't know a thing about horses," she confided.

Noooooo, no kidding. Even an ordinary farm horse had hooves that could trample her or kick her into next week, plus inch-long chisel-like teeth that could sink into her. The Jersey Devil, being a meat eater, had even nastier teeth. Customized. *Want to see my fangs?* But he did not show them to her.

"Except that I read *The Black Stallion*," the girl added. "Can I ride you, black horse?" she asked wistfully.

Oh, for the horned god's sake…

He was already breaking all the rules. If a human did not run from his scream, he was supposed to screech and snort and rampage and glare fire until the human did run, and if those tactics failed, he was supposed to traumatize the human with his hooves. But poop on all that. Poop by the scoop. He just didn't feel like it.

Fine. Whatever.

He stepped away from the pine, arched his neck and lowered his head in a fairy-tale gesture of equine acquiescence. Apparently, she knew enough about fairy tales, if not about horses, to recognize the body language. Immediately, she grabbed his mane and scrambled onto him. Those soft feet had usages after all. Her monkey toes climbed his foreleg and withers. Lightweight, she settled behind his withers, her knees hooked around the junctures of his wings.

"Ooooh," she said, her voice worshipful and delighted, "It's high up here."

The Jersey Devil set off at a sullen, jarring walk, plodding down the berm of the highway. So what if cars came by. So what if people saw him. His job description was shot to hell anyhow, and he wasn't sure what would happen to a minor monster who was doing some major screwing up. His boss would have a few things to say, that was for sure.

"Oh, thank you," the girl said, although it was not clear for what she was thanking him. "Thank you. Nobody else cares."

Shut up.

She did not shut up. "Nobody believes me," she said more softly. "Not even my BFF. Nobody wants to believe he's doing those things to me."

Whatever she was complaining about, the Jersey Devil did not want to deal with it either. *I've got my own problems.* He walked faster, slamming his heels into the ground with each step.

But his stride eased as the girl's slight warm weight massaged him. A mile passed, then another. On his back she had gone into a trance of glory and was wordlessly singing. "I'll call you Blackie," she said suddenly. "No, that's stupid. I'll call you, uh, Black Angel." She said the name like an apotheosis.

Until that night, the Jersey Devil had experienced humans only superficially: screech at them, and they ran. He had not had occasion to deal with the nearly religious fervor of a horse-besotted girl. Her unquestioning adoration put him far off balance.

"Where are we going?" she asked with utter faith.

Going? The Jersey Devil had not been thinking in terms of going anywhere. She wanted a horsie ride, so he was giving her a horsie ride, dammit. But now she had called him Black Angel, and she wanted to know where they were going… She expected him to take care of her? The realization caused a large explosion in his small brain, expressed in a terrific snort. Okay. Okay, he knew where they were going. They were going to get her something to eat, and they were going to plunge him all the way into deep manure. They were going somewhere he had never been in his entire three-hundred-year life.

They were going to McDonald's.

§

His belly had been growling before they started, and it had grown mighty in borborygmus by the time they arrived at the golden arches. He saw at once that the puny doors were not large enough for him. Too bad. Like a Mack truck relentlessly in reverse, he backed up to the glass, feeling the girl grab his mane as she divined his intentions; he kicked. She shrieked with glee as if on an amusement park ride. Other shrieks, not gleeful at all, sounded from inside, and the Jersey Devil snorted, excited by the screams. Warming to the sound of crashing, shattering glass, he continued to enlarge the entrance as the restaurant emptied, cars zoomed from the parking lot, and the girl on his back laughed in harmony with the tinkling glass. Such an intelligent child; she was not afraid. Not afraid at all.

When he had opened almost the entire front of the establishment, he carried her inside. There was no need for her to risk her bare feet on broken glass. He took her clear to the cash registers, where he stopped as if at a mounting block. She slipped down from his back to stand on the counter top, wobbling a little and hanging onto him until she got her legs back.

"There's nobody to wait on us," she said, still laughing.

The staff had disappeared from the kitchen area, as the Jersey Devil knew quite well; he had seen people in clownish uniforms running through the parking lot.

"I guess it's okay for me to help myself, since they ran away." She sounded serious now, wanting to know whether it was morally correct for her, a starving child, to take food, and she seemed to decide that since her guardian angel had brought her here, it was all right. "Are you hungry?" She folded to her bony bottom and scooted down off the counter, heading for ranks of paper-wrapped hamburgers. She grabbed an armload of them, unwrapping several and placing them on the counter before the Jersey Devil before she bit into one herself.

Ick. Cooked meat. No better than possum that's been three days in the sun on asphalt.

Still, the Jersey Devil ate. The bread was not too bad, although squashed. The dill pickle slices tasted interesting. But he soon diverted his attention from the burgers to the leavings on the tables. A good grease smell emanated from many small cardboard containers, and thereby he discovered fries. Salty fries, he decided, were almost as good as fresh raw chicken with the feathers on. He munched them cardboard and all. Behind the counter, the girl had gulped down three burgers and was swilling a drink of some sort from a huge plastic cup.

In french fry gestalt, the Jersey Devil only gradually became aware of an annoying noise: sirens. Louder, nearer. The next moment, several police cars screeched into the McDonald's parking lot.

Her bare feet thwacking the floor, the girl came out from behind the counter, stood near the side door, and looked at the Jersey Devil as if awaiting directions. He was her bat-winged, equine angel. She would do whatever he indicated.

Go away. Let me alone. He just wanted to eat fries. He was not afraid of the cops, whose bullets could not dent his black, supernatural hide. His fear was of other authorities.

The police had scurried and deployed themselves. "Come out with your hands up!" a cop bellowed.

If I come out with my hooves up, you're not going to like it, fella.

"Captain," one of the other cops yelled from near a side window, "I see him. Holy shit, it's some kind of big animal. Holy shit!" He sounded like a youngster, his voice and probably the rest of him shaking as if with buck fever. Having just discovered Chicken McNuggets *en papier*, the Jersey Devil did not even bother to glare as the rookie leveled his gun barrel and fired. Glass flew with a soprano song. The bullet ricocheted off the Jersey Devil and shot harmlessly into a Ronald McDonald effigy grinning in the corner, but the interruption of his feast annoyed the Jersey Devil. He screeched and reared. Red lightning flashed in his eyes.

"Don't! Don't shoot at him; you'll hurt him!" The girl came running to place her skinny body between the Jersey Devil and the excitable cop.

Too late the Jersey Devil realized that bullets, although they could not kill him, might very well kill her. He had to get her out of there.

It was a thought that upset the order of his universe, throwing a three-century lifetime's worth of assumptions into confusion matched by that of the night. He heard shouts, another gunshot, yells— "Don't, idiot; you'll hit the kid!" He clattered across vinyl flooring and knocked tables cockeyed in his haste to stand by her, and she seemed to comprehend his wish; she scrambled onto him. Her hands felt firm on his mane. She seemed to be okay so far.

He wheeled and leaped through the wide-open front entry. Instinctively, as whenever his adrenaline soared, his bat-like wings spread and beat the air. With his softly furred patagia vibrating like drumheads, he surged upward. His forehooves struck the roof of the nearest cruiser; he tucked them and rose steeply, tidily clearing the ornamental pear trees.

"Oh," the girl squealed, "we're flying!"

She was not the only one who was impressed. The manly shouts below achieved new heights of frenzy.

"Black Angel," the girl said with hushed rapture, "this is wonderful. I've always wanted to fly."

Just hang on. If you splat, I'm not going to be the vulture that eats you.

The hoarse vociferations of the police and onlookers faded away behind them. Flying at about five hundred feet over the lights of town, lugging a bit under the unaccustomed weight of a passenger, the Jersey Devil wheeled sluggishly southward toward the friendly darkness of the pine barrens. Now that his belly was approximately full, all he wanted was to get home, ditch this kid, and rest.

Sirens. Blue-red-blue lights flashing on the roads below. The cops were following.

"Black Angel," the girl said with a panicky catch in her voice, "don't let them get me. Please don't. They'll send me back to—*him*, and—he'll just do it again."

It was the first time he had discerned fear in her. She was not afraid of him, a grotesque denizen of the night, yet she feared—what? It had to be a monster beyond imagining.

With a rolling, white-rimmed eye on the police cruisers below, the Jersey Devil saw that they were following easily. Despite his bat wings, The Jersey Devil did not dart like a bat. Due to the bulk of his body, his air speed was modest, and he was too unwieldy to attempt sudden directional changes. Too bad. If he could swoop, maybe he could lose the kid.

"Please," she begged, her voice thin with terror, "I can't go back there."

Unquestionably, there were ways he could get rid of her. A mid-air bucking spree—but even as he venomously thought it, he knew he could never forsake her.

"Please, Angel, do something."

Resigned to being her champion, he grumbled, *I could bomb their windshields.* But he knew that all the horse crap he had in him would not help for long. *All right, okay!* He did not like it, but he knew he would have to do it sooner or later anyway. Might as well take her with him. Maybe she could help plead his case.

To the watchers on the ground, looking up at his grotesque underbelly and wings and at the frail child riding him— "Write it up as a stranger abduction," the captain was telling the cop stuck with that unenviable job—to the watchers looking up at the bizarre bat-winged horse clearly visible in the moonlit sky, it was as if the apparition vanished in midair, rider and all.

But to the Jersey Devil, a very minor nighttime manifestation in an unlikely place at an unsympathetic time, it was not that he had vanished. It was merely that, with a sigh and a sour-tempered rolling of his eyes, he had gone to face his tribunal.

§

This was not a nighttime place. This was a place where it was always light yet never light. A place forever aglow in lambent rainbow mist.

"Fool! Three-hundred-year upstart! A mere sprout! Who are you to dare to extemporize?"

It was the World Tree who spoke, she whose crown towered forever veiled in mist and mystery, she for whom "goddess" was too lowly a title. Even had the Jersey Devil not been kneeling before her, nose to the ground, even had he been standing, he would have been able to see only the very least and lowest of her mighty branches far overhead. Perching on the visible branches and looking down with a certain smug satisfaction (or so the Jersey Devil sensed) were various of the lesser mythical birds: the Gillygaloo (which laid cubical eggs and wept constantly), the lop-winged Whangdoodle, the ass-backed Smollygaster, and many others, but no manifestations of any importance. Major mythological personages such as the Phoenix or the Roc were far overhead, swaddled and haloed and glorified in fog, along with other winged beings, such as the Pegasus. If indeed the Pegasus were flying anywhere in the neighborhood, the Jersey Devil would never see him.

"Do you understand what you have done?" the World Tree continued to scold. "This girl, what are we to do with her? Now that she has seen us, she can never return."

"I don't want to return," the girl spoke up, her piping tone so brash in this empyrean place that the Jersey Devil winced and trembled.

"I don't care what happens to me. It can't be any worse than what was happening already."

"Nonsense. What can possibly be worse than exile from your people?"

The girl told her. She told her in words that were perhaps not the technically correct terms for the act described. Nor were they street words. Rather, they were the words of a child struggling to describe the unspeakable.

"His front—my bottom."

As she spoke, and as the Jersey Devil began to comprehend, he felt an unfamiliar burning sensation within his chest, a hot pain that heaved his ribs and surged upward to block his throat and sting his eyes. Without leave from the World Tree, he arose from his knees to step closer to the girl. What was this punishment taking hold of him, this saltwater tide of misery? His eyes were so blurred he could barely see the child as he reached with his gargoyle head to nuzzle her. The anguish ran out of his eyes and down his long, ugly face.

She turned to him and hugged him around his neck, hiding her face in his mane, and his tears dripped down her back and shoulders. There was silence.

"Well," the World Tree said at last, quite softly for such a presence, "that is indeed worse."

The girl did not reply, but her head lifted from the Jersey Devil's neck and behind her thick glasses her eyes were wide and shining. She gasped, "Wings!"

At the same time the Jersey Devil saw them budding, sprouting from her shoulders, pushing through her cheap clothing—fabric wet from his tears—the way spring flowers push through last year's leaves. Wings worthy of a skylark. Airy, uplifted wings the color of raindrops.

Humbly the Jersey Devil turned to the World Tree and said it first. "Thank you, Mother."

"Nonsense. I gave her nothing. You gave them to her."

"I— I can fly?" stammered the girl. "Oh! Oh! Thank you! I've always wanted to fly." She jiggled, jumped, stood on tiptoes with her skinny arms outstretched.

"In a moment, little one. Patience. You, Black Thing, come here."

The Jersey Devil bowed his head and took a few steps forward. He sensed that it might be politic to kneel again. But he did not.

"I am going to give you a change of assignment," said the World Tree. "Decide for yourself whether it is an advancement or a demotion. I'll never tell."

It was hard to know how to react to the World Tree when she got that quirk in her voice. One did not quite dare to joke with her. The Jersey Devil said nothing.

"The pine barrens are a lost cause since the Turnpike went through," said the World Tree in resigned and contemplative tones. "Confine yourself to them no longer. Your new task is this: You are to seek out those who do vile things to children. By whatever means you choose, make their lives painful and short. Perhaps you would enjoy an alternative form of fresh meat. Do I make myself clear?"

The Jersey Devil's head rose higher with each word. His upper lip wrinkled in the equine equivalent of a smile. His fangs showed. He bowed low, then wheeled away, eager to get started.

"Begin with this little one's tormentor."

As if she needed to tell me. As if I wasn't going to do that anyway.

"Little one," the World Tree concluded in bored tones, "you had better fly along with him to make sure he gets it right. He is rather stupid."

"All *right*!" The girl sprang into the timeless air. Her thin face grew rapt with the astonishment and glory of flying. Her glasses shone like rainbow mist. "Come on, Black Angel!" she cried.

He leaped to fly beside her. When her wings grew tired, he would take her upon his back. He would soar smoothly so as not to joggle her, and perhaps she would lay her head on his neck and sleep.

My name is not Jersey Devil anymore.

Perhaps the girl had named him rightly. Black Angel, avenging angel. What is an angel but a strange creature with wings?

Thanks for reading!

Thanks for reading. If you enjoyed this book, please consider leaving an honest review on your favorite store's website.

§

About the Editors

Kelly A. Harmon is an award-winning journalist and author, and a member of Science Fiction & Fantasy Writers of America. She is a former newspaper reporter and editor, and now edits for Pole to Pole Publishing, a small Baltimore publisher.

A Baltimore native, Ms. Harmon writes the *Charm City Darkness* series, which includes the novels: Stoned in Charm City, A Favor for a Fiend, A Blue Collar Proposition, and In the Eye of the Beholder. A stand-alone novel, Blood Soup, was winner of the Fantasy Gazetteers Award. Her short fiction has been nominated for a Pushcart Award and short-listed for the Aeon. It can be found in The Pale Leaves and Gallery of Curiosities magazines, Beyond Steampunk, Occult Detective Quarterly, The Best Indie Speculative Fiction Volume 1, and more.

She is co-editor with Vonnie Winslow Crist of Pole Publishing's first three Dark Stories anthologies: *Hides the Dark Tower, In a Cat's Eye, and Dark Luminous Wings, and* Pole to Pole's first four anthologies in the Re-Imagined series: Re-Launch, Re-Quest, Re-Terrify, and Re-Enchant.

Visit her website at http://kellyaharmon.com, or connect with her on Facebook.

Vonnie Winslow Crist, MS Professional Writing, has had a life-long interest in reading, writing, art, science fiction, fairy-tales, folklore, and legends. An award-winning author and illustrator, she is a member of the Science Fiction & Fantasy Writers of America,

Society of Children's Book Writers & Illustrators, and Pen Women. Her books include The Enchanted Dagger, Murder on Marawa Prime, Owl Light, The Greener Forest, and Leprechaun Cake & Other Tales. Her speculative stories can be found in Chilling Ghost Short Stories, Faerie Magazine, Killing It Softly 2, Chaos of Hard Clay, Fae Wings & Hidden Things, Amazing Stories, Cast of Wonders, and elsewhere.

Editor of The Gunpowder Review, Ms. Crist co-edited with Kelly A. Harmon Pole to Pole Publishing's first three Dark Stories anthologies: Hides the Dark Tower, In a Cat's Eye, and Dark Luminous Wings, along with the first four anthologies of Pole to Pole Publishing's Re-Imagined series: Re-Launch, Re-Quest, Re-Terrify, and Re-Enchant. For more information, visit her website: http://vonniewinslowcrist.com/, blog: http://vonniewinslowcrist.wordpress.com, Fb page: http://facebook.com/WriterVonnieWinslowCrist, or http://twitter.com/VonnieWCrist

Now Available!

Re-Launch
Science Fiction Stories of New Beginnings

Beginnings are always messy. ~ John Galsworthy

Spacecrafts hurtling toward alien worlds. Second chances for civilizations. First contact. Rebirth. Non-humans looking for a new life. Opportunities for fresh starts and do-overs far from Earth. These stories and more explore the theme of Re-Launch.

Send your imagination into orbit with 18 science fiction tales from an international roster of authors.

Featuring fiction from Douglas Smith, James Dorr, Kris Austen Radcliffe, Eando Bender, Wendy Nikel, Stewart C. Baker, Meriah Crawford, Gregory L. Norris, Jennifer Rachel Baumer, Jonathan Shipley, Vonnie Winslow Crist, Lawrence Dagstine, CB Droege, Jude-Marie Green, Steven R. Southard, Calie Voorhis, Anthony Cardno, and Andrew Gudgel.

Re-Launch reminds readers that new beginnings rarely go as planned and danger waits for the unwary on all worlds.

Read More: http://poletopolepublishing.com/books/re-launch/

Other Books in the Re-Imagined Series:

Re-Quest
Dark Fantasy Stories about Magic and the Fae

Home is behind, the world ahead. - J.R.R. Tolkien

Old gods outwitted by heroes. Magical weapons that bring good and evil. Dragons winging over the city or walking upon the earth. A wizard witnessing endless battles. These stories and more explore the theme of Re-Quest.

Leave home behind and wander magical worlds in these 16 fantasy tales from an international roster of authors.

Featuring fiction from Robert E. Howard, Douglas Smith, James Dorr, Lillian Csernica, Gregory L. Norris, Jonathan Shipley, Kelly A. Harmon, Doug C. Souza, Jennifer Rachel Baumer, Dale W. Glaser, CB Droege, Jeremy Zimmerman, Christine Lucas, Dennis Mombauer, Bradley Sinor, and Chris Kuriata

Re-Quest takes readers on fantastical quests filled with adventure, magic, and danger.

Read More: http://poletopolepublishing.com/books/re-quest/

Re-Terrify
Horrifying Stories of Monsters and More

With Stories by: Nancy Springer, Douglas Smith, James Dorr, Eric Choi, Darrell Schweitzer, Steve Southard, Gregory Norris, Gustavo Bondoni, Jonathan Shipley, Vonnie Winslow Crist, Meriah Crawford, Nicole Kurtz, Phillip Chamberlain, Kelly A. Harmon, Lisa Lepovetsky, Winston Marks, Geoff Gander, and David M. Hoenig.

Read More: http://poletopolepublishing.com/books/re-terrify/

Books in the Dark Stories Series:

In a Cat's Eye
In a cat's eye, all things belong to cats. - English proverb

Cat stories set in ancient Egypt, pre-history Mexico, Victorian England, space stations, grim magical worlds, during the zombie apocalypse, and a typical neighborhood give a glimpse into the mysterious lives of felines. And each cat, whether friend or fiend, believes In a Cat's Eye, all things belong to cats.

Cat-lovers and readers of science fiction, fantasy, mystery, and horror will find a tale to sink their claws into from an international roster of authors. Featuring fiction from Jody Lynn Nye, Gail Z. Martin, A.L. Sirois, Sir Arthur Conan Doyle, Doug C. Souza, Oliver Smith,

Jeremy M. Gottwig, K.I. Borrowman, Gregory Norris, Christine Lucas, R.S. Pyne, Steven R. Southard, Joanna Hoyt, Elektra Hammond, A.L. Kaplan, and Alex Shvartsman.

In a Cat's Eye is purr-fect reading for a dark night—just beware of paws on the stairs.

Dark Luminous Wings

From Icarus to Da Vinci to tomorrow's astronauts, humans have dreamt of flight. Feathered wings. Mechanical wings. Leathery wings. Steel wings. Stories of winged creatures set in graveyards and churches, bustling cities, fantastical worlds, alternate histories, and outer space reveal the shifting nature of Dark Luminous Wings.

Take flight with 17 science fiction, dark fantasy, and horror-filled tales from an international roster of authors.

Featuring fiction from: Brian Trent, Nancy Springer, Gregory L. Norris, Steven R. Southard, D.H. Aire, Evan J. Osborne, Claire Davon, Nemma Wollenfang, Jason J. McCuiston, Rebecca Gomez Farrell, Trisha J. Wooldridge, Maxine Kollar, Jeffrey G. Roberts, Adam Millard, Michael M. Jones, Todd Sullivan, T.J. Perkins.

Dark Luminous Wings will set your imagination soaring—but watch out for sharp beaks, piercing talons, and gravity.

Hides the Dark Tower

Mysterious and looming, towers and tower-like structures pierce the skies and shadow the lands. Hides the Dark Tower includes over two dozen tales of adventure, danger, magic, and trickery from an international roster of authors. Readers of science fiction, fantasy, horror, grimdark, campfire tales, and more will find a story to haunt their dreams. So step out of the light, and into the world of Hides the Dark Tower—if you dare.

Featuring fiction by Richard Chizmar, Alex Shvartsman, Rie Sheridan Rose, Jeff Stehman, Jonathan Shipley, Robert E. Waters, Evan Dicken, Anatoly Belilovsky, Brad Hafford, A.P. Sessler, Larry C. Kay, Jeremy M. Gottwig, Steven R. Southard, Kelda Crich, M.J. Ritchie, Edward McDermott, Ray Kolb, Andrew Gudgel, Jeremy Zimmerman, N.O.A. Rawle, Meg Belviso, Daniel Beazley, Briana McGuckin, Kane Gordon, Peter Schranz, G. Scott Huggins, Vonnie Winslow Crist, and Kelly A. Harmon, and featuring a poem by Laura Shovan.

http://poletopolepublishing.com/series/dark-stories/

www.ingramcontent.com/pod-product-compliance
Lightning Source LLC
Chambersburg PA
CBHW030304200626
46816CB00002BA/756